I0601804

Swallows of Mostar
Neira Fazlovic

NineStar Press

Contents

A NineStar Press Publication

www.ninestarpress.com

Swallows of Mostar

eBook ISBN: 978-1-64890-903-0

Print ISBN: 978-1-64890-922-1

© 2025 Neira Fazlovic

Cover Art © 2025 Mandy Porto

Edited by BJ Toth

Published in November 2025 by NineStar Press, New Mexico, USA.

This is a work of fiction. Names, characters, places, and incidents are either the product of the author's imagination or are used fictitiously. Any resemblance to actual persons living or dead, business establishments, events, or locales is entirely coincidental.

All rights reserved. No part of this publication may be reproduced in any material form, whether by printing, photocopying, scanning or otherwise without the written permission of the publisher. To request permission and all other inquiries, contact NineStar Press at Contact@ninestarpress.com.

NO AI TRAINING: Without in any way limiting the author's [and publisher's] exclusive rights under copyright, any use of this publication to "train" generative artificial intelligence (AI) technologies to generate text is expressly prohibited. The author reserves all rights to license uses of this work for generative AI training and development of machine learning language models.

CONTENT WARNING:

This book contains fade-to-black sexual content, which may only be suitable for mature readers. Depictions of falling, heights, deep water, and past parental death.

To all of us who need to take a leap of our own

Chapter One

Čudna jada od Mosta grada

The morning sun was warm against Franka's skin, and the pleasant summer wind ruffled her hair. Her lungs eagerly took in the first wisps of fresh air after weeks of being stuck inside with nothing but textbooks and math equations to keep her company. She leaned against the cold, stone wall of the ancient street that led to the Old Bridge, as the sweet and nutty taste of her ice cream caused her brain to produce some much-needed serotonin. With the River Neretva carrying away her worries, Franka looked up at the bright sun and smiled for the first time in weeks.

The scene in front of her was a common sight in this part of Mostar. The lanky guide was probably barely out of high school, with a subtle Slavic accent in his English and a vocabulary that could use a bit more work. Still, his flock of tourists (Canadian retirees, if Franka was correct) seemed interested in what he had to say about the city of Mostar, the often overlooked jewel of Southern Europe, as he called it, even if they probably could have read most of his speech on Wikipedia. Today, Franka didn't mind because, only moments ago, a miracle happened: after two years of living in this city, she finally effortlessly understood a single sentence of the language.

The sentence was uttered, or to be more precise, yelled, through a thick accent by a tall young woman in a traditional Bosnian costume who sold trinkets to the tourists at the store closest to the Old Bridge. To be perfectly honest, the sentence wasn't overly complex, but it was more than a hello or a plea to buy some souvenirs Franka would have recognized even before she was so cruelly punished by the gods and forced to live in Mostar. It wasn't even directed to Franka or any other tourist, but to Ado, a short young man (at least, short for the land of giants that was Bosnia and Herzegovina) who was now running past Franka in only his bikini bathing suit, sporting a very smug grin on his youthful face. The sentence was simple, but it might as well have been poetry to Franka. *"Ado, idiote, ne naginji se na ogradu, neki kreten ju je jučer razvalio!"*

1

Some jerk busted the fence yesterday, and Ado was a fool for leaning against it. What a lovely statement!

Croatian was needlessly complicated, in Franka's humble American opinion. So was Bosnian. And Serbian. Mostly because they were the same language with a few subtle differences, no matter what the native speakers would like to argue. Declinations, verb changes, and grammar cases, not to mention genders were all entirely unnecessary. Who decided "river" was female and "bridge" was male, and can their descendants pay for making Franka's life in the city of Mostar somehow even more miserable?

But on this sunny summer morning, as she made her way to the Old Bridge, Franka at least got this one sentence correct. Maybe Mom was right. She really needed to leave the house.

***

"Franka, I just heard from a reputable source that it is summer outside. Can you believe it?" Mom had announced last night. She had walked into Franka's, what could in the most generous terms be called "room," without knocking and skipped over a pile of textbooks on the floor.

Franka sat behind her desk, a few days away from being completely taken over by the chaos that spread far and wide. Math, chemistry, and physics textbooks covered most of the available surfaces, other than the bed with messy covers that were probably supposed to be changed a few weeks ago. The seemingly endless quantity of mugs and bowls of cereal that kept appearing, but never disappearing, were very close to developing their own civilizations in this hot and moist environment. Franka didn't have time to care. She had more important things to worry about.

She had finished studying chemistry for today (the urea cycle) and turned to math practice, littering her desk with scraps of paper filled with math formulas she understood perfectly. In English. Croatian was a different story.

"Really?" she asked, not even looking up at her mom, checking her result in the back of the textbook instead. It was correct, as was every single result she'd gotten for days had been. "I haven't noticed," she added in Croatian when she remembered this was her "no English summer."

"Go out, please," Mom said, switching back to English. "I beg of you. You have been in this house for a month! You will pass your exam."

"I thought so last time, but here we are now!" Franka said. She was so lucky Bosnian colleges worked differently than the American ones, giving her an opportunity to retake her entrance exam in September and actually get in. The whole schooling system was unlike the one she was used to, where specialized colleges for pharmacology (as well as anything else) allowed her to skip undergrad studies and become a pharmacologist in just five short years. That was, if she could pass her exam.

"You have been stuck in this filth since June! That's not healthy," Mom continued, looking around as Franka suddenly became aware of the mess, the faint smell of stale air, and the boxes of stuff she should have unpacked two years ago. Still, she shook her head "no" and picked another math problem to focus on instead.

"Neither is not getting into college," she said and tried to get back to her linear systems with two variables. Every list of questions from previous entrance exams for the Faculty of Pharmacy at the University of Mostar had at least one of those. If she wanted in, she had to be proficient, so god help her! "Very bad for the thyroid gland."

"So, you want to cram two years' worth of studying that you didn't do into two months?" Mom asked, perfectly aware Franka might pull it off by any means necessary.

"That's the plan," Franka said and turned back to her math problem, but Mom wasn't quitting.

"Go out. Please," she begged again, but Franka wasn't listening. "One hour?" she asked. "Can't you spare one hour, so I don't think you are losing your mind with all that science? One hour and you can get me off your back for at least a week."

Franka paused for a moment. She was wasting time arguing right now, as she did for the past few days. It probably added up to an hour or so in total. Maybe this was the solution.

"You are in one of the most popular travel destinations in Eastern Europe. Enjoy it for an hour," Mom continued. "Pretend to be a tourist. Grab some ice cream. Please. Mostar is a beautiful city. I promise you."

"Very overrated," Franka scoffed. When she was a kid, Franka had loved coming to Mostar for a few weeks every few years. Then she would go back home to Atlanta and tell her friends she went all the way to Europe and to this small country called Bosnia and Herzegovina in the Balkan Peninsula where her mom was born. Now that she was stuck here, it was hell. The city didn't change, but everything else did. Mostar was a picturesque town, filled with history, world-famous for the sixteenth century Old Bridge that connected both sides over the gorgeous River Neretva that divided them. It was also too hot, too touristy, and too small (both in its size and the mentality of its people).

"Because our suburban hellhole in Atlanta was so much more fun," Mom said, making Franka frown. If nothing else, Mostar was a living, breathing, organic city, even if half of the buildings were destroyed in the War and never fixed.

"I have to study. I don't have time to mess around," she continued. Tomorrow was the time to tackle the Krebs cycle again. Last time she lost at least ten points on that question. She knew it in English, but when she tried to explain it in Croatian, panic took the wheel of her brain and drove them both straight into a ditch.

"You want to practice the language? Go out, talk to an actual Herzegovinian other than me! It will do you wonders," Mom continued, closing the textbook right in front of her.

That was the second argument that had given Franka pause. Coming to Mostar with barely any knowledge of the language despite her mom being born and raised here and then going to a school that was in English for two years really didn't make any of this easier. Every time she thought she had the hang of it, someone would drop a new slang word or speak too fast and she would get lost again, so it was easier not to try at all.

"And you know, Isabella would love a selfie from the bridge. You know she loves bridges," Mom added in her sweetest voice because she knew bringing up Aunt Bella would work.

And it did.

***

So, today, around eight, Franka put on her baggiest black T-shirt and jeans, smeared on some eyeliner, and finally left her house for the first time in weeks.

She could have gotten to the Old Town much faster if she came in from the west side of the city, but the morning was too nice for a shortcut. Mom's assessment of how much Franka needed to leave the house was spot-on. That first whiff of fresh summer air caused her body to take one step after another without her input because it missed movement so much. She walked past the ancient trees of the Zrinjevac Park, and to the Spanish Square and the objectively gorgeous but undeniably bright orange Mostar Grammar School that so generously hosted her Unbounded High School that she would hopefully never have to enter again. She crossed the Neretva River and reached "their side of the town," as Mom occasionally slipped up and called it privately. If anything, despite the few more mosques, the east side of Mostar didn't belong to the Bosnians more than it did the Croats like her mom. It belonged to tourists and tourists alone.

For the next hour, she decided she wasn't the Franka Garcia who lived here for two years and hated every minute of it. She was Franka Garcia, on vacation to her Mom's hometown for a week or two, who would go back to her home in Atlanta, where she would get into a prestigious college because her life wasn't in shambles. That Franka could enjoy the Old Town and pretend for a little while she was okay.

She turned right, past Musala Park, and made her way to the bridge, hyping herself up to be as excited as she was when she was a kid.

Her fellow tourists weren't here yet. It was the middle of the week, but August was still the peak of the season, so they would probably swarm the city soon. For now, it was only Franka and a few stray cats.

As she got closer to the bridge itself, the street narrowed. The smooth white stones were replaced by aesthetically pleasing but very slippery and jagged cobblestone that made her feet ache through her sneakers. A rookie tourist mistake on her part. But that was okay. Today, she was a tourist.

The Mostar stores that had songs written about them lined the walls of the narrow, stone streets. Colorful trinkets awaited the mobs of tourists who would spend their hard-earned money on "made in China" magnets and babushka dolls (because any Slavic country is apparently Russia). Not wanting to waste her money on something she didn't need, Franka filled her tourist quota with something sweet.

"*Uživaj, sine,*" the middle-aged lady said, handing Franka a scoop of walnuts and figs ice cream. "Enjoy, son."

Franka smiled and said thanks, keeping the observation of how Balkan people always called you "son" regardless of gender to herself. Weird. She was still not used to it, even if she'd been hearing it her whole life from her family in Mostar. For such a gendered language and people who cared deeply about what constituted a girl or a boy, everyone could be a son.

The ice cream was creamy, sweet, and absolutely delicious. Despite her objections, she was still half Herzegovinian, so anything with figs was bound to taste great.

She took a few photos by the Old Bridge viewpoint, where the white stone arch that spanned both sides of the river was in full view. When a few more people tried to do the same, she moved on quickly. They were all too loud and cheerful for her taste.

The street that led to the bridge was narrow and crooked, filled with vibrant colors of the souvenirs. Salespeople beckoned her to buy their things with their friendly smiles and kind words. Well, except for the girl who chased away the half-naked Ado. She looked like she was forced to be here at gunpoint, glaring at Franka and a group of tourists she got swept up in.

"You chose a spooky day to visit," the overly enthusiastic guide told his flock who followed him at the same pace Franka was walking. "It is said that on this day, the second of August, if you swim in the Neretva River, it will pull you into its depths and you will drown!" he said in an exaggerated creepy voice like it was Halloween. "But that is just an urban legend, right?" he asked to spook his captive audience.

"Three people died last year!" the same girl yelled from her storefront, making Franka chuckle, even if she wasn't sure the story was true.

The girl glared at the tourists with a look usually reserved for finding a toenail in a perfectly decent slice of pizza, fixing the red fez hat that covered her golden hair like it was a nervous tick. Or she hated wearing it.

Her costume consisted of pale-pink harem pants that Franka was happy to know were called *dimije*, a white shirt, and a matching pink vest the same cultural class at her high school taught her was called *jeleče*.

For a second, their eyes met. Had Franka seen her before? A face that gorgeous was hard to forget. Full lips, straight nose, sun-kissed olive skin, and brown eyes carrying a look of rightful anger.

But Franka's train of thought was derailed as she and "her group" finally reached the bridge itself.

Built in the sixteenth century, destroyed in 1993, and rebuilt again in the 2000s, as the guide so kindly pointed out, it towered over the cold river like an oasis in the middle of a desert. It should have been so simple to rebuild, as it was just one arch, but it was anything but. Two forts on each side were there to watch over it. Almost a hundred feet long, the bridge was made of large blocks of white stone carved by hand, the same way they were hundreds of years ago. The surface was covered in sparkling white cobblestone, slippery from the morning dew, surrounded on both sides by a stone fence. Designed and built by some guy named Mimar (weird name, probably Turkish), the bridge really was something special. No wonder this was one of the symbols of the whole country.

Franka reached the top of the arch, leaned over a stone wall at the top of the bridge, and stared at the green river flowing over sixty-six feet below them—Neretva, the coldest river in the world.

Some people jumped from here! On purpose! For fun! And they have been doing it for centuries.

People of Herzegovina had no chill. Maybe chill couldn't grow on this harsh terrain.

If she stayed here long enough, she would probably see them perform their stunts sooner or later, as young guys would gather money from tourists who wanted to witness a dive, but Franka had no desire whatsoever to wait that long. What was the fun of jumping off a bridge and risking your life anyway?

Her wire-framed glasses threatened to fall into the abyss, so Franka returned to safety again. She barely needed them. Her prescription was tiny, but she liked them. They made her feel safe—another barrier between her and the world.

Leaning against the stone wall of the bridge that didn't seem like it could even be busted to begin with, Franka finished her ice cream. The tour guide rambled about the history of the bridge with the undying passion of a true *Mostarlija*, a denizen of Mostar.

But Franka made a promise last night: a selfie for Isabella. It was one of the most photographed places in the country, and the hipster part of Franka had deemed it basic, but her aunt would like to see her smile. Besides, today, Franka was a tourist.

So she did a stupid thing.

She nudged herself up and sat on the stone fence, guarded by the dark metal spikes (added later by the Austro-Hungarians, as the guide noted). After two years of hibernation, she was out of shape, but she was still strong enough to lift herself up with no hassle.

She took her phone from her pocket and turned on the camera.

The selfie view revealed how desperate she was for a break. Her blue-green eyes were perfectly complemented by the giant dark bags underneath them and the pale, greenish tint in her usually light-brown skin. Every strand of her wavy, black hair declared independence from one another, making her resemble a feral, scared cat. But nothing a few hours of extra sleep couldn't fix.

She would get them on the fifth of September, after her exam.

When she leaned back to get a good angle, an awful, screeching sound of metal breaking apart made it painfully obvious that what the shopkeeper girl was saying about the fence was true. But by that time, it was already too late.

Franka was falling from the Old Bridge.

The fall took less than three seconds. That is what they say, but it sure felt so much longer.

People had been seriously injured jumping from the bridge fully prepared, so for the first half second, Franka was sure she would die. She was falling backward; her spine would turn into mush from the strength of the impact if her heart didn't give up when she hit the ice-cold water.

In the next half second, her years of gymnastics training kicked in, along with one undeniable fact: she had an exam to take!

What was the best way to land? Headfirst? No, that would cause her brain damage, and then she would definitely flunk. Swallow dive, with her chest out and arms spread? No, that was a thing for professionals. She couldn't write if her arms were broken.

Feetfirst! That was the answer. Even if her tibia were smashed into minced meat, she could still hold a pen.

So, she rotated her body midair like she had done a thousand times before as the water below her came closer and closer.

And then it was over. Her feet hit the water surface like it was concrete, but she just kept going, deeper and deeper, until the blue surrounded her completely.

Chapter Two

Ostala je pusta bašća od jasmina

All that for a *jebeni* selfie.

Mirna would spend the rest of the day wondering why she did it. It was a stupid idea, but one moment, the black-haired girl was on the bridge, and the next she was gone. No one noticed. She didn't even have the decency to scream.

Only when Mirna sat on the large white stones of the riverbank, wrapped in a towel that didn't belong to her, did she finally realize what had happened.

After years of dreaming and practicing and arguing, Mirna Lakić had finally jumped off the Old Bridge.

As the adrenaline wore off, the image in her head came into focus: the feeling of the ice-cold river as she hit the water, barely remembering to keep her body as straight as possible and her buttocks firmly clenched, like she had done a million times on the practice board but never off the bridge; the girl struggling to keep her head above the water as the strong current pulled her under; the look in those blue-green eyes as Mirna finally dragged her to safety. She wasn't scared like one would expect from someone who was currently breathing only because of sheer dumb luck. No, the girl seemed full of life, just like Mirna was.

The ambulance came and took the uninjured girl, leaving Mirna to process what had happened.

"Go home, child. Get some rest," Grandpa told her, patting her on the back for a job well done. "I'll take over the store until your mom comes back," he promised. For once in her life, Mirna didn't argue.

However, when she got home, she didn't rest. She took a shower, put her wet clothes and the rest of the hamper load in the washing machine, and then changed the light bulb in the kitchen. Someone had to do it, and she was, as was so often the case, the best candidate for the job.

That same afternoon, she returned to the store because she couldn't make her mom leave work and potentially lose a client or let Grandpa work the whole day in the middle of the season, especially not when the adrenaline made her feel she could lift up the bridge herself. At least she didn't have to wear the costume as it was still drying, so she put on a yellow cotton dress and got to work.

It turned out that was the best decision she had made in a long time. In only a few hours, seemingly everyone in Mostar had heard what happened.

"Mirna, you queen!"

"Woo-hoo! Our swallow!"

"Proud of you!"

Praise rained down on her, and she soaked it all in. Everyone saw her rush over and jump off the bridge. She was a hero!

Not even working at the shop could ruin her mood. Everything was going too well for the sea of tourists to bother her, even if they were here for one day to say they saw the famous Old Bridge without understanding the city of Mostar.

Yes, come to our shop, Mostarske Džidže, and give your money to the Lakić family. Mirna needs college textbooks.

Thank Allah for clueless tourists.

"Franka has actually lived in Mostar for two years," Ado said, trying to kill her buzz as they sat in front of their store that same evening.

She finished recounting her courageous, yet ever so slightly embellished story of how she saw this poor, defenseless maiden fall and jumped to her rescue. It was all basically true, said with a little more dramatic flair. She may have added the detail of a vengeful spirit of Neretva grabbing her ankle and trying to drag her to the abyss. On the second of August, it was expected. A man with initials F. Č., age seventy-eight, actually did drown that day, but it was in the town of Konjic, so it really didn't count.

Ado brought her a box of her favorite cookies—long thin wafers with hazelnut filling—the best! "For bringing honor to the family because I sure as hell won't," he said, but he treated himself to half of it.

"You went to the same building for two years, you goof. Are you that unobservant? That girl attended the Unbounded High School. You know, the third floor of your own school?" he asked to rub in his superior observation skills even more.

Unbounded High School was a worldwide chain of schools that mostly rich or very smart kids attended. The branch in Mostar shared parts of the building with Mirna's regular public high school.

Since they declined Mirna's application two years ago (based on one teeny, tiny incident of breaking Izmir's nose), she was too pissed at their whole institution to notice their students when she ran into them. But come to think of it, she had a vague recollection of the black-haired, goth-adjacent girl occasionally walking down the same hallway as her.

"Her mom grew up here, but she moved to America before Franka was born. She's a teacher there too," he continued. "Her dad was, like, Hispanic or something."

"How do you even know all those things, you little *mahaluša*?" she asked him, rolling her eyes, but not surprised one bit because her brother was born to be a local gossip girl. And she wasn't that opposed to hearing his intel, for whatever reason.

"I get around," he simply said. "Now, excuse me, those lovely ladies from Belgrade might need my Old Bridge expertise," he added, fixed his hair, and left her to pester a new, unsuspecting group of tourists by pretending to be a world-renowned cliff diver.

Ado had never actually jumped off the bridge. He was too much of a coward to even look down from it on most days. But that did not stop him from going around in his swim briefs and with his hair wet from tap water and pretending he'd just jumped, but, oh, how unfortunate, they must have missed it.

The guys who actually jumped for a living usually tolerated him for three reasons:

a) He was like twelve (actually fifteen), and what were they gonna do? Beat up a tween?

b) He never took any money people would give to see a jump.

c) For the same reason they tolerated Mirna's involvement in the whole scene: Grandpa Džemal.

According to a reliable but unconfirmable source, the ever-present choir of the city gossip, Grandpa Džemal had made more jumps off the Old Bridge than anyone else. Mirna suspected at least twelve old men in Mostar had the same story, but only one of them was on Wikipedia, and it wasn't her grandpa. Still, he was a legend in diving circles, always there by the bridge, giving advice to everyone who tried to dive, even if he hadn't jumped in decades. His stories were the reason behind Mirna's unorthodox hobby.

She had been swimming and diving since she was old enough to keep her head above the surface. Her summers were spent mostly in water or on her way to it from the diving board. After a while, the guys she trained with accepted she was a girl and that if they continued to be jerks to her, she would either punch them or steal their girlfriends, depending on her mood. But if they wanted to see her dive on equal ground with them, the unofficial politics of this sport were not in her favor.

When she was seven and came back from the playground crying, when some boys told her she would never jump off the bridge because she was a girl, Grandpa made her a promise.

"If you train hard enough, one day you will be the first female competitor," he said. She'd wiped the snot off her face with her sleeve and looked up at him.

"Really?" she asked.

"Of course. I can tell. I'm a diving legend for a reason." And she never let it go. He, of all people, knew what he was talking about.

"Mirna, son, you did well," Grandpa told her when she came to take his place at the store that afternoon. He spent his days in retirement under the bridge, eating figs and talking to tourists. He would often help at the store (and was so much better at it than Mirna), but Mom didn't want him to work too hard in his old age. "Your landing could use some work, and you know it. When you jump on your feet, you need to disturb the water as little as possible, but you splashed us at the shore," he said, something she already knew.

"I was wearing *dimije*!" Mirna tried to argue. When it came to experts trying to teach her stuff, she was the "shut up and listen" kind of student, but this really wasn't fair.

"Well, that girl was dressed too, and she did a somersault midair and landed without a splash," he said, giving Mirna one of his cryptic smiles. Mirna attributed that observation to his old age. That girl couldn't even swim, for goodness' sake!

When Ado left her side, she sold a few more trinkets to the last remaining tourists. Mom was right. Her sales pitches really did work better when she actually smiled.

Before she could pack up the shop for the night, a man approached her. She knew him, of course. Everyone in Mostar did: Emir Kapo, a living legend.

A few years ago, he retired from competitive diving, at the ripe old age of twenty-nine, because he decided he had reached the peak and should now be in charge of the whole sport. He looked like he was a part of the Old Bridge come to life. Not exactly tall, as much as he was strong, like he could carry the whole city on his back. He had dark eyes, a buzz cut, and olive skin that he shared with Mirna and many other people on their side of the city. He appeared with the friendly smile he usually reserved for very important visitors, like celebrities and politicians who wanted to know more about bridge diving, so Mirna was caught off guard, especially given how their last conversation had gone.

Two weeks ago, the day Mirna turned eighteen, she marched up to him and told him she was going to dive off that bridge, even if she had to pay to do it. He laughed her off, and she said what her mom would describe as some unladylike things. Seeing him here with a smile on his face was a minor miracle.

"I've heard an extraordinary piece of gossip today," Emir said, looking at her, a bit playfully now. "A tourist fell off the bridge, and our Mirna jumped after her and saved her life. How peculiar!"

"You heard correctly," she said, unable to wipe the smug smile off her face.

"Amazing," he said, and Mirna knew he was being honest. This was the kind of thing that could go viral and promote bridge diving to even more people, and that was all he cared about. "I knew you, of all girls, had it in you." He probably thought he was giving her a compliment, so Mirna bit her tongue and kept smiling. "How did it feel?" he asked, moving around the cheap magnets that sold like *halva*. Mirna would have stopped anyone else as she had arranged them exactly how she wanted, but she needed him more than she needed order.

"You know. You do it all the time," she said, but now her smile was the real deal. She didn't want to tell him the whole truth of that feeling being the best she had ever felt in her life. For a few moments, she was unstoppable. But playing it cool worked best when dealing with these kinds of people.

"It's addicting, isn't it?" he asked. "How would you like to do it again?"

"Me? Poor little girly girl Mirna?" She let her snark come out for a moment.

The Old Bridge was home to two big cliff diving competitions. The first one was the famous Blue Stallion Cliff Diving World Series, which had divers from all over the world (including women!), held at the end of August, a few weeks from now.

The other one was what Mirna really cared about: the local championship, the one that had been happening for over 455 years. Officially, it began in 1968, but they all knew people had been diving from the bridge for as long as there had been a bridge. As soon as the bridge was rebuilt, the first thing they did was get someone to jump off. It was the Mostar way.

"Was one jump too much for you?" Emir asked, taunting her because he knew it would work.

She had been begging them to let her dive for years! Until this year, they had an excuse of her being a minor and needing parental permission (that her mom would never ever give), but now they had to go back to their real argument: girls simply could not dive.

That was, unless they were one of the professional cliff divers who compete every summer with the Blue Stallion World Series. They, of course, didn't count, because they were foreign? Here with the Blue Stallion? Mirna did not understand. A few local women did jump from time to time, but they never competed.

"She's a firefighter, Mirna! You are a twerp!" Emir brushed her off when she brought up a local woman who dove a few times.

"I think I'm just getting started here," she teased him back. "I plan to be a local legend. Emina, but way cooler." Emina was a real Mostar woman who was turned into a legend by a local poet, Aleksa Šantić, when he wrote a poem about her in 1902 that every single person in this country probably knew by heart.

"I'm in luck, then," he said with a chuckle. "And so are you. The competition has been moved to Saturday, but it works perfectly for the two of us. I know we haven't always seen eye to eye—What an understatement!—but how about you join us?" he asked. "You have been training all your life. I don't know of a better woman to represent us."

"Yes!" Mirna yelled, scaring off an elderly Asian couple who put down the snow globe with the Old Bridge inside it and slowly backed away. "One hundred times yes."

He smiled and squeezed her hand like he was trying to break her bones, but she returned the favor with the same amount of force.

"Okay, see you Saturday. Unless you have to work here?" he teased, like he didn't know Mirna would burn the store on a good day if it wasn't her family legacy, let alone for an opportunity like this.

So, on Friday, Mirna smiled at every single customer and didn't even mind wearing the costume. Hell, yeah, she was representing her culture! Her good mood resulted in fifteen euros worth of tips that she was, of course, allowed to pocket. Gym membership for September? Paid! In the afternoon, Mom came to take her place so she could practice, and Mirna all but floated from the bridge, took off her costume in one fast swoop to reveal the pink suit underneath, and went to the small jumping board next to the bridge to practice, landing everything perfectly. It was a great day to be Mirna Lakić.

But the downfall of the Mirna empire came on that warm Saturday that was supposed to be the best day of her life, and it came swiftly, but in three parts.

That morning, Mirna woke up at seven, ready to win this whole thing.

Jebeš ga, she would run for mayor after. And reunite the city. And make them have a city council again. Why not? She was on a roll!

"Mirna, love, I ironed that shirt that you like. The blue one. For the interview," Mom said. She peered into Mirna's room, where Mirna had laid out all her bathing suits on her neat bed and was choosing the right one to jump in. She'd bought most of them in thrift stores because she wasn't about to jump in a bikini, for goodness' sake. She chose the pink one last night, but maybe the black one looked more intimidating in the daylight? Or the yellow one?

"Yeah, yeah, thanks..." she mumbled. Or maybe the green one? It would offer her the most protection from the impact and, since she was going to jump a swallow, she needed all the protection she could get. "Wait! What interview?" she yelled, now chasing after Mom, who must have predicted Mirna's reaction as she was already hanging laundry to dry in the backyard. Some of it was theirs, but a lot was from some of the apartments she cleaned in her spare time. People who rented to tourists didn't usually feel like cleaning up after their temporary tenants, and that is where her mom would swoop in. That's why Mirna spent most of her summer in the store. Winter meant fewer tourists and less money, so like bears, they had to gather as much as they could now.

"The local TV station said they wanted to do a story about you and Franka," Mom said like it was something they had been talking about for days. "They are all coming here after the competition. It's not gonna take a long time. I promise."

"Mother, I did not agree to this!" Mirna insisted.

"But it will be so good for the store, love," she said like she wasn't aware that not one local ever bought a single thing from their store. "Come on, it will be so much fun."

"But Moooom..." Mirna whined, but a part of her knew she'd lost this battle before she had the chance to fight.

"And, if you agree, you will have my blessing to dive," Mom said, hanging the freshly washed sheets.

"I'm eighteen," Mirna reminded her. "I can drink, drive, and jump from wherever I want." This gave her mom a pause as she hung Ado's bright orange sneakers.

"Well, if you behave nicely, you don't have to wear the costume in the store," she said, finally making a foolproof argument after a few moments of contemplation.

Mirna really hated that costume. Not that there was anything wrong with traditional *dimije* pants or anything else, but they could only afford the cheap ones made from polyester that looked terrible on her and felt even worse against her skin.

She could not pass up the opportunity to get rid of the outfit by any means necessary. If she played her cards right, maybe she could burn them in a cleansing ritual to rid the city of their foul vibes.

"No gushing about me too much," Mirna finally said when she weighed her options.

"But we're so proud of you!" Mom said, when Mirna was halfway to her room, her mood already on a decline. "Also, while you're at it, check on the *japrak* please; we're having Franka over for dinner."

Japrak. No wonder this country was cursed for a thousand years for killing Franz Ferdinand and putting minced meat in grape leaves.

But Mirna would still compete with other divers. If one interview and *japrak* was all it took, she would take it with a smile on her face. She chose the green suit in the end. It reminded her of Neretva.

Before any jump, with the exception of accidental ones, divers were subjected to a medical examination to make sure they wouldn't fall dead upon impact. That was why most competitors poured cold water on themselves before the dives, trying to prevent a heart attack. Mirna would pass her examination, of course. She was into sports and healthy food. She would even cut down on stress once she started college and didn't have to work at the store anymore. Yes, pharmacology was a difficult field of study, but it didn't involve a single tourist, so what more could she ask for?

Like every test she ever took in her life, Mirna aced her medical examination.

"Healthy as a horse," the nurse told her, probably unaware how messed up horses actually were, medically speaking. Maybe she wasn't as much of a scholar of useless trivia as Mirna was.

It was very fortunate the examination ended when it did because if it had lasted for a few more minutes, Mirna would have failed it.

"There she is, our swallow!" a familiar voice yelled at her as a strong hand tapped her shoulder, with enough force to cause pain. But Mirna was used to hanging out with the boys, so she turned to face Emir, in his best swim shorts (one with the Old Bridge spanning both of his butt cheeks) as he would be doing the opening dive even if he wasn't competing.

Hiding in his shadow was a kid, maybe five years old, whom Mirna recognized as his son, obvious from the fact that they looked almost identical. But the kid, named Emil, because his ex-wife refused to name him Emir, kept staring at the ground and shifting in place like he would rather be anywhere else.

"Emil, one day, you'll compete here too. Isn't that right?" he asked, but Emil didn't answer him, rubbing the back of his neck instead. Emir shook his head in disappointment. Mirna tried to smile at the boy, but he was still staring at the ground.

"Are you excited?" Emir turned his attention back to her.

"*Normala*," she said in a fake casual tone, even if she was about to combust from pure, undiluted joy. "Ready to kick your assess."

The last part made him chuckle, but not in the "like hell you will" way, but more like she was an overconfident child who fundamentally misunderstood the state of the world. Without saying anything, he handed her the program. The pressure inside her rose at the sight of a thick line separating her name from the last contestant, Miloš Zokić, from Serbia, and labeling her as a show act.

"I thought I was competing," she said in the calmest tone of voice she was capable of. He laughed.

"Mirna, honey, you are a girl," he said. "A very strong one; one I admire, but you can't compete with us. You are a teen." He used the same voice he had when she was an actual twelve-year-old who wanted the same thing.

"So are most of the other contestants!" she insisted. The youngest person to dive was nine! It was before the War, on the old Old Bridge, when the concept of child safety was still sci-fi, but he did it, and he was fine afterward!

"It's different, and you know it," he tried not to say what they had all wanted to for years: it was all about her gender and nothing else.

"Are you scared I would win?" she taunted him now, playing with fire, and the derision ended exactly how she knew it would: with him flaring his nostrils and looking like he regretted ever giving this ungrateful snot-nosed teenage girl a chance.

"Look, it's either just a show dive or nothing," he said, without a trace of that lightheartedness from moments ago. "If you refuse me now, you will never dive off that bridge again. Not even your grandpa can change my mind. I guarantee you that. You want to jump again. I know that drive." He read the hunger in her eyes, and she hated him for it.

Mirna took a deep breath. That feeling of freedom was unlike anything she had ever felt. She wasn't scared of dying, or of the depth. She wanted Neretva to embrace her again. If this was what it took, she would have to swallow her pride. It didn't mean she would like it. But this was a big step forward. Maybe next year, they would let her compete.

"Okay, I'll do it," she said.

"That's our girl," Emir said in the most condescending tone of voice imaginable, making Mirna bite her tongue so she wouldn't punch him in the face. "And no swallows or head dives."

"Fine," she agreed, burying her great plans along with her triumphant good mood.

"Can't wait to see you there," he said and got lost in the crowd, his kid following, leaving Mirna to try to get her blood pressure back to normal.

Mostar was overwhelmed with so many people that a younger Mirna would often worry the bridge would collapse under their weight. This was the only day in the year she actually liked seeing swarms of tourists. They could see something amazing.

Still, this year was different. In between grumbling about the actual fifteen-year-old child competing today (not Ado even though Mom would have probably let *him*!) and realizing she was only allowed to jump today because the firefighter canceled at the last minute, she found herself looking through the crowd, trying to find someone. And she hated it.

That someone was also apparently interested in finding her. Before the competitions began, Franka politely asked her way through the crowd (and probably used her tiny size to squeeze through) until she popped up in front of Mirna's store, the final blow to her good mood.

She was as comically overdressed for the hot summer day as she had been before. Black sweatshirt with anime eyes on it and black jeans with a black bucket hat on. Her eyeliner was smeared on thick, without much artistic effort, like she was trying to look goth but ended up more like a panda.

"Hi! Mirna, right?" she asked, with a bit of an accent in her speech. Most foreigners spoke Bosnian like Croatian, Mirna concluded, even if she didn't understand why.

"Yeah," she said, trying to avoid eye contact.

"I'm Franka. And I wanted to thank you for what you did. You saved my life," she said. Mirna didn't want to mention that she wouldn't have drowned. Someone else would have saved her.

"Yeah, yeah, you're welcome," Mirna mumbled. She was never this flustered, for goodness' sake. So what if her eyes looked like Neretva? That was bullshit. She was just annoyed! That was it. Without saying anything else, Mirna turned around and left.

She needed to get in the zone. This was her chance. If not to compete, then to prove she was good enough. She wouldn't be the first woman to jump, far from it, but it was still a big deal.

Over the last few years, by pure chance, the generation of divers in Mostar switched, so most of the ones competing and training were pretty young. A few older guys in their late twenties or thirties were also there, but no one from Mostar came close to what Emir was doing in his peak. No wonder locals hadn't won in a while. They wouldn't win this year either. The competition from other cities was blowing them out of the water. Mirna watched enough competitions to be able to perfectly predict the results. One of the Montenegrins would win the swallow, while no one could come close to the feetfirst dive the competitor from Slovenia made. Well, maybe she could, but no one would let her, even if her dream was always the swallow. It was what Mostar was famous for.

She didn't want to mingle with other divers as she didn't feel like pretending she was her usual happy-go-lucky self, and if someone accused her of being on her period, she would have no choice but to drown them. It was the law.

In the crowd that gathered under the bridge, Franka stood out for her awful clothing choices and her brown skin. Mirna couldn't help but stare down, no matter how much she didn't want to.

"And now, please welcome the heroine of this great city, a young woman who jumped from the bridge to save a stranger, Mirela Lakić!" the announcer yelled, as they were done with the official competition and were waiting to crown the winner. (Later she learned Danilo Bulatović from Montenegro won gold for his swallow dive, while among the feetfirst divers, Boris Franko from Slovenia was the clear winner.)

It took Mirna a moment to realize they were calling her. No one had called her Mirela in a decade. She was always Mirna.

"Mirela is a member of our local diving club, and she has been training for most of her life. She is here to show us that girls can jump almost as well as the boys."

Mirna wasn't listening to him anymore. She climbed up over the fence and stared down at the Neretva River.

The crowd turned silent. Or maybe Mirna couldn't hear them anymore. It was her and the bridge.

Was Neretva always this far away?

No, Mirna, this is your Neretva. Jump and it will all be okay.

She took a deep breath and made the mistake of looking down at the crowd again. Franka was staring at her, with her hands covering her mouth in fear and excitement.

It all suddenly made sense. Later, she would be both yelled at and congratulated, often by the same people. Later, she would have to contend with a painful bruise on her shoulder from a terrible landing. Later, Emir would tell her she messed up their deal, and she could kiss diving goodbye.

But now, she spread out her arms and flew like a swallow.

The river embraced her like her own child.

Chapter Three

Neka ljubi se istok i zapad

Just like Franka's, Mirna's house was very nice. Once, a long time ago. But time, war, and probably a lack of money took their toll on both of them. Only traces of their intricate facades were left, leaving crumbling stone underneath, a sign of the times (and possibly bombings). That is where the similarities ended. Franka's house was an old mansion, built in the late 1880s, in the Austro-Hungarian style, while this house was a smaller, typical Ottoman home, probably even older. Still, this place felt lived in, filled with old family trinkets and smells of delicious food, in opposition to Franka's house that, even two years later, still looked vacant. Unlike the Garcias, the Lakić family obviously took great pride in their home.

Despite the ball of anxiety at least three feet high that followed her here, Franka found herself enjoying Mirna's garden a lot. It was, if nothing else, very green. Fig and pomegranate trees, with fruits on them close to being perfectly ripe, and grape and kiwi vines formed the green ceiling of their outside sitting area with a wooden table covered in a red-and-white checked tablecloth. She almost felt at home here. The mint juice Mirna's mom made was simply amazing.

If only the news crew wasn't here.

Franka had arrived before they did. She was here even before Mirna returned from her dive. The funny thing was that they lived a ten-minute walk from each other, but their paths never crossed, probably because Franka never left her house.

Mirna's mom opened the doors, visibly flustered but gleaming with pride. She was a short woman, probably a full head smaller than her daughter (still taller than Franka because everyone in this godforsaken country was a giant), plump, but with a kind, motherly face. Her light brown hair was tied up in a messy bun at the back of her head, and she wiped her callus-covered hands against her red apron.

"Welcome. To. Our. House. Franka," she said in very slow, very deliberate Bosnian, word by word, to make sure Franka understood her.

"*Hvala*," Franka simply answered with a smile. She may have been a shut-in mess for two years, but her dad would haunt her from above if she forgot her manners, so she handed Mrs. Emina a decorative paper bag with half a kilo of ground coffee, a box of sugar cubes, a liter of fruit juice on the expensive side, and a box of chocolates, as instructed by her mom who had some passing knowledge of the customs, no matter how American she pretended to be ("Towel! Do we put in a towel?" They chose not to because it seemed like a superfluous expense to Franka.). "My language skills have really improved. We can speak normally, but thank you for trying to make me feel welcome," she added as politely as possible, as Mirna's mom led her through their cozy house and into the backyard.

Before she could properly sit, a familiar teen was already by her side, now wearing a freshly pressed shirt, with his hair perfectly styled, and smelling like entirely too much cologne.

"I'm Ado. Remember me?" he asked as if anyone could forget him. He and Mirna looked quite alike, with their olive skin and brown eyes, but his hair was black, as opposed to his sister's golden waves, and he was almost a head shorter like his mom. "Mirna's far more awesome brother."

"Are you sure? She is the one who jumped a swallow from the Old Bridge," a familiar old man asked as he sat opposite Franka like he was about to interrogate her.

"Grandpa Džemal," Ado introduced the man who helped get her out of the river, with the tone of dismissal only a fifteen-year-old was capable of. "One of many, many old men who jumped from the tower next to the bridge, or won most competitions or whatever he claims that day."

Franka frowned at Ado's snark. Something about this man, even if he was pushing seventy, made her think he had done all those things and might do them again if he set his mind to it. Even if he didn't help save her life, Franka would have liked him, mostly because she always wanted a proper, nice grandpa of her own. She only had a few, vague memories of Grandpa Matej during the very early visits to Mostar, along with the distinct image of her mom, the first night after they moved here, burning every single photo of him in a fireplace when she thought Franka was asleep.

"Don't mind my grandson," Džemal said, brushing him off. "I know who I am and what I did. But tell me, child, is Franka perhaps short for Fikreta?" he asked, making Franka snort through her nose and almost choke on air.

"Are you asking me about my nationality? If so, my mom is a Croat." Franka knew there was no way in hell anyone in Herzegovina, or Bosnia for that matter, would think Franka, a very Croatian name, was short for Fikreta, an extremely Bosnian one, so she didn't exactly tense up at Grandpa Džemal's inquiry—the man was being snarky—but it wasn't comfortable. The awareness that one could only belong to one of the two sides of the city, and that one's name was the determining factor in deciding which one, made her insides twist into a coil. To her, they all looked the same. She was the only one who stood out. Her Croat mom made her an outsider with the Bosnians, while a small and very radical percentage of Croats on "their side of the city" considered dark skin (or to be more accurate *olive complexion* because all of these people were still very Caucasian!) to be typical for Muslims because they "interbreed" with the Turks. Thank God, that was one cultural thing she knew all about, so she only had to google the pop culture giants such as Moomins the cartoon and Brena the singer if she wanted to follow a basic conversation. "I hope that's okay."

Franka didn't grow up in Bosnia or in Mostar. To her, War was what her mom fled thirty years ago and not something related to her. It really was terrible, a tragedy, but not her own. It was a selfish way of thinking, but the whole history here was so messy and complex that she couldn't wrap her distinctly American mind around it. She wasn't much more Colombian either, even if she knew the language. Dad's side of the family was here for longer, so they lost a part of their culture and became mostly American, like Franka. As a child of two immigrants from vastly different parts of the world, that was the easiest thing to be. But pretending she didn't know what Džemal was talking about was stupid. Of course, she knew. Two sides were at war and even if the fighting stopped, the divide between them never disappeared. To some people, it really did matter if she was Franka, the Croat, or Fikreta, the Bosnian. But judging by the warm and welcoming smile on his face, Džemal wasn't one of them.

"It's more than okay!" another voice yelled, this one female and completely new. "It's going to make our story so much more special!"

The TV crew consisted of a smiling, larger-than-life hostess, with chestnut brown hair styled into a smooth bob and long, dark red nails that should have qualified as a weapon, and her cameraman, who might have been recently dug out from under a *stećak* tombstone where he probably wished to remain.

"Bisera," the hostess introduced herself, shaking Franka's hand with unnecessary vigor. "It's so nice to finally meet you."

"Likewise," Franka lied. She was mostly here to appease her mom and to try to figure out how on earth she was still alive. It really was a miracle.

When she had fallen and finally reached the river, the water had been unlike anything she had felt before.

Every nerve ending in her body had been on fire with cold, like she had landed in liquid nitrogen.

Franka had suddenly remembered she was a terrible swimmer. She might have survived the fall, but Neretva always took what belonged to her. She was still conscious, but her pathetic swimming moves were no match for the strong currents of the river that began to drag her under. Her soaked clothes made her too heavy to float on her own. Her lungs began to fill with water because she couldn't keep her head above the surface.

But she wouldn't drown.

"*Jebo ti selfie mater!*" a female voice yelled at her as a strong hand grabbed her shoulder and began to drag her to the shore.

The panic subsided and Franka stopped struggling and let what must have been a foul-mouthed Vila, the forest fairy, take her to safety. She had a basic knowledge of Balkan swear words, but she was in near-constant awe of how creative they could be with the different combinations of the F-word and many different subjects it could be used on. This one, encouraging a selfie to do inappropriate things with her mom, was a particularly juicy example.

"Are you okay?" her rescuer asked in much calmer English as she placed Franka on the nearest rock that stuck out of the water down the stream from the bridge, while she stayed in the river.

"*Jesam, jesam,*" Franka said, confirming her "okay-ness" in Croatian to make it obvious she understood her. Her heart beat so fast against her wet clothes she expected to start panicking, but instead, she only felt more alive than she had in years as the cold water washed away any traces of exhaustion from her body.

Her rescuer was the tall young woman, still wearing the cheaply made *jeleče* vest and *dimije*, but her fez must have been on its way to the Adriatic Sea, along with Franka's glasses.

She stared at her like she was a strange beast before their eyes met, and then she suddenly looked away from Franka.

By that time, a small rubber boat that did the rounds for tourists finally reached them, as this part of the river wasn't accessible by shore.

"Mirna, is she alive?" the captain asked in Bosnian. Franka was now trying to sit up on the shore, but wet clothes that weighed a ton made it so much harder. Maybe baggy, oversized shirts had their downsides.

"Alive, but a fool," Mirna said, glaring at Franka, even if she now knew Franka spoke the language. Without asking her, Mirna picked her up like she was a toddler and put her in the boat, but Franka didn't object, because she was pretty sure she was too flabbergasted by the last few minutes to get in on her own.

"Did you... Did you jump after her?" the man asked, looking at Mirna who now sported a smile that encompassed her entire face and at least half of the Old Town. The look of pure joy suited her much better than the murderous frown she had back at the bridge. This was the true Mirna, in all her beauty and glory.

"It was amazing!" she yelled.

Later, as Franka waited for the ambulance she insisted she didn't need, wrapped up in a blanket and sipping hot tea from a local coffee shop, she had to agree with Mirna.

It really was amazing.

Mom picked her up from the ER not even half an hour later, bringing a change of dry clothes and crying and apologizing. For what, Franka wasn't sure, but she still hugged her back as hard as she could. They all remembered the similar phone call that had brought much worse news two and a half years ago.

Franka couldn't get herself to study. She could barely talk for most of the day, so they stared at the TV screen in their living room as reruns of some local sitcom about a wacky family played without either of them paying much attention to it. They ordered takeout chicken sandwiches that Franka barely touched, prompting Mom to offer to take her to the ER again. But Franka was fine. She was more than fine, really. She was alive again. She wasn't sure how to deal with that particular sensation. Suddenly, the drowsiness that followed her since they got here was gone, and she was finally awake.

In the evening, someone knocked on their door. Kids did that from time to time, because this house, like many in the neighborhood, was abandoned for a long time, and they still hadn't gotten the whole garden thing under control, so it presented a challenge for the younglings to prove their bravery. Still, the kid standing in front of her was too old for such childish games.

"I'm Adnan, but everyone calls me Ado. Nice to meet you," he said, shaking her hand before she could object. "I'm the brother of the girl who saved you."

"Mirna! Is she safe?" Franka yelled. She didn't even get to thank her when they reached the riverbank. Mom wouldn't let her out today to try to find her or learn anything about her except her name.

"She has been looking for an excuse to jump off that bridge for a decade. I think you might now be her best friend for providing her with one," he said. "Anyway, since your phone is currently polluting our lovely river, our mom sent me to find you and to invite you over for lunch at our place on Saturday. Mirna will dive off the bridge again—she just told us—and a local TV station wants to interview you two."

"But..." Franka was about to refuse him, citing her inevitable and crucial date with her math workbook, before Mom ran to the door.

"She accepts. She accepts!" she yelled before Franka could say anything.

So what could Franka do but sit in her room the whole Friday and study her ass off to make up for the two whole days she took off? Still, it was different this time. The "Uvod u Organsku Kemiju" textbook finally made sense to her. She understood it—in English, Croatian, Bosnian, Serbian, even Spanish. She really did know this.

Franka didn't drown in Neretva on that second of August, but something else had: her self-doubt. She would crush this interview, and she would crush that exam. She had spent years paralyzed in fear. Fear of failure, fear of talking and embarrassing herself, fear of taking any sort of risk. And even now, as she spoke to Mirna's family, she talked slower, feeling the discomfort of being around so many strangers creeping up from behind her, but for the first time in a long while, she didn't let fear consume her. Maybe she wouldn't have the strength to fight it off like this again tomorrow, but right now, it was a victory she wouldn't trade for anything.

In Mirna's garden, her mom offered them all juice and coffee which Bisera refused, but Franka was more than happy to accept as they waited for Mirna. She could never say no to free food or drinks.

"She got a bit swept up in the crowd," Ado assured them, reading the message she sent, apologizing for her absence. "She can't say no to people congratulating her."

"Our Mirna is very charming when she wants to be," her mom said as she poured more pomegranate juice into a cup for Franka who drank it all way too fast to be subtle about how much she loved it. It was even better than the mint one.

"Except with the tourists," Džemal said, making Franka smile at the thought of Mirna in her costume.

"Best student in her generation," her mom said like she didn't hear Džemal's words. "She would have been a valedictorian..."

"If she hadn't punched a dude," Ado finished her sentence, sounding impressed with his sister for the first time, before his mom gave him a look only a mother could give. He smiled and shut up.

Come to think of it, Franka had seen her before. A girl like Mirna, tall, blonde, objectively gorgeous, and friendly with everyone was hard to miss.

She would see her in their joint STEM labs from time to time, chasing every extracurricular under the sun, but Franka had paid little attention to her. After two years, she barely knew the people she went to class with either. Most of them were foreign, here to attend the fancy international school. Some were like her, but a lot of them were children of rich and famous people (an heir of a big candy empire asked her on a date but she refused), and they lived in dorms together. Franka was spared from that horrible fate by her house which was like five minutes from the school and her mom being a teacher. She kept her grades at the minimum that wouldn't make her a target of forced tutoring and kept to herself whenever possible. She didn't want to make friends in this godforsaken city anyway. Most of them had left Mostar already to start their new lives somewhere better or return to their old ones. But Franka remained.

They were silent for a few moments as the half-dead cameraman set up his equipment. Without warning, Bisera approached Franka, smiled like only a middle-aged white woman could, and removed her hat.

"Much better," she said in her sweetest voice because she knew she was being rude. "Oh, my, what lovely eyes you have," she added. Franka smiled back at her, even if internally she screamed for justice. Yes, the hat was stupid, but it made her feel safe, goddamn it.

Sounds of footsteps from the house alerted them all to the presence of another person before Franka had the chance to freak out.

For a few moments, before she noticed everything that was happening in her garden, Mirna's flared nostrils and glare full of hatred for the world made it obvious she was ready to send everything *u tri lijepe* and call the whole thing off. When her eyes met Franka's, she scrunched up her face into a grimace like she'd encountered a particularly nasty bug. Still, the next moment, she was back to the same smiling young woman Franka expected her to be.

"And there she is, our hero of the day, our Swallow of Mostar!" Bisera said, as she got up and ran to Mirna, who kissed her on both cheeks like they knew each other for a long time, even if they'd just met. "Your dive today was really something special! We can't wait to hear more about it."

"Thank you," Mirna said as her smile returned to her most charming one. Her voice was casual but confident like she had done this a million times before. "We are so honored you chose to tell our story. It's a very important one. This city is too divided. We all know it. We young people must bring it back together."

She sounded so cool and self-assured that Franka's heart began to beat faster. That feeling was familiar from before, but she hadn't felt it in a long time: competitiveness.

This was a battle of wits and charm from now on. Whether Mirna liked to or not, it was on.

Bisera sat them down behind an old wooden table in the most picturesque part of the garden, next to each other, and chased everyone else away. It was just the two of them and the electricity in the air Franka hadn't felt in years.

Even so, Franka caught a glimpse of grandpa Džemal, who obviously decided this to be the perfect time to work on the garden, pruning shears in his hand, an expression of a man who was trying very hard not to be noticed on his face. Franka had no doubt Ado was hiding behind some plant or listening to the conversation from the open windows of the house.

"I will ask you many questions, and you can answer however you like. Take your time. We won't use everything, of course, but the more, the better," Bisera said. "We really want to show you off as an example to people of your generation. They need to see how unified we can be if we only try, despite our differences. That is the main angle of our story here. Can you do that for me?"

"Of course," Franka said, with her most charming smile.

"No problem. We will be speaking the truth," Mirna added, turning to face Franka, a purposeful challenge.

"Is it okay if we use the footage of your dive today?" Bisera asked, seemingly oblivious to the real extent of the scene playing out in front of her.

Mirna's smile went back to the fake one for a few moments. It was really easy to spot her eyes turning cold in an instant if one paid attention, which Bisera did not.

"Of course," Mirna said in her most polite tone, even if she still looked like she would rather burn the whole TV station to the ground.

"Mirela Lakić, a perfect grade point average student, recently graduated from Mostar High School, and a freshman-to-be at the Pharmacology Faculty at the Džemal Bijedić University," Bisera announced what she had researched (or maybe the whole of Mostar knew already) as the camera began to roll.

Franka had to stop herself from glaring at Mirna in complete awe. Golden child, of course. And they were studying the same thing. Or, they would be, once Franka passed her entrance exam.

One point in Mirna's favor. Despite her last two years of high school being in English, and not to mention her mom working there, Franka still barely passed the exams. It turned out that one needs to either open a book or at least not spend their classes doodling on their notebooks if one wants to absorb any information. When she had finally gotten serious this spring, it had been far too late.

"Please, it's Mirna," she said. "That's what everyone calls me. They kept telling me to be calm so much that it became my name," she revealed with a scientifically proven perfect chuckle. Yes, Mirna means calm, even if it's pronounced differently, Franka reminded herself, still in awe of how skillfully Mirna talked to that camera.

Now, it was time for Franka to use the knowledge from those few debate team meetings she attended back in Atlanta.

"How come you moved to Mostar from America? Isn't it usually the other way around?" Bisera asked her with a chuckle at her own joke.

"My mom was born here, and Mostar has always been a second home to us," Franka lied with her best smile. "When she got a job at the Unbounded High School and our family house was standing unused, it made the most sense for us to come back to the city she grew up in," Franka simply said. It was a true story but condensed as hell.

They wanted to stay, both of them. Despite all the shortcomings of "the greatest country in the world," they'd built a life there. Franka wasn't always the hermit with bad grades Mostar had turned her into. She was a great student with lots of friends, people she liked, gymnastics practices, Isabella; everything she needed. And most importantly, she still had her dad.

But after he was gone, his medical bills stacked up, and they lost their house. As tragedy always struck more than once, Mom lost her job. But someone Mom grew up with offered her a teaching position at a prestigious private high school in Mostar, a city Franka had visited only a few times, and only for a few weeks in total. They had a house here too. No one had lived there since her grandma died a decade ago. But it was still in decent condition. When choosing between imminent homelessness and spending their last cash on a plane ticket, Mom knew what she had to do. The rational part of Franka didn't blame her for it. Dad would have done the same thing. But the rest of her couldn't help but be overwhelmed with resentment for having to live in this small, conservative, shitty town where no one was her friend.

Still, not a single one of those things was Bisera's business, so Franka gave her all she could, then turned the conversation in a direction that would make her look better.

"When I came here, the language barrier might as well have been impenetrable. I'm fluent in Spanish, like my dad, but I only knew basic Croatian, so

I had to learn the language almost from scratch. While it was very difficult, I think I finally got it," she said, holding her head up high. Every single word was perfectly pronounced and every case was correct.

Dad always wanted her to learn Croatian like she had learned Spanish from him. He signed her up for cultural classes and made her interact with her cousins in Croatian when they were here. But Mom never spoke it around the house, hating the sound of it, so Franka didn't have a chance to learn it well. While many US cities had a substantial ex-Yugoslavian diaspora she could interact with, Atlanta wasn't one of them, and Franka suspected that's how her mom liked it.

"You most certainly have," Bisera said in an equally charming tone of voice. "Mirna, you have been cliff diving all your life; is that correct?" She switched her focus again. Mirna nodded her golden head.

"Yes," she said. "I have been with the diving team ever since they let me. My mom is worried, of course, especially since our store Mostarske Džidže is right next to the bridge, but like my granddad before me, my love for Neretva was greater than any fear."

"Were you scared when you jumped after Franka?" Bisera asked. Mirna looked directly into the camera.

"I didn't have time to be scared. I saw someone who needed help. I would do it all again if the situation was the same," Mirna answered like she was reading off a script.

"How brave of you," Bisera said, but Mirna smiled.

"It's not bravery per se," she said. "Only a simple desire to do unto others as you wish to be done unto you. That is from the Bible, correct? We can all learn things from one another. It is only together that we can move forward."

She turned to face Franka and continued smiling, even smugger than before. She won this round, even Franka had to admit that.

"Franka, was that your first time diving?" Bisera switched her attention.

"Yes. I don't make a habit of falling off national monuments of any country," Franka said with a chuckle that sounded ten times as forced as Mirna's was.

"And yet, the witnesses said you did a somersault in the air and landed like a pro?" she asked. The very subtle change on Mirna's face from a genuine smile to a fake one fed Franka's ego through the next statement.

"Probably because I've done gymnastics for four years back in Georgia. In gymnastics, like in diving, you need to land well or you will crack your neck. My muscle memory took over and saved my life. Along with Mirna, of course," she added, turning to her right and smiling at Mirna who was courteous enough to return the smile. "I'm a terrible swimmer, but she saved my life, and for that, she has my eternal gratitude." And she still had an exam to take. She couldn't die. Not until she earned her degree. "She didn't know if I was Bosnian or Croatian, Serbian, or American or Colombian. She just did the right thing," Franka said. "One day, I hope I can pass the same kindness to others." She took one quicker glance at Mirna and decided to go for it. She might not win this "whatever the non-phallic version of a dick-measuring contest was," but it didn't mean she couldn't make a few blows to her opponent.

"I hope the two of us can be an example for other people our age. Don't let the bridge be a dividing line between Croats and the Bosnian. We've lived together in this city for centuries, and we have to come together again. That is our only way forward," Franka said in her politician voice. If Mirna could spin the whole "unification narrative," so could Franka. If this is what they were after, it was exactly what they would get.

"Do you think you will stay in touch?" Bisera asked.

Her brain working overtime like it hasn't in years, Franka put her hand over Mirna's shoulder. Mirna's gleaming smile dissipated for a moment, replaced by a wince like Franka was poison to her. Still, the next moment, the smile was back. Mirna upped her game and pulled her into a hug, making Bisera say, "Aw" and setting every single nerve ending in Franka's body on fire with the unexpectedness of her gesture.

"I think this is the beginning of a great friendship!" Mirna said.

Franka knew Mirna probably never wanted to see her again. She was the stupid American who fell off the bridge for a selfie. Mirna probably jumped to make herself the hero. After this dinner, they might see each other in passing sometimes, but they would go right back to being strangers. Still, Franka wouldn't deny herself the fun of this one conversation.

"Franka, a bit of an unorthodox question for the end, but I'm sure our audience would love to know: Despite how it happened the first time, would you ever dive off the bridge again?"

Franka didn't answer her right away.

At the forefront of her mind was a vision of Mirna, in her green wetsuit that hugged the contours of her inhumanly perfect body. She stood at the ledge of the bridge, ignoring the world. It was just her and the river.

The next moment, Mirna was flying, like the inevitable downward trajectory of her dive would somehow miss her and she would soar high over the river and straight to the sun. Franka finally understood why they called it a swallow dive.

Mirna was a bird: the Swallow of Mostar.

The crowd was quiet for a few moments as she hit the cold water. A few seconds later, she swam out, smiling as she climbed up into the boat they sent out for her, even though she could have swum to the shore easily. She raised her left hand in triumph and yelled, "Thank you, everyone!"

Even though she almost drowned, Franka would give anything to dive off that bridge again! She wanted to be that swallow too. She hadn't felt so alive in years! Adrenaline was her drug of choice, and she was chasing that high again.

"Yes, I would love to dive again," she said. "In some better, more controlled circumstances," she added with a small smile, trying to hide that her heart was now beating so hard at the mere thought of a do-over. "That fall was one of the most exhilarating experiences of my life."

"Great!" Grandpa Džemal yelled. "Mirna, you have a new student!"

Chapter Four

Go u gostima

"Yes, I would love to dive again," Franka had said in answer to Bisera's question, and for the first time, her words weren't part of the game they were playing. Mirna tilted her head as she stared at her, speechless for the first time since this conversation started. Franka's words sounded like they might as well have been her own. "In some better, more controlled circumstances. That fall was one of the most exhilarating experiences of my life."

"Great!" Grandpa Džemal said, springing out of nowhere as only an old man could. "Mirna, you have a new student!"

"WHAT?" Mirna had yelled, breaking all the pretenses of the golden child she had been trying to maintain for so long.

Grandpa had been silently lurking behind the cameraman, all but invisible until he decided to wreck the image Mirna had been trying so hard to present.

She should have brushed Franka's comment off with a smile. For anyone else, she probably would have, but something about this girl made her throw all composure out the window. Maybe because she was American.

Apparently forgetting he was interrupting the interview, Grandpa said, "If both you and Franka want to dive again, I don't see why you couldn't work together. Under my supervision, of course." His eyes were full of excitement like he was a little kid who had a brilliant idea of how to create an infinite supply of chocolate. "You have years of hard work, and she has natural talent. It's a God-given combination."

For years, she had begged him to teach her what he did! He made his last dive before the War, on the old Old Bridge, but she could still learn so much from him if only he wanted her to. He taught her to swim when she was a kid and helped her become one of the best swimmers in the city, but when it came to diving, other than a few vague tidbits, he kept his techniques a secret like it was alchemy, not bridge diving.

"You have to discover how to do it on your own," he would always say, but that clashed so much with Mirna's science-oriented mind. If any of them wanted

35

to get better and make sure this sport outlived all of them, they had to improve on what those before them did. That was the scientific method; standing on the shoulders of giants, and whatnot.

And now he wanted to train this little girl who couldn't even swim? Bullshit!

"No way, not a chance!" Mirna said, too loudly, like she always did when her temper got the better of her. She tried to keep it under control, but she would fail too often.

The sound of Mirna's voice attracted Mom, who came out of the house in her apron and gave her that "not now, sweetie" look that never, ever worked.

"Okay, I think we have everything we need here," Bisera interrupted, her perfectly styled eyebrows raised and her mouth slightly open in disbelief. "Srećko, are you ready?" The cameraman nodded and gathered his equipment at an ungodly speed. "It was nice meeting you, girls. Thanks for the story. I hope we do another one soon." In an instant, they were both gone, probably afraid Mirna might literally blow up and take them with her.

"Dinner is ready," Mom said in her sweetest voice before Mirna could lose it again. "Mirna, love, I made *ičija* pie too. I know you hate *japrak*. Come on, we don't want it to get cold."

Mirna took a deep breath and moved from the garden table. If nothing else, she had to at least try not to upset her mom, even if she was pretty certain she would fail. Franka remained, rubbing her neck and frowning, too shell-shocked by whatever had happened to move.

"Come on, let's eat," Mirna said in as much of a monotone as she could muster. She didn't want to look at her, so she focused all of her attention on the patch of grass that sprung from between the cracks of the cobblestone.

"In this house, when Mom says it's dinner, we eat. Together," said Ado, who, as per usual, was summoned by whatever sounded like a possibly interesting gossip. He offered Franka a hand, wearing his smuggest smile, and Franka accepted it.

They ate in the living room. The Lakić home wasn't one of those American houses with way too many rooms, so they had to make do. On most days, Mirna liked her house with its creaky floors and slightly too low ceilings designed for her much shorter ancestors. It was filled with history, just like their store next to the bridge. Long gone were the days they were a wealthy merchant family. Three wars made sure of that, but this was still her home.

Now, it might as well have been a wooden box. She tried to calm down, rationalize everything that was happening, and come up with some solid arguments about why it was a bad idea, but her mind had as many whirlpools as Neretva did.

Mom made bey's soup, a lovely white, thick stew with chicken, okra, potatoes, and so much veggie, one of Mirna's favorite dishes. Mirna prepped the vegetables last night. She didn't want her mom to overwork herself, but Emina Lakić was a typical Bosnian woman who didn't know how to stop, especially when she had guests.

"She can't even swim!" Mirna said, as they all sat at the table and dug in. She glared at Grandpa, ignoring those piercing green eyes staring at her. The soup was sadly delicious, even if Mirna could barely hold the spoon with her right hand. *My kingdom for an ice pack!* She took a deep breath and transferred all the anger at herself for her shitty dive into this situation, certain it would somehow, in some way, ease the pain.

"Neither could you, but I taught you myself and look at you now," Grandpa said, still too calm for a man from Herzegovina, slowly eating his soup, very much enjoying himself. "You would teach her those basic things. And after she's ready, I would help you both improve your technique. By next year, I guarantee you will be better than any of the guys who jumped today."

"And she's out of shape!" Mirna said, pretending she didn't hear a word he said.

Mom glared at her for being rude, but Franka didn't say a thing. She ate her amazing soup in silence like this had nothing to do with her.

"Like that can't be changed," Grandpa scoffed. "Weren't you complaining you didn't have anyone to go to the gym with you?"

As a matter of fact, she had been. Mirna loved exercising, the feeling of endorphins taking over her body that got stronger with each push-up she did. It made her heart pump and her mind feel stronger. She could take out all her frustrations about every single snobby tourist or sexist douche on those poor punching bags. But only weeks out of high school, her friend group was falling apart. That's what she got for being friends with everyone, but no one's best friend. Some were already in other cities, while others were on vacation. Selma was in Mostar and free, but she made it explicitly clear she would only run if, Allah forbid, someone chased her.

The guys from the diving club weren't much better either. In theory, she was "one of the guys," but the practice was a whole different story. Ever since they started diving, she was left behind, too stubborn to give up or join the swim team, more appropriate for a girl, because she had to believe she would eventually be allowed to compete. Otherwise, her efforts would have all been for nothing. All the practices, all the study of the technique, even that time she punched Izmir and lost a chance at a scholarship that would have changed her life. No one dared to say a mean thing to her, especially not after that, but she could read the room, and she wasn't welcome in it.

Instead of dwelling on the injustices of the world, she would go to the gym alone, with her headphones on, listening to the kind of music no one could ever know she listened to, pretending that was how she liked it.

She allowed herself one quick glance at Franka, who now stared at her plate like it was the most amazing thing in existence. She said she trained in gymnastics for a while, right? That would imply at least some basis for athleticism. Maybe she could do it all again if she wanted to.

Still, Mirna stayed silent and focused on her meal, before Mom could kill her for being rude, which she objectively was. She wasn't even close to done being rude and upsetting her mom, but she had to pace herself.

After the soup was gone, Mirna helped Mom serve the main course. *Japrak* was as awful as it ever was, but *ičija* pie, made of chicken and crusts of crunchy dough dipped in broth, was awesome.

"Okay, how about this? Train her until next year and I will make sure both of you can compete," Grandpa said, disturbing the uncomfortable silence that could only be replaced with argument. Mirna scoffed and stabbed her pie with a fork like it was to blame for today.

"If you assassinate Emir Kapo and replace him with someone who doesn't personally hold a grudge against me, then maybe," she said.

He was the reason she was late to the interview and the family dinner. As soon as she was done with the dive, she had tried to get away from the crowd. Her shoulder was already starting to hurt and she couldn't let them see anything was wrong, but she hadn't been fast enough to escape.

"I told you to dive feet first."

Emir's voice hurt almost as much as her shoulder did. He came up behind her, nostrils flared, eyes cold and full of fury. A few feet behind him was Emil, his eyes wide, and for a moment, Mirna forgot to feel bad for herself and instead pitied that little kid who had to live up to the great Emir Kapo one day, whether he wanted to or not.

"Well, I didn't listen to you," she said, to say something, even if she had no excuses or any way to defend herself. She had gotten too cocky and confident in her skills. She'd practiced the dive a million times, but it was different from such a height, especially when she wasn't thinking clearly. Now she would pay for it. It was just that simple.

"You stubborn child," he continued. "Others didn't notice how much you messed up your landing, but I did. How badly did you hurt yourself?"

"I'm fine," she insisted. Not even for all the money and fortune in the world would she confess to him that even the feel of her wet suit against her upper torso was painful. Of course, he noticed. He was a legend for a reason. But that didn't mean she would confirm his suspicions of her weakness.

"That's what happens when you don't listen! If you were seriously injured, you would have ruined the whole competition for everyone," he said. "I never should have let you dive. You are not good enough. And you never will be. Emil could have done a better job than you!" he yelled. Behind him, the kid shook his head no, but thankfully Emir didn't see him. "For as long as I'm in charge, you will never, ever dive off that bridge again. You had your chance and you blew it." He didn't say anything else, turned back, and disappeared into the crowd, followed by Emil.

She knew that would happen; of course, she did. But even if it was the most perfect landing anyone had ever seen, she had still disobeyed his orders. Emir was a true Herzegovinian, stubborn to his core. Unless a miracle happened, she would never dive off that bridge again.

"Believe in me," Grandpa promised, but Mirna shook her head, not wanting to even entertain the idea.

"You are not the problem here, Grandpa," she said. "Mr. Kapo is. I don't think he'll allow me to compete while he makes the decisions. I won't waste my time on this for such a promise," she said, even if it hurt to admit more than her shoulder did. "School is starting soon, and Mom needs help at the store until then."

A pragmatic argument—that would work. Mirna rarely worked at the store during the school year. Mom had fewer cleaning gigs and when she did, Grandpa could cover for her. Mirna's job was to focus on school, but as much as she complained, she couldn't let her mom work herself half to death when she could help in some way. She was the eldest, and she had to do her part to keep the family going.

"What if I promised you will never have to work in that store again?" Grandpa asked, making Mirna stop in her tracks.

No store! Ever again! Freedom from haggling tourists who didn't mind paying thousands to get to Bosnia but drew the line at three-euro novelty cups. Freedom from screaming toddlers and prima donnas of all genders who thought a ten-minute walk around Old Town was too much of a hassle. Freedom from jerks who tried to pick her up with jokes as old as the bridge.

But that was impossible. Mom really did need her help, at least during summer. As much as Mirna hated working at Džidže with the passion of a thousand flaming suns, she would never quit. With her dad in Germany for most of the year, Mirna had to step up and make sure Mom didn't have to raise two kids and work two jobs on her own. If Mirna needed to work at the store, she would. If she had to attend college in Mostar instead of Sarajevo because the money was tight, that was what she would do. Good grades, good behavior, selling useless crap to tourists, cooking, cleaning, fixing everything around the house (or calling someone if she didn't know how), making sure Ado didn't oversleep and miss school, and everything else that was needed was her job, by her own choice. She might complain about it, but she would never let it all fall on her mom.

"You can't do it," Mirna said. "You can't work full time instead of me. Mom won't let you work that much." Mom nodded in agreement. He was old, and a man, so it was better to have Mirna do it.

"But she *will* let me," Ado said. He stood up in front of her, like a brave knight or a very proud peacock—it was hard to tell the difference—but Mirna scoffed at the idea.

"You?" she asked. "Mom won't let you. I've asked her a million times to have you help out." Younger child privileges, Mirna understood. It wasn't fair—that was for sure—but "pwecious wittle Ado" could not be asked to help or to clean up after himself. Still, Mom didn't react with outright rejection, like Mirna expected. Instead, Mom chewed her piece of *japrak*, staring at the discussion in front of her with great interest.

"You know I can get her to agree. I'm her dad," Grandpa said. "Isn't that right, Emina? You know it's a great idea. You have been worried that Mirna was working too much, right?" he asked. Mom's expression didn't change at all as she put one more *japrak* on Franka's plate.

"And you want to work at the store?" Mirna asked Ado. He nodded, with the purest, yet the most punchable smile on his face, like this was the best day of his life.

"It is my dream come true!" he said. "I get to talk to cute tourists all day and earn a little extra cash. I will bring us profit, Mirna. We're gonna be millionaires!" he promised, making Mirna believe, if only for a moment, that he could pull it off.

How long had they been planning this? Since she jumped after Franka? Or was Ado trying to find an excuse to play dress-up and show the whole family he was "on that grind" or "hustling" or "a sigma male" or whatever he learned on the internet that week. Maybe that's why he'd spent the whole summer so far at the bridge, talking to the tourists and advertising the store.

"What do you say, Mom?" Ado asked. Mom gave him a long and hard look, her eyes narrow and full of suspicion.

"Aren't you—" she began, but Ado cut her off.

"Too young? Mirna was younger when she started working. Not cut out for this job? Which one of us is in trade school for tourism?" he asked. "And do you really think I can be much worse than she was? Just because I'm a guy doesn't mean you need to shield me from work other than, like, chopping wood. I want to help," he insisted.

Mirna didn't want to remind him that last year she was the one who chopped most of the wood for the winter. Instead, she smiled at him. Deep down, he really was a good kid, and she knew he would be pretty good at the job. Or at least better than Mirna, which in all honesty wasn't a high bar to clear. But Mom was raised by her mother to think that men are both to be listened to and that they were kinda useless and couldn't do anything for themselves. When Dad was home from Germany, she would never let him cook, let alone clean, even though he had been providing for himself for a long time and could do all those things.

But Mom now looked at Adnan, so much like her, and smiled.

"You have a one-month probation period," she said. "And after, if your grades start to slip, you are out, understood?"

He bowed and removed his imaginary hat from his head.

"As you wish, my lady," he said, grinning from ear to ear.

All that time, Franka had been silent. She politely ate her food, and the few times Mirna caught a glance of her, she appeared to be enjoying it, smiling at Mom from time to time as if to say, "Yes, this is very tasty." Other than *japrak* being *japrak*, that was to be expected. It really was delicious. But she didn't say a word, like she had forgotten Bosnian again.

"Okay, that is settled then," Grandpa said.

Even Mirna couldn't argue anymore, as she finally finished her mental calculations:

a) It was too good of a chance to be missed.

b) If and when Franka failed, Mirna had the gloating rights.

c) It's not like she would especially go out of her way to train her. Franka would follow her while Mirna did her own thing.

But they all forgot an important side to this discussion.

"Does anyone care if I want this?" Franka finally asked, her voice calm, but cold like Neretva herself. Both Mirna and Grandpa finally shut up.

"Do you want it, child?" Grandpa asked in his most polite old-man voice.

Mirna froze as she stared at those eyes as green as Neretva. It never occurred to her that someone might not want this opportunity. She would give anything for someone to train her one-on-one to become a better cliff diver. But because she was a girl, she could barely train with regular divers, and that was only because she was Mirela effing Lakić, and she didn't take no for an answer, no matter how many times they offered it. How could Franka refuse this opportunity? And why did Mirna care? She just spent all this time arguing against the idea!

"Yes," Franka finally said. Mirna let out a breath she didn't realize she had been holding. Franka looked at her and didn't let her look away. For once, Mirna didn't want to. "I know you think I'm a stupid, useless tourist, but I have the background. I've trained long enough that I know what it takes. I'm willing to try again. When I saw you today, something inside me changed. I want to soar like you did."

Against her better judgment, Mirna smiled.

"Seven a.m., the gym by the train station, don't keep me waiting!" she said, pointing her finger at Franka's face.

"But Mirna, you never went to the gym that early in your life!" Ado said. The cost/benefit analysis of feeding her little brother to the angry spirits of Neretva turned out slightly too costly for Mirna's liking a long time ago, so Ado knew he would get away with his remark.

"Eight!" Mirna said, as her heart began to beat faster. Why was this so exciting? "And then the pool. And then the gym again! Until nightfall! You will be in shape for the Olympics by September!" she promised. She really didn't want to get into this idea, but like the competition they both silently agreed to with Bisera, it was starting to be kind of fun.

"Mirna, you have a year," Grandpa said, back to his calm voice. "You don't need to train like maniacs."

"One small issue, Mirna," Franka began, looking more scared than she did when Mirna dragged her out of the river. "I-I have an exam I need to study for. And it's really important. I can't spend all my time exercising, no matter how much I want to."

"What exam?" Mirna asked, just realizing she knew next to nothing about her. She was pretty sure she graduated high school this year like Mirna, but that was about it. She should have listened to Ado more.

"Entrance exam for pharmacology college," Ado said quickly. Long gone were the days Mirna even bothered to ask how he knew things like this. He would tell her she wasn't observant enough, but she was starting to suspect supernatural forces.

At Ado's words, Mirna smiled again. She and Franka were the same age and she was a future fellow pharmacologist; that was a good sign.

"Ooh, that's a piece of cake," she said. "I was the first one on the list," she added for reasons of absolute maliciousness. It really wasn't that difficult, especially since Mirna and STEM went together as well as Mirna and Neretva. "Džemal Bijedić University?" she asked.

"University of Mostar," Franka answered.

"Oh," Mirna said. It made sense, of course. Two different pharmacology colleges in the same city, because it was Mostar, *jebeš ga*, and that was how they did things: two bus stations, two puppet theaters, and two universities. "Why would you go there, for goodness' sake? Džemal Bijedić is so much better!" she argued, even if she wasn't sure why, but Franka scoffed at her.

"Like hell it is!" she said.

"We'll see about that!" Mirna turned to her grandpa. "Grandpa, throw in 'Adnan has to wear the costume at the store' with your deal, and I will tutor Franka until her exam for free!" she promised. "I want to see what her third-rate school is all about!"

"Come on!" Franka said but, notably, didn't refuse her offer. "It's better than yours, at least!"

"Both of you are going to second-rate schools," Ado announced, standing up. "And Mirela Lakić, I will wear those *dimije* pants, and I will make them work in a way you couldn't have even dreamed of!"

"I was going to give you my old costumes from before the War," Grandpa said, visibly on the verge of laughter, along with Mom, who had not stopped smiling for minutes on end.

"Oh, okay, that works too," Ado said, sounding slightly disappointed he wouldn't get to wear the *jeleče*.

"Does that work for you, American girl?" Mirna teased, now filled with a concoction of emotions she couldn't quite sift through. In reality, she was quite terrible at reading her own emotions. Anything negative, she would bury until it bubbled out in the form of anger sooner or later. But this wouldn't. Her heart was beating fast, but somehow this discussion was almost as exciting as the dive off the bridge.

43

"Maybe I can teach you a thing or two," Franka said, now so close to her their noses were almost touching.

"Can we please eat some *smokvara* now?" Mom pleaded.

"I would love to, Mrs. Lakić," Franka said in her most polite voice. And just like everything else, the fig cake was delicious.

The plan was simple.

They would go to the gym or swimming in the morning, and during the day Mirna would study with Franka, which would be very beneficial to her own classes later on, so it was a win-win situation.

The next day, at 8:30 a.m., Mirna ran five kilometers at the gym, just to flex on Franka, running on the treadmill next to her. For once, Franka was dressed in a normal T-shirt and yoga pants, which fit her very well. And, worse, she kept up. Not perfectly, as she chugged along at half of Mirna's speed and distance, but for someone supposedly out of shape, she was doing too well for Mirna's liking. She did fifty squats and sit-ups without that much hassle, even if it looked like she was going to eject her left lung out of her chest. How was that even possible?

Ado started his shift this Sunday morning too, as Miss Samira's rental property had been all but destroyed by drunk Belgians, and she really needed Mom to help keep her ratings high.

"This is awesome!" Ado said, sending Mirna a selfie with a famous local rapper duo who stopped by their store.

Mirna's shoulder still hurt like hell. Overnight, a gnarly shade of purple took over a large part of her upper torso. Even the most basic hand movements caused her to wince. But she wouldn't tell anyone about it. Nothing was broken or strained. It was the force of the impact at the slightly wrong angle. The bruise would fade and heal in a few weeks at the most. Until then, she had her ice pack, her button-up shirts to hide it, and an occasional painkiller.

People didn't notice how sloppy her landing was so they congratulated her wherever she went. In Mostar, diving off the bridge changed how people looked at someone, even among those who weren't into the sport. It was a big deal to be brave enough to dive, especially if one could pull off a swallow, which she could as far as the amateurs were concerned. If they knew how much she'd messed up, she could ruin it for every woman who would ever think of diving again. If one failed, then the others would too, right? At least, that's how these people thought. That's why she kept smiling at them and shaking their hands, even though Franka couldn't keep the look of bafflement off her face.

The ever-present choir of city gossip was still mostly convinced Mirna saved an actual tourist, so they paid no attention to Franka, but Mirna knew that would change as soon as Bisera's report came out. Even falling from the bridge and surviving to tell the tale was pretty impressive and would probably earn Franka a handshake or two.

After the gym, they went to a haunted Victorian mansion—Franka's house—sitting at a table surrounded by her books and notes, as the posters of long-dead bands looked down on them. Franka lived on the other side of the river from Mirna, in one of the old houses Mirna had thought were abandoned. Inside, the house really wasn't that bad. It was spacious, albeit a bit creaky and definitely infested with ghosts. Franka's room was in a small tower on the top floor, which was great for aesthetic reasons because it looked like a perfect mad scientist's lair, but terrible for everything else, as it was so incredibly hot. It was pretty barren for a room someone had lived in for two years, having just a few posters and textbooks, with no knick-knacks. A few unpacked boxes, covered in dust, sat in the corner, presumably since they'd arrived here from the US.

To Mirna's great and utter disappointment, Franka was actually really smart. Like, almost as smart as she was. She solved equations with ease and understood the principles behind physics and math on a deep, fundamental level. And it was only their first day of studying together.

Goddamn it.

As Mirna listened to Franka explain the difference between carbon bonds in organics versus inorganic molecules, she had to accept the fact this might not be that bad.

"Why are you smiling?" Franka said. "Did I say something wrong?"

"Alcohols have at least one hydroxyl functional group, not carboxylic acid. Those are amino acids," she said in as much of a serious voice as she was capable of, trying to wipe the smile off her face.

"And they also need an amino functional group," Franka added. Sadly, once again, Franka was correct.

Chapter Five

Što je danas lijep i sunčan dan

At 8:10 a.m. on the fifth of September, Franka found herself in front of the building that would be her second home for the next five years: the Faculty of Pharmacy University of Mostar.

The pit of anxiety in her stomach grew and grew with every minute. She had to get in. Not only so she could study what she wanted or follow in her dad's footsteps. She also had to stick it to Mirna.

A message arrived on Franka's phone (Mom's preemptive gift for getting into school) just as they were about to enter the exam hall and she had to put away her phone.

> **Mirna**: "Hey, good luck with your clown college."

> **Mirna**: "If you think you passed, join me this evening. We're going diving."

The message was accompanied by a selfie of Mirna at the local beach, in an honest-to-God bikini, with sunglasses on and a wicked smile on her face.

Franka turned off her phone and shoved it into her backpack. Now she really had to pass.

And she would. Mirna had made sure of that.

The past month was, without a doubt (or without much competition), the most active one she had since she'd arrived in Mostar. Mirna was a surprisingly good tutor, both when it came to her entrance exam and for fitness. Every morning, at 9:00 a.m. (they'd both agreed on the time), they were at the local gym, ready to do their first rounds. While they ran on the treadmill or lifted weights, Mirna would ask her questions from a list of questions from previous years' exams.

"You said anxiety and language got to you the last time? This is how we fix both of those issues," she said as Franka did the fifty squats assigned to her for this session. "Now, what is Kepler's Third Law?"

After those first few days, Franka's entire body was on fire with pain. Other than mandatory gym lessons she mostly skipped, she had not so much as run for the past two years. But that didn't mean she would give up. Spite was a powerful motivator, as she had learned recently.

They practiced written problems wherever they could: from Franka's house, Mirna's garden, and any coffee shop that didn't chase them away. With every single day, both science and sports got easier and easier.

Mirna also refused to talk to her in anything but ex-Yu languages.

"I know it's easier, but I see how you speak our language. It takes you time to translate everything you say. If you want to study something as challenging as pharmacology, you really need to be fluent. So, *hanumo moja, deder ti mi kaži kako ide od Bernoulli-age jednačina?*"

It took Franka at least five minutes of googling to figure out Mirna asked her to recite Bernoulli's principle.

Every time Franka would slip and go back to the sweet, loving embrace of English, Mirna would up her local dialect until she was using words such as "*hajvan*" (animal, but more commonly used as an insult for a person), "*kijamet*" (very bad weather); "*šuhveli*" (suspicious) and *ušpatiti* (after extensive research, Franka was pretty sure Mirna made this one up) until she became completely incomprehensible. Franka only learned the language in the academic setting (plus the swear words, ingrained in her DNA).

And it worked. Franka was no longer too anxious to go to the store on her own or to call locals on the phone in fear of messing something up because she didn't know the words. Now she only got lost because she didn't get the references.

The first time Mirna came to their house, Mom was ever so slightly apprehensive. Sure, she welcomed her and thanked her for saving Franka's life and for volunteering to help her study, but she was eying her with the suspicion of a sheep who wasn't sure if it was seeing one of its own or a different large quadruped with sharp fangs merely wearing the skin of its brethren.

Franka didn't want to start a fight later when Mom reminded her how dangerous cliff diving was and how maybe she should consider a different hobby in a voice that made it obvious this had nothing to do with the sport itself. It was then that Franka realized the precise bush where the proverbial rabbit lay. Mirna was a Bosnian, from the other side of the city and a part of Mom was halfway convinced the War was still not over. Franka didn't mention that Bosnians weren't the ones who destroyed the bridge in the first place. But they did kill her great uncle Franjo, who was the only person from Mostar that Mom ever talked about in a positive light. She loved him so much that Franka was named after him, and that was the important part.

Romana Garcia was not racist or xenophobic; Franka knew that for sure. If Mirna were a Muslim from Lebanon she wouldn't have said anything, but the scars of war still lingered on. She would have to get used to Mirna and her evil Bosnian agenda to teach Franka to jump off bridges and solve math equations.

"I really thought you would be a terrible teacher. Or at least that you would try to just get this over with as fast as possible," Franka confessed to Mirna after the first week. They were done for the day and when Mirna suggested they get something sweet, Franka didn't protest. Ana sold them the crepes ("I had such a crush on her in elementary school," Mirna said, making Franka choke on her pretty decent hazelnut and chocolate pancake), and they sat in the Zrinjevac Park, in the shade of ancient trees and enjoyed the view.

"You think too low of me, Franka," Mirna said in a dignified voice. "I am, in fact, a nerd, and I would never jeopardize your education. Also, I would love to be a college professor one day, so I consider this my first real gig."

"I could see you pulling that off," Franka said. Mirna gave her a genuine smile that had become more and more common over the last few days. The difference was subtle, but the way her eyes lit up was unmistakable. "But when are we going to jump off something? Isn't that what all of this is about?" she asked. Her body yearned for a new, fresh dose of adrenaline. She had watched so many videos of jumps from all over the world, especially from the Blue Stallion competitions and all she wanted to do was try them out for herself. Something in her soul knew she would be really good at it if given the chance.

"My tiny apprentice, you are still not ready for that step," Mirna said in a grown-up voice. "We must first build up your stamina and teach you how to survive the dangerous journey into the river herself. I am afraid you are yet to reach that level."

"I can actually swim," Franka assured her, breaking Mirna's devotion to her bit.

"Oh, can you?" she asked, raising her eyebrows. "Because it looked like you were drowning in Neretva."

"It's different!" Franka insisted. Dad taught her how to swim when she was a kid, while her mom preferred to stay at the beach and read a book. She remembered all the basic techniques, but the water she was used to was calm and

49

warm, in complete opposition to Neretva. "I can swim in normal water! That river is crazy!"

"And we love her for it," Mirna said, smiling at the thought of the river like it was her family. "You need to be a good enough swimmer to resist its currents easily."

"Then teach me, oh wise and powerful one," Franka said. Mirna didn't answer her right away. Her smile disappeared as she looked down to her right side like she was looking at her own right hand. "Did you hurt your arm?" Franka finally asked. It suddenly made sense how Mirna wore shirts that showed as little of the upper torso as possible, despite the warm weather, even at the gym. Thinking back on it, Mirna had been saving her right side in the gym too, doing fewer series with it when she thought Franka wouldn't notice. Given how much Franka stared at her to make sure she was keeping up, it was hard to miss.

"I wasn't good enough," Mirna simply said. "But it's nothing. I'll be okay."

Franka wanted to push for more, but that cold look in Mirna's eyes told her to quit it. Franka didn't argue. She didn't want to do anything that might break this little thing they had going on, but it was obvious what must have happened: an imperfect landing that resulted in an injury that Mirna was too stubborn and too proud to admit. To Franka, and the rest of the audience, it looked amazing.

"Come on, let's take a selfie!" Mirna distracted her, taking out her phone. "My social networks have been in a drought recently." Who was Franka to say no to that smile? "No, no, I have an even better idea!" she said as she took Franka by the hand and made her run with her. "Bruce Lee could use a visit!" she squealed at the excitement of her own brilliant idea.

For reasons Franka never, ever understood, Mostar had the oldest statue of Bruce Lee in the world. It was right there, in Zrinjevac Park, in all his golden glory, a bit shorter than in real life, but still taller than Franka.

"A lot safer than the bridge," Franka joked at her own expense as Mirna took out her phone. "Should we kiss him on the cheek?" she suggested, aware of how unsanitary that might be, but Mirna was too excited for Franka to back out of her proposal. And the photo turned out great.

That night she finally caved in and made a Quickgram (@Columbian_bowtie), all so she could follow the @thicc.pharma account, full of Mirna's selfies and photos of Mostar, and fewer followers than she expected to find because Mirna kept her account locked. Franka was more of a Birdie (now Z) person herself and she didn't have much to post on Quickgram, given that she so rarely left her house, but now that might change soon.

For the next week, they continued their gym and tutoring that got easier and more fun by the day, until Mirna texted her on a Wednesday.

"Swimming time," was all she said and sent her the location of the local swimming pool because she wasn't "ready" for Neretva.

Franka had not so much as dipped her toes in the water in the two years since she arrived on this cursed continent. And back then, she was a different person, a person who would wear a bikini. And a pink one at that. Nothing too "risky," but not her current style at all. Since it was too late to go shopping (and it was still in usable condition, so she technically didn't need a new one), she wore the suit to her meeting with Mirna, who showed up in a wetsuit again.

"That is dangerous," Mirna said when she saw her. She stared at her like she had never seen a woman in a bikini. Bosnia was a majority Muslim country, but that didn't mean it followed sharia law or anything like that. Most girls at the swimming pool wore bikinis too. Why was Mirna so shocked to see Franka in one?

"For diving?" Franka asked, trying to blend into the tiles behind her, regardless of how futile her plan was.

"And for distracting the coach," Mirna added, but for some reason, Franka didn't think she was talking about grandpa Džemal, which made her stand up straight again, now trying to hide her smile instead. "We're going shopping before you jump off anything. At least a one-piece suit. I really hate that we have to pay attention to that, but if you were to lose a piece of clothing during a dive, they would never, ever let you forget it. We're not risking that," Mirna explained, back to her professor persona. "Also, it is safer. It softens your impact, at least a bit." Franka nodded in agreement. As far as she was concerned, she could hoard all of her money under her mattress for safekeeping, but just like gymnastics required special equipment, diving needed its own equipment, so she had to part with at least some cash.

"Now, show me how you swim," Mirna said in her coach persona. Franka got in the water, feeling Mirna's judging stare on her back, and swam her heart out. The afternoon water was warm and filled with kids who got in her way, but she tried to focus on her form. The crawl seemed like the appropriate technique. Something told her Mirna would consider everything else subpar.

Franka thought she did pretty well. Training her strength and stamina with Mirna for a month really did wonders for her, and the videos taught her how she needed to grab at the water and how exactly to breathe. All she wanted was to impress Mirna, but that was easier said than done.

"You are going to drown," was all Mirna said as she awaited her at the other end of the pool, her arms crossed, like a celebrity chef judge commenting on an underseasoned sauce.

"I, in fact, did not drown," Franka corrected her, even though she was already out of breath and trying desperately to hide that fact from Mirna.

"In a pool filled with kids, of course not," Mirna said, shaking her head. "Let me show you how it's done."

In one quick move, she took off her wetsuit to reveal a very well-fitting, yellow one-piece suit underneath, and she simply jumped over Franka and straight into the pool.

In water, Mirna was a wonder. This was her element, in a way it would never be Franka's. She glided through it like a mermaid, as if she belonged there more than on land.

"That was amazing!" Franka squealed when Mirna returned in less time than it took Franka to reach the other side of the pool. "You really should have been a swimmer."

Mirna smiled, fixing a strand of her golden hair that had escaped from her neat bun at the back of her head.

"You know, you are not the first one who told me that," she said. "But I promise you, I can make you as good, or even better. I'm just that good of a teacher and a swimmer."

"We'll see if your claims hold up if and when I get into my school and then compete in the dives," Franka said.

"No doubt in my mind about either; we just need to practice," Mirna promised. "Now, tell me, Franka, which gas is toxic due to binding to hemoglobin, creating a stable complex that prevents the transfer of oxygen?"

Later that week, after the Blue Stallion diving competition that they watched together ("That's my wife!" Mirna yelled when the contestant from New Zealand won again. Mirna, apparently, had many wives, even if they weren't aware of her existence), they went to Mirna's favorite thrift stores and found a semi-appropriate suit for Franka. It was black and pretty simple, even if it might have been made for kids, which would explain the turtle pattern on the back, but it would serve her well.

From then on, they practiced swimming and basic diving one day and went to the gym on the other. Franka started to gain speed and precision in water. She was still miles away from what Mirna could do, and she would probably never reach her level, but she was more and more confident in her ability to not drown, which was all she needed to accomplish.

Two days before the exam, Mirna decided they should focus on studying 100 percent of the time.

"You really don't have to do this," Franka said as they sat in her house, drowning in a sea of reduction and oxidation equations she was now totally sure she could do in her sleep. Why did they ever seem so difficult in the first place? "You've been working with me every day for a month now. Don't you have some friends to hang out with?"

"I have you, my rival," she said as dramatically as possible, making Franka smile. "I made a promise and *inat*, or spite, as you would call it, is a powerful motivator. I want the best possible Franka to get into that school so that it's more fun when I destroy you academically later."

"You're a weirdo," Franka said with as much care as her voice was capable of conveying.

The last time she took the exam, she forgot everything she knew, including the language, the moment she entered that hall—anxiety, plain and simple. She had needed to not only pass but do amazingly well to make up for her terrible grades. And she wasn't able to do it. She had known she would fail not even ten minutes into the exam. The moment she left that classroom, she remembered answers to most of the questions, but it was too late, and she scored below the cutoff.

This time she knew she wouldn't be. The questions were easy now that she knew what she was doing, trivial even, as she circled the correct answers or applied the correct formulas and got the right results.

"Okay, pencils down," the professor said after the time ran out, but Franka was already done at that point, and she was checking her answers. As the professor came to gather her test, she smiled at Franka, and Franka knew she would pass.

Franka texted Mirna as soon as she was in the clear September air.

> **Franka**: Nailed it!! Can't wait to kick your ass when the actual exams start.

> **Mirna**: Oooooh, I would love to see that :P Meet me down by the bridge. I promised you a reward, and you have earned it!

Franka ran back to her house, changed into her swimsuit, and packed a towel. The school year for high school students had started, so Mom was already at work. She left Franka lunch money, which was nice, even if Franka was still too excited to eat anything.

She took the quicker route from the west side of the Old Town, passing the Church of Sts. Peter and Paul, and entered the small, densely packed street filled with vendors, other than the Lakić family. A set of fairly clunky, large stairs led to the area under the bridge, and when Franka finally laid eyes on her, the River Neretva had never seemed so beautiful.

Mirna waited for her at the top of the diving board on the other side of the river. She had on a pink one-piece swimsuit, and when she saw Franka she smiled, waved, and simply dove off the board and into the cold river below. How can a human fall with so much grace? It wasn't fair. Like when she jumped off the bridge, for a few moments, it looked like Mirna would never even fall, but when she did, it was with ease, like the river awaited her.

"Congrats," Mirna said, swimming out to the other side of the shore.

"Thanks," Franka said as her smile took over most of her face. Weird. She hadn't been this happy since forever. The muscles at the sides of her face were starting to hurt a bit because she hadn't used them in two and a half years. "I assume we can't practice on the actual bridge?" she asked, making Mirna chuckle.

"Sure, go ahead, see how it goes," she said. Something told her Franka wasn't the first one to ask her this stupid question. "Will Emir Kapo kill you first? Or the fall?"

"Soon," Franka said, looking up at the bridge that might as well have been miles away.

"You need permission to dive, and they don't give it out to everyone. Just bored tourists who want to give them fifty euros," Mirna said with an unexpected dose of bitterness in her voice.

"Can we pay them?" Franka asked. Fifty euros wasn't an insignificant amount of money, but it wasn't actually that much in the grand scheme of things. Given that she had done nothing but sleep and watch anime for two years, Franka had enough savings to cover the cost of a few dives, if that's what it took.

"Emir laughed me off the bridge when I tried to do it on my birthday," Mirna said. She sounded like she was ready to drown Emir in cold blood if given the chance, and the beaten but pissed look in her eyes made Franka want to join her in her efforts. "But that permission thing is here for a reason," she added in a more businesslike voice. "This sport is no joke, Franka. You got to understand that before we do anything," Mirna said, back to her coach persona. She retied her long golden hair into a bun but kept looking Franka in the eyes.

"I didn't think it was," Franka assured her. If it wasn't for Mirna, God only knew if anyone would have saved her when she fell.

"You were very lucky that one time," Mirna continued. "But people have been seriously injured diving. Not only from up there." She pointed to the top of the bridge, where Ado was frantically waving at them. They finally waved back at him.

"Do you know why he has never jumped off the bridge?" Mirna asked.

"I guess because he's too young," Franka said, but she wasn't sure of her answer. In the US, this would likely have been correct, but Mostar was different. Some of those divers looked like very tall toddlers in Franka's mind. Mirna shook her head no.

"He wouldn't even be the youngest one, not even close," she said and sighed. "He was into diving as much as I was. He trained and worked hard. When he likes something, he puts his heart and soul into it, and Ado really liked diving. Then, a few years ago, he wanted to do a swallow off this board. But he didn't do it right. He ended up with a broken arm and bruises on most of his body," Mirna recounted. "Ever since then, he hasn't even thought about diving again. I don't want that to happen to you."

"It won't," Franka promised, although it was something she couldn't guarantee, no matter how hard she tried. She remembered the yellowish discoloration on Mirna's shoulder the first time they went swimming. And that was after two weeks. God only knew how it looked in the beginning. "I've watched all the videos you sent me. I'll be okay."

"Okay, I believe you," she said. "But just to be sure, no experimenting today. You will be the Swallow of Mostar some other time."

Franka nodded, even if a part of her really wanted to do what Mirna did on that day. She wanted to fly. But Mirna was right. She'd had a long and stressful day. It really wasn't time for experimenting.

"You need to make as little splash as possible," Mirna clarified what Franka had already learned in theory. "The way the divers from Blue Stallion jump is different from how locals do it, and it's different from Olympic diving. This is an extreme sport, so it makes sense."

"Mostar people are a lot less...refined," Franka said, finding the right word that made Mirna smile.

"True," she said. "Because most of them aren't professionals. Very few of them are as obsessed with it as Emir Kapo, so they do it mostly for fun and street cred. But Grandpa sees something in you. Maybe it's because you're so tiny."

"I am not actually that small! I'm five foot three. It's not my fault you Bosnian people have obviously been genetically modified!" Franka insisted. People here were genuinely taller than in the US. Even Dad noticed that when they visited. Franka subscribed to his theory that it was because of all the pie they ate.

"Sorry, don't speak American, but I do think it translates to '*prcoljak*,'" Mirna teased. *Prcoljak*: something or someone very tiny, unfinished. Franka stuck her tongue out like a child, making Mirna burst into laughter. "But while you can be halted by putting the things you need on a higher shelf, your tiny frame is very good for diving, as you won't make a big splash."

"You're jealous because you're a giantess," Franka said, holding her head up high. Mirna really was exceptionally tall, even for a Bosnian. "Now, let me show you how it's done."

Franka climbed up to the diving board, leaving the smiling Mirna behind. It wasn't nearly as tall as the bridge was, but she might as well be miles above the water.

When she was a kid, she was fearless—or stupid, however you'd like to put it. She jumped off every diving board when they were at a pool, did pirouettes when ice-skating, and jumped off her bike mid-drive for fun. Nothing scared her. But that was before she understood how fragile the human body was. It'd been years since she had done anything quite so reckless.

"Don't look down too much," Mirna yelled. "It's not good for your nerves. Relax and go for it. I'll be here if anything goes wrong." Franka smiled at that thought. Mirna had saved her once; she would save her again.

Franka listened to her. She didn't think about the technique at all, so she took a step forward and let herself fall. Neretva was so far away and so cold, but Franka knew she would be safe. For a few moments, she flew. Not as gracefully as Mirna did, simply falling feetfirst, but the adrenaline rush made her think she could take over the world.

Neretva was as cold as it ever was. For a split second, she opened her eyes in the water and found herself surrounded by the green-blue paradise. An inkling of panic appeared in her brain, but she didn't let it bloom. Instead, she moved her hands and feet like Mirna had taught her until she surfaced again. She swam back to the shore where Mirna was waiting for her.

"Good job," she said as they high-fived.

"That was amazing!" Franka squealed, moving wet strands of her hair from her face, making Mirna smile like a proud parent. And she had a lot to be proud of. If it wasn't for her, none of this would have been possible.

"Wanna do it again?" Mirna asked. "Be careful about the position of your feet when you land. I know you have experience landing on your feet when doing gymnastics, but here, you should land on your toes. It's going to make less of a splash. And be careful under the water. You need to break the bubble you create. It should look like the water is boiling."

"Okay," Franka said, trying to keep all the information at the top of her brain for quick and easy access. She got out of the water and climbed up to the diving board again.

She would land feetfirst. She promised Mirna that much. But she didn't say anything about what she would do midair. As long as her arms were up, her body straight and her buttocks firm when she landed, she should be fine.

It was simple, really. After years of practice, she could still do a somersault in her sleep. That's what had saved her life a month ago. And now, she would do it again. But this time, she would know what she was doing.

She leaned forward and curled her body into a ball in the air. It was so different from doing it in gymnastics when she would land on the floor. Now, she was in the air for far longer than she was used to and she would land in water that was getting closer and closer every moment. She got back into the correct, straight position, with her hands up in time for Neretva to take her.

This time, swimming out came easier, like Mirna taught her. The water didn't feel quite so cold, like both she and the river were getting used to each other.

"That was fun," she said, back on the surface, moving a strand of hair that was again stuck to her face. Her heart was beating so fast now she felt like she could really fly if she just tried hard enough.

Mirna didn't say anything. She stared at her, her mouth slightly open in shock, almost cartoonish in her appearance.

"Yeah, I know. My landing wasn't perfect," Franka said. She had grabbed one leg, still underwater. The impact of the water was particularly hard on her right foot, probably because it wasn't completely straight when she hit the surface. It wasn't broken or sprained, but it would probably be sore for a little while.

"Is this what you did when you fell off the bridge?" Mirna finally managed to ask. Franka shook her head no.

"I think I did a somersault in reverse because I was falling on my back," she recalled. "It all happened so fast. I mean, you saw it, didn't you?" she asked. Mirna shook her head no.

"I saw that you fell, but I didn't see what else you did. You were taking a selfie one moment, and the next you were gone. By the time I ran to the top of the bridge, you were already in the water," she said. "No wonder Grandpa was impressed," she added in a quieter voice like she didn't want Franka to hear her.

But Franka did hear, and she couldn't help but smile. It really was a great day to be Franka Garcia.

Chapter Six

Jesen stiže dunjo moja

Very soon, the pomegranates and the clementine ripened on their trees and most of the tourists finally left town. Fall was here and it was glorious. Mirna always liked fall. Maybe it was because of her love for the colors it brought or the smells of *ajvar*, the delicious spread made of peppers, being cooked in every household. She knew it was her favorite season, even if it meant the diving was about to come to an end.

"Classes start tomorrow," Mom told her that Sunday morning like it wasn't the only thing Mirna had thought about for days. Mirna had just got back from cleaning their furnace for the winter, so she was covered in black soot and dust. The last time Dad was here he forgot to do it, so she took it upon herself and did a pretty decent job, thank you very much. Winters here weren't as cold as in the northern parts of the country, but cold winds would come any day now, and they had to be prepared. "Are you excited?" she asked.

"It's going to be okay," Mirna promised, more to herself than to anyone else as she washed her face in the sink.

"Franka is starting tomorrow too, right?" Mom continued to pry. Mirna smiled at the thought of her protegee.

"Yep, her clown college also has an introductory gathering for freshmen," she said when she was finally satisfied with her reflection in the bathroom mirror. To be perfectly honest, Franka's college was not lame at all. Mirna had planned to attend it a few years ago before she changed her mind. Still, this rivalry was too fun to be so easily dismissed for the sake of something as boring as facts.

Colleges in Bosnia usually started their school year in late September or early October, with the first semester lessons ending in January. The second semester usually began at the beginning of March, lasting until early June, and followed by exams. During the semesters, they would have midterms, but the real exams would take place between them, in January and February and June and July.

When Franka got the results of her entrance exam, officially becoming a fellow freshman, they took a break from their training and celebrated with ciders at a local pub.

"I keep forgetting I can get legally shit-faced here before I'm twenty-one," Franka said, even if that sour look on her face revealed she wasn't really enjoying her blueberry cider.

Ciders were the first alcoholic drinks for most girls here, because they tasted like slightly alcoholic juice, while most guys went straight to pretending beer didn't taste like it had gone bad before it left the store. Of course, a significant number of people here didn't drink at all, as Islam forbade it, but over the last four centuries of being Muslims, local Bosnian people made some adjustments to the rules as they deemed necessary.

"A lot of people I know started drinking when they were like fifteen," Mirna said. "Me included, at least a bit. You, my rival, are a late bloomer."

"You Balkan people are a different breed," Franka dismissed her, sipping her drink through a straw, while Mirna chugged hers right from the bottle, like it was apple juice, to look marginally cooler. She actually wasn't much of a drinker either. She didn't want to get in trouble while drunk, but Franka didn't need to know that.

"You can pretend to be American all you want, but we will make you one of us sooner or later," she said. Franka smiled, probably aware that was the biggest compliment Mirna was capable of at that moment. Which was a shame because Franka deserved nothing but to be fawned over.

Now that she broke the seal, all she wanted to do was jump. Mirna wasn't complaining. Neither was Grandpa Džemal, who would join them on the beach and comment on their technique. They could witness a genuine talent bloom.

Grandpa's friends, a gaggle of other old diver legends, were less than impressed by this new development.

"You have gone senile in your old age," Safet told him. He was a few years older than Grandpa and sported an impressive mustache and a cane he mostly used to point at people and yell. His new favorite pastime seemed to be pretending the two of them weren't perfectly capable of hearing what he was saying, with the tone of dismissal only spending seventy years as a well-off man could provide. "Training girls. You were always the weird one."

"What's wrong with girls?" Grandpa asked, winking at Mirna. "My granddaughter dives better than your grandson, and you know it," he said, and Mirna loved him for it.

Mirna couldn't help but think how unfair it was to keep Franka away from this sport for so long when she was so good at it. She was a natural in a way Mirna could never be. She did things people practiced for months, if they ever even learned how to do them, and made it seem like a child's game.

After Mirna taught her the basics, Franka spent her free time on the internet, reading about techniques and looking at videos of dives at every major competition, from the Olympics to the Blue Stallion and everything in between. She kept asking Mirna questions about the technique, the history, the rankings, everything.

Having someone to gush about diving with was so amazing! It was a rare passion, even in Mostar. It was especially weird for a girl to have posters of cliff divers like they were pop stars, but Mirna would rather dive off the space station than tell a living soul she was also really into K-pop. Encyclopedic knowledge of every Blue Stallion diver and every place where they competed was slightly less embarrassing.

Franka could do things that were supposed to be impossible for a beginner. She did somersaults and spins and pirouettes like she was born on that diving board. Her swimming style was still barely good enough to keep her from drowning–Mirna had to intervene a few times–but she was a wonder to behold.

"Why am I so bad at this?" Franka yelled at herself this afternoon as she got out of the water after a dive. Mirna stared at her, lost for words. She had done two somersaults midair and landed perfectly on her head. How could that be considered anything but *jebeno* brilliant?

"Bad at what, exactly?" Grandpa asked. He joined them on most of their practices, full of helpful advice and harsh-but-honest criticism. Finally, after all those years of begging, he was sharing his secrets with her. And while he was far from his peak, years of observation taught him what made a good dive and what could be done to improve it.

"My landings are off, and I can't do a swallow to save my life," Franka said, her eyes filled with determination like the competition was tomorrow.

"You have been doing this for a month, Franka," Grandpa said. Mirna remembered that same tone of voice from when she was a kid and couldn't get the hang of butterfly-swimming style on her first try. "And you are already better than most of the guys who got paid today to jump. Son, you have to be kind to yourself."

"You are doing great," Mirna said, even if she feared it might have sounded insincere because she was still too shocked. Is this how she sounded when she complained she got a 97 percent on a test?

61

"No, I can do so much better," Franka said. "I want to be as good as Mirna!" Mirna barely managed not to burst out laughing. Maybe she should have been jealous of this Mozart of cliff diving, but she would rather enjoy the music than be her Salieri.

"Yes, you can do better," Grandpa Džemal said. "You still have to work on your swimming and your movements after you land. But please, cut yourself some slack. I refuse to work with two perfectionists. It will be bad for my health," he added in an overdramatic voice. Franka was still frowning, so Grandpa went into phase two. "Okay, that is it for today. You have classes soon, and you need to get your mind away from diving for a little while. Go, get some food or something. It's good for you."

Mirna and Franka were, as usual, unable to resist the offer of food, so they left Grandpa to discuss the history of the bridge with the interested tourists and went to get pizza slices.

"I didn't take you for a perfectionist," Mirna said. They were back in Zrinjski Park, pretty close to Franka's house, ignoring the screaming children running through the grass, as they bit into their red and yellow bread. Few things in life could beat the simple pleasure of cheesy tomato bread, even if Franka refused to try hers with mayo, the proper Mostar way of eating pizza.

"I didn't think I was one either," Franka said with a chuckle, her mood substantially improved already. "I guess I haven't found something I was so passionate about in a long while so it all bubbled out of me."

"I mean, you were a gymnast for a while, weren't you?" Mirna asked. In the air and on the board, Franka moved differently than any of the locals. She had more control over every muscle fiber in her body, and she made sure she used them all correctly. That is something only years of intensive training, which no one else in this city had, could give someone.

"I was, but that was middle and high school. I was never that serious about it. I knew I wasn't going to the Olympics. I wanted to have a good time and hang out with my friends, and as long as my grades were good, my parents encouraged me."

Whenever she talked about the US, Franka's eyes turned glassy with nostalgia, like it was the promised land of some kind. Given everything she knew about it, Mirna had her doubts about that idea, but for Franka, it was the truth.

"And..." Mirna tried to ask a question.

"Yes, Mirna, I was a pretty decent student in Atlanta. I probably would've had less trouble getting into college if I had continued there," she said. They knew each other well enough for Franka not to take Mirna's question too personally, even if it was a bit tactless.

"Why didn't you return to the US to go to college?" Mirna asked. She would have loved that opportunity! Heck, she would be happy to at least go to Sarajevo, where the colleges were better, but since she could study the same thing here, she didn't want to burden her folks with the cost of living somewhere else. This was good enough.

"Capitalism, my rival," Franka answered. "*El problema es el capitalismo.* I think the prices of our colleges are a meme by now, and I didn't want to go into debt for the rest of my life," she said. "Dad was still paying his off when he died." She said the last part quietly like she wasn't sure she wanted to say it out loud.

After two months, Mirna knew next to nothing about Franka's dad. She only saw a photo by Franka's bed of her with a dark-skinned man who resembled her. Franka's smile never seemed so genuine as it did in that picture. Maybe Franka thought talking about him too much would make his passing more final.

"I'm glad you escaped from that brutal third-world country," Mirna said, as serious as she could be. To be perfectly honest, both countries were equally messed up, but at least no one in the whole of Bosnia or Herzegovina actually thought this was the greatest country in the world.

"When my mom moved, I had to go with her," Franka explained. "I was a minor and I didn't have anyone to stay with. But honestly, if I had any sort of opportunity to go back, I would. Without hesitation. I want to go home."

Mirna didn't say anything to her. Despite everything, Franka would never love Mostar enough to consider it a home. One day, she would find a way to leave, Mirna knew that. But for now, she was stuck.

"Didn't you mention an aunt?" Mirna asked. "The one you were taking the selfie for?" Franka smiled.

"Auntie Isabella is more like an older sister to me," Franka admitted with a smile. "She's dad's younger sister and she's like ten years older than me. You know, stereotypical 'cool aunt,'" she said.

"Yeah, like Aunt Ramiza, who brings us Swiss chocolates whenever she comes," Mirna said, but the slightly confused look on Franka's face reminded her she was the one in the diaspora. She was the one bringing chocolate.

"When we were moving here, she was in grad school. She's studying civil engineering, and she really couldn't take care of me back then, even if she wanted to. We couldn't make it work, and I really didn't want to be a burden on her."

"And what does she say about your new hobby?" Mirna asked. A part of her wanted to evangelize to every single person on this planet about the religion known as "diving from the Old Bridge."

Franka took out her phone and showed her a message Isabella sent in response to a video of one of Franka's more impressive jumps, the same videos Mirna published on her Quickgram to great success.

"Ah, Dios mio, you are one crazy kid, Franka! Do I need to calculate diving possibilities into every bridge I design?" she wrote. "But in all honesty, that looks rad. I wish I had the guts to do it myself!" followed by a gif of a cartoon piggy gracefully diving into a pool.

"She said the Old Bridge is really cool and super impressive. She can't wait to see it in person. You can give her a proper tour of the place. I know you know more than most about the bridge." If it was a tactic to get Mirna to like Auntie Isabella, it worked. Despite her hatred for tourists of Mostar, if they were actually interested in the history, and the bridge itself, then Mirna could make an exception. She mostly disliked those who came to Mostar to check it off the list of cool places to visit, without much thought about what they were visiting. In reality, she wanted everyone in the world to come and see the Old Bridge and Neretva. As long as they were respectful.

"Yep. Bridge and I share our birthday, July 23rd. My dad joked I'm the reincarnation of the old Old Bridge," Mirna said, gleaming with pride. She loved that chunk of rock like it was her family.

"You know, I can see that," Franka said, playing Mirna like a fiddle, which she was very well aware of. "I am so happy you shared some of that love with me."

"Always," Mirna promised. "If you are willing to teach me that kickass somersault you do."

"You have yourself a deal, my rival," Franka said. "I can't wait to teach you a thing or two, for a change."

Soon, Mirna walked Franka back to her house. It was still sunny outside, but they needed some time alone to gather their thoughts before the big day.

"Good luck tomorrow," Mirna said in her most serious voice. "And let the better pharmacologist win."

"It's college, Mirna, not *the Hunger Games*," Franka teased her with a smile.

"Well, it's pretty close to me," Mirna assured her as they hugged and waved goodbye.

Mirna decided to walk back through the Old Town. The decreasing number of tourists in the afternoon meant she had most of the town for herself. Or so she thought.

She heard them long before she saw them. The guys from her diving team were all there, on the bridge, in their brief suits and being as loud and obnoxious as they ever were.

"Mirna!" they yelled. "*Carice naša!*"

She was, in fact, not their empress, but their mascot at best, but she wasn't going to mention that.

"Come jump with us!" Aca Aleksandar called, the friendliest of them all as per usual, only to be shushed by the rest of them.

"Hi, guys," she said in the most casual tone of voice possible as Bakir jumped off the Bridge with less grace than Franka had fallen off it. Still, she kept that observation to herself.

"Mirnice, darling, how are you?" Emir Kapo stood in front of her, squeezing her hand like it and it alone disobeyed his orders as his gaze moved down her body, colder than Neretva herself.

"Doing okay, just passing by. It's nice to see you all," she added, at least partially a lie. She grew up with these guys. Since they were kids, they had all worked toward the same goal, a goal that was easy for them to achieve, but that she had to fight for. Instead of supporting her, most of them adopted the same attitude as the previous generations, leaving her in the dust. She wanted to be happy to see all of them, but they made that increasingly more difficult. "I dropped Franka off, and I really should be going too," she added to try to get away from them and their "bro" ways.

"Franka, the girl who fell?" Aca asked. Mirna nodded, even if calling Franka "the girl who fell" after what she had seen her do was such a simplification of a much cooler truth. But no one but Mirna and Grandpa knew that, so she couldn't blame him.

"Oh, I've seen her dive a few times," Emir said in that voice that was supposed to sound smooth but ended up slimy. "She really is something else. A real natural talent for the sport. Maybe next year, because you can't follow simple directions, she can be our show act," he said.

In a second, his intentions became crystal clear to Mirna. He wanted to make her jealous of Franka's natural abilities, to make her doubt her own worth, and thus sow a rift between them. Divide and conquer.

Well, tough luck. She was already super jealous of Franka, but that wouldn't stop her from helping her. If Mirna couldn't do it, then maybe Franka could show them girls can compete, and Mirna could then piggyback off her success. She never said she was the wunderkind of this sport, just that she was good enough to compete.

"That sounds like a really cool idea, Emir," she said with her friendliest smile. She was really good at faking her emotions. "Franka would love it. Have you seen her somersaults? She is better than, like, any of us." She baited him on purpose, but he fought back.

"It's so amazing, in only a few weeks, she reached the same levels you practiced for years to achieve," he said. The other guys stared at them, seemingly without blinking, like it was an intense tennis match, but they didn't say anything. "Maybe girls can be as good as the guys. Just not all of them."

"Well, not all girls, of course," Mirna said, refusing to give him the satisfaction he wanted. "Just like not all guys. It is a dangerous sport, Emir; you are the one who keeps warning us about that. You told me that, like, half of the guys here weren't nearly good enough to compete," she said. It was the truth, and even if she made an enemy of half of the divers here with that one statement, she also managed to mess with their heads, and that was all the victory she could get at the moment. "Franka's success doesn't invalidate my own. You know, us girls; we have to stick together. Maybe we'll paint the bridge pink and jump on our own," she added, a tad dreamily, to mess with them even more. "Now, raja, I do have to leave you here. Have a lot of fun with your diving."

She smiled and waved goodbye to them, leaving them to squabble.

The war was far from won, but she at least put a slight dent in their troops.

Chapter Seven

Računajte na nas

Whose bright idea was this wake-up call at 7:30 a.m. on a Sunday?

Yes, Mirna's, of course. She was the morning type. As far as Franka was concerned, the world shouldn't start before 11:00 a.m., especially not on the weekends. But Franka couldn't say no to Mirna's puppy eyes and pure, undiluted excitement, so she dragged herself out of her bed and got dressed.

October passed by them, just like November. But December arrived in full force. In this part of the country, winters were never that harsh, but the air was cold and the jugo wind could chill her to the core. Even Mirna had to retire her crop tops and replace them with full-length shirts. Many mourned when that day came. Franka more than most.

Every week, their classes became more intense and asked more and more of them, but so far it was going reasonably well. The first partial exams were already behind them.

This time, Franka decided she would actually try from the beginning. She wouldn't leave studying for the last possible moment. With a college like pharmacology, she couldn't afford to. And one more important fact: Mirna wouldn't let her.

Mirna was, in fact, a nerd who studied every single day from the start of the semester, at least a little bit, and Franka's pride made her follow in Mirna's footsteps. So she, too, read through every lesson before and after it was done, consulted study guides, and watched videos on the popular internet website where overenthusiastic hosts described the issues at hand. She made herself pay attention in class and ask questions like she was learning cliff diving, but a bit more important to her future—and significantly less risky.

"I will not let you have better grades than me at your lame-ass school," Franka said as they studied cell biology together. They didn't have all the same subjects, but when they did, it was easier to have a study buddy (or study rival, as Mirna insisted on being called). Also, on the days they didn't see each other, something was missing from Franka's life. That smile and the sound of Mirna's voice made the cold autumn days a tiny bit brighter.

"Go ahead, American girl, show me how it's done," Mirna challenged her.

The Q&A part of their exercise routine was now updated, as Franka wasn't the only one answering questions. They would take turns asking each other questions and checking the answers in both sets of textbooks they had. Mirna had the perfect voice for explaining complex cellular mechanisms, as they ran their 5K, or did squats.

The river was declared too cold for swimming by Mirna's mom, who had one word for the two of them: ovaries. Any "ovary owner" in the Balkans knew what she was talking about.

Mirna did make them both sign up to the official diving team, where they got a certificate that they jumped off the Old Bridge. It didn't actually mean anything in the grand scheme of things, but Franka immensely enjoyed listening to Mirna argue that, while she had no intention of diving, her near-perfect landing (as witnessed by a local legend that was Grandpa Džemal) despite having no training made her worthy of being a part of the club that numbered a few thousand tourists.

"I want it on paper," Mirna told her later, holding the paper in her hand like it was the map to El Dorado. "I want them to know you already jumped, so when the time comes, you and I can do it again." Franka had to agree. A paper trail meant everything.

They would come back to diving in the spring. Some people still swam or jumped, but Mirna and Franka didn't want to anger the gods or their moms, so they had to call it quits. A local hotel had a closed pool they could use, but it was a bit pricey, so they went only once a week.

"More than enough," Mirna assured her as they returned from the gym. "But if we clear our exams now, we will have the whole summer to practice, so don't slack off with your studies. Now, can you explain the sodium-potassium pump to me?"

Franka, of course, could.

She was still getting used to all the differences from American colleges she was supposed to attend. Everyone studying to be a pharmacologist had the same classes, mostly at the same time (except for practical lessons). She didn't have to study English or Bosnian or art history, only subjects related to pharmacology, like biology and chemistry. If she passed all her exams, in five short years, she would be a master of pharmacology and could start working already. In the US, her studies would take so much more time. And not to mention money.

After a while of suffering, Franka finally got a new pair of glasses. The frame was almost the same as the last one, a simple round wireframe. She liked the freedom that an existence devoid of glasses brought, but she didn't like the headaches from reading or staring at the laptop screen. She could see well during practice and swimming, but academia was a bit different, and it created enough migraines even with 20/20 vision.

They both had their last exam from this first session that Friday. Franka was happy with how she did, while Mirna was the one who had bit her nails to the bone and swore she would fail. (For the record, she got 98 percent.) Now, they could slow down for a few weeks. On Saturday, they both went out with some of their colleagues from college, but Mirna had great plans for Sunday. Sadly, they did not involve sleeping in and nursing the very slight hangover that could only come from three ciders.

On this cold morning, fog had descended over Mostar. No one should have been outside, but Franka sneaked out of her house so she wouldn't wake Mom up to follow whatever extravagant idea Mirna had. Mirna was, of course, already waiting by the statue of Queen Katarina at the end of the park because Franka was a few minutes late, even though her house was so much closer than Mirna's.

"Buenos dias, mi rival, Franka," Mirna said when she saw her. She must have still looked like a corpse, while Mirna was smiling, her long hair tied in a stylish, yet casual, long braid that stuck out of her red beanie. She wore a puffy vest and a comically oversized backpack.

"Buenos dias, Mirna," Franka answered automatically, even if she hadn't used Spanish in way too long. "Wait, are you learning Spanish?"

"You know something that I don't," she simply said, her head held high because it meant the world to her. "I cannot allow that. So, I installed an app on my phone."

"But I'm a native speaker, Mirna. The app is not going to help you. You'll never catch up to me," Franka teased her in Spanish, for the satisfaction of seeing Mirna's face scrunch up in frustration and concentration as she tried to parse her words. Her dad had taught her Spanish, along with Aunt Isabella. She had taken it in school too. She had pretended she couldn't speak it, so they wouldn't make her take French. No wonder she knew it better than Croatian. Also, Spanish was so much easier. That and the food were the only things she knew about her Colombian side, but it was more than mostly nothing (and baklava) from her Balkan side.

Franka would give anything for some vaguely Latino food that wasn't a subpar tortilla, but her new countrymen didn't have the right ingredients. She loved Balkan food! It was homey and delicious in its simplicity of ingredients, but she would trade all the *musaka* in the world for one really good *aborrajado*. But luck was not in her corner. This country didn't even have plantains!

"Not to worry, Mirna," Franka finally said in English. If Mirna continued her language studies and got even decently good at them, Franka would return the "favor" that was intense Bosnia-fication of every conversation, but that was a long-term deal. "If anything, I'm a true American at heart."

"The bald eagle of Mostar," Mirna said, chuckling at her own joke. "Now come on, we have a city to save."

"I'm not doing any more interviews," Franka quickly said, making Mirna smile. Mom loved every second of Bisera's report, and it also resulted in complete strangers stopping Franka on the street to congratulate her on her great success of falling off a bridge, but it was an experiment she had no desire to repeat. "I did my part in the unification of this great city when I fell off that bridge."

"Not to worry," Mirna said. "This is between me and you. No Biseras will be involved," she promised. "Have you ever been here?"

"I mean, my house is right there." Franka pointed, making Mirna frown before she realized that she hadn't actually told Franka where she was taking her. She was too excited to actually elaborate when she called her last night, and Franka didn't have the heart to tell her.

"At the Partisan Cemetery, you tourist?" Mirna asked. Franka shook her head no. She had heard of it. Mom told her it was pretty cool, but she couldn't find the time to go. It looked too far away. "I'm not that surprised. We don't advertise it enough."

It turns out that the Partisan Cemetery was like a five-minute walk from her home, but if Mirna wasn't there to guide her, she wouldn't have been able to find it. It was hidden in the middle of a green forest on the outskirts of the urban area of the city, but not actually that far away from the places tourists visited. Mostar had a lot to show, but if tourists dared to leave the Old Town, it was to visit the Kravice Waterfalls (Little cows, how adorable was that?) or the Dervish house in Blagaj, neither of which Franka actually saw with her own eyes.

The cemetery was once a monumental creation when people actually cared for it. Now, it reminded Franka of a post-apocalyptic world. These massive cement walls must have been sparkling white once, but now they were gray, often covered in moss and wild grass. A few swastika graffiti, as well as the "*Ustaše Mostara*," reminded her this still was the same Mostar it always was.

"Some kids who probably don't actually know what those words even mean," Mirna commented, her face crushed up in a grimace of disgust.

"Assholes," Franka simply said, not interested in justifications for hate symbols, no matter how old the perpetrators were. They might not have known the full extent of what a symbol like a swastika represented, or they might have had the wrong image of *Ustaše*, a literal fascist organization, but even an outsider like Franka knew enough not to make any excuses.

They walked up the stone path that slithered like a snake and led them to the actual graveyard. Four massive levels of graves of the partisans who died fighting the Nazis in the Second World War lay all but abandoned, covered in grass, forgotten by the people and the time.

Most of the dead weren't actually buried here. They died all over the country, fighting for their freedom and the freedom of their loved ones. Here, rows and rows of tombstones stood, with their names and years and places they were born and where they died. That was all that remained of them.

"The graves are supposed to symbolize a tree being cut," Mirna whispered, her voice quiet which Franka was thankful for. These people deserved their peace. When they reached the final, fourth level, Franka knelt next to one of the stones, wet morning dew from the green grass seeping through her jeans. Age ate away at the name, but the years were still visible: 1922-1942.

"He was just twenty years old," she said. Not even two years older than her, and gone before he had the time to actually live. Mirna sighed.

"You'll see that most of them were that young. They were kids, like you and me," she said, her voice heavy with sadness. "Can you imagine dying for freedom, to build a better world for those who stayed behind, and then, not even a century later, they kill each other again?"

"Not even fifty years later," Franka corrected her. "And they desecrate their grave too," she added, as she tried to put one of the tombstones back where it belonged. It was a symbol of a real person, the minimum of respect they deserved in death.

"It's a lot better than it was before. I mean, after the War," Mirna explained. "But no one is taking care of it. You know, it's Mostar, and we are just like that. Neither side cares about the partisans enough to respect their graves, even though some Croats were partisans and some Bosniaka were Ustaše," she continued with her history lesson that Franka didn't mind one bit.

"And what are we doing here?" Franka asked, still a bit confused. Was this a history lesson? "Except bumming me out?"

71

"We are going to be the change we want to see in the world," Mirna said, gleaming with pride. She took off her backpack and presented Franka with a stack of trash bags and yellow kitchen gloves: small size for her and medium for Mirna.

"Cleaning trash?" Franka asked, her eyes narrowing in suspicion.

"Yep," Mirna confirmed, giving her a big black trash bag and gloves. "Teens come here to get drunk on the weekends, and no one cleans up after themselves, so that is where we come in," she revealed like it was the most logical conclusion anyone ever came up with. "Come on, it's going to be fun. And it will get us into Grandpa's good graces. He is a Commie like no other," she added with a devious smile. "As a reward, I packed some cheese pie Mom made yesterday so we can have breakfast here."

"Now you've sold me completely," Franka said as every bit of skepticism escaped from her body in an instant. She would do anything for Emina's amazing food.

They started from the top, at what might have once been a fountain, now filled with brown stale water. Trash was everywhere, mostly plastic bottles of water and soda and cans of beer, as well as packets of snack food. They worked in silence, but Franka occasionally heard Mirna curse the "*kreteni i idioti*." They filled the bags pretty quickly as the nature around them began to wake up. Birds sang their morning song. The sun was already out, and it started to warm up the world around them. Soon enough, the last of the fog was gone, and they were left with a beautiful Sunday morning.

As she picked up the trash, Franka's mind wandered back to her dad's grave, back in Atlanta. Aunt Bella brought flowers and cleaned the weeds every few months like she promised she would, but Franka wanted to see it again for herself. With his physical body now empty, the records they collected together were as much of a reminder of him as his grave was, but Franka still wanted to sit by his side again and tell him everything that had happened. He wasn't here to comfort her anymore, but she liked to think Dad was still somewhere, watching over her.

In the end, she and Mirna collected four large bags full of trash from only the main part of the monument. The forest around it remained impenetrable and, no matter how Mirna said it, Franka was still not 100 percent convinced it was free of landmines. Not in a million years and a trillion pleas from Mirna would she enter those woods.

"We did a good thing," Franka said as they threw their garbage bags in a dumpster just outside the gate and came back to the cemetery, now cleaner, but still as desolate as it was before.

"And we are doing it again in a few weeks," Mirna announced as if she were talking to Bisera again. "Some new kids will leave their litter here, but I guess we won't have this much work to do. On an unrelated note, didn't I promise you a reward?" she asked with a wicked smile.

"Oh god, please!" Franka said. "My mom can make eggs on a good day, and I'm not much better. I'm craving a homemade meal!" Dad was the chef in the family and both she and Mom had gotten too complacent with his cooking to learn to do anything but order takeout on their own. Thank God for a new source of delicious nutrition.

Mirna set the whole thing up. She brought a plastic container filled with small handmade rolls of *sirnica* cheese pie, made with homemade filo dough and cottage cheese filling that may have been cold but still tasted divine.

"Your mom is amazing!" Franka said after her third chunk of pie that tasted so sweet and so salty and amazing. If she could marry it, she would—without hesitation.

"I will let her know," Mirna mumbled, her mouth full of pie. "I'm sure she'll appreciate the offer."

They sat on the stone wall and ate their pie in silence. In front of their eyes, the city came alive, waking up after a long sleep, like Franka had a few months before. She took a quick photo of the view and published it on her Quickgram, which had been a little empty since she had no more videos of impressive dives to share. Most of her followers were her colleagues from college, but some people she knew in Atlanta had also found her account. She'd lost contact with most of them over the last two years.

To be honest, her isolation began even before she moved to Mostar. With Dad in the hospital and then gone and Mom trying desperately to make sure they had a roof over their heads and a meal on the table as debts piled up, things like "school friends" sounded like something from a different life, a life that she simply didn't have the strength to pretend to live anymore. When she had moved, for the first few months she sent some of her friends messages to assure them she was okay, even if she wasn't, but sooner or later their lives got in the way of answering with anything but a few words or emojis, which was true for her messages too. After a while, their communication came down to likes on posts and an occasional reaction. Now that she was feeling better, sharing good things in her life didn't feel like such a chore.

"I am always surprised how nice it feels to hang out with you," Mirna said, making Franka laugh. For someone so brilliant, she was really dense in some areas.

"Mirna, you have to accept one simple fact: we are actually friends," Franka said. Mirna's mouth fell open in shock that, while exaggerated, was at least a bit real.

"I mean..." she tried to argue, but she had nothing to argue about. They had spent almost every free moment they had in the past few months together, and they both liked it. What on earth could they be other than friends at this point?

"You could've asked Selma, or even Ado to help you with this," Franka simply said, taking the last piece of the pie, rules be damned.

"But it's a part of training," Mirna simply said, but Franka shook her head no, trying not to burst into laughter with all that pie in her mouth. "I guess you are right. I was never a friendly person."

"You? Mirela Lakić, the golden child?" Franka said. "We can't walk ten meters through the city without someone saying hi to you!" It seemed like everyone in this city knew her name and her story. No matter who they were or if she even knew them, Mirna smiled and said hello in a way that made her seem like the biggest sweetheart in the world. The moment they were done with the conversation, she would turn back to her initial mood and continue what she was doing, like she was never interrupted.

"Yeah, they are saying hi to me," she said. "And we go out sometimes, and we have fun. But I never let it get to the real friendship stage. I never let them get close to me. My relationships weren't much more in-depth either. They just see the golden child, the perfect Mirna." She looked away from Franka, her breathing heavy and her head bowed.

"I like the imperfect Mirna too," Franka said. "The one who gets too much into fake rivalries because she really wants to LARP, the one who knows useless trivia about cliff divers from all over the world, the one who jumped off a bridge to save a person who she thought was a stupid tourist." Mirna turned as pink as a pomegranate.

"That is very nice of you to say," she said, still blushing and looking away. Making Mirna blush was a difficult task only a few had ever accomplished. It was the perfect time to strike.

"Now, tell me, Mirna, the cell membrane consists of which classes of lipids?"

Later, Mirna would swear she didn't hear the question right and that she obviously knew the answer to such a basic and simple thing, but Franka was proud of herself because, for once, she was the one who caught Mirna off guard.

Chapter Eight

Nova godina kuca na vratima

On the last day of the year, Mirna woke up super early, as usual. Today, however, there would be no gym, no studying. She didn't even have any chores to do around the house. A miracle indeed. It was a day to celebrate. And a day to contemplate one's choices. Mostly in the fashion department.

She spent the better part of the day in her bedroom, trying to get ready for this party. She had to look stunning. Her best dresses were neatly laid out on her bed. Now it was up to her to pick the perfect one.

Her first choice was the silver cocktail dress she got at the thrift store for ten marks. Around noon, she walked out of her room to check herself out in the big mirror in her parents' bedroom, sure she made the right decision.

"You look like you're representing our country on Eurovision with a subpar pop song." Ado's insult was so specific and so true that the silver monstrosity was suddenly out of the question. And the pink one wasn't working for her because her boobs didn't look their best. She could do better.

In the end, she chose the yellow cocktail dress, in the fifties style, absolutely adorable—five marks at the thrift market. What a bargain! By the time she finally made this crucial decision, it was already 7:15 p.m. She barely managed to do her hair in loose curls, which she put up halfway, and do her makeup in a way that looked cute, but like she hadn't spent the whole day prepping for this. This was as good as she would look. And she looked great.

If only she could rationalize to herself why she was trying so hard. It was just a New Year's Eve party. She didn't even care for this made-up holiday.

Selma had invited her and a few other girls from their year a few weeks back. Her uncle owned the club, so they would get unlimited drinks all night for only thirty marks each.

"Can I invite a friend?" Mirna had asked after Selma made her offer. "You know, Franka?" For whatever reason, she couldn't picture not having her around for that night, even if she didn't know how Franka would like to spend her night.

She seemed like the type of person to call it a bullshit holiday but still stay up in her pajamas, eating food and watching a movie.

"Of course! A friend of Mirna is a friend of us all!" Selma assured her. They had met a few times over the last few months, and while Selma approached Franka like she was meeting a princess of some exotic, far-off land who probably knew nothing of the local customs, Franka generally grew to like her. Or at least, like her enough to take her up on her offer of cheap drinks and good music. "And if she has any other pharmacologist friends, she can invite them too! We can make a whole thing of it!"

Franka, in fact, did have a few more friends to invite, and because Mostar was a tiny city, most of them knew Selma or someone else she invited already, and they were not about to pass on an opportunity for a bargain of a party. So, six of them would gather tonight to celebrate the end of this awesome year.

"I did not know the Oscars were tonight," Ado teased her again as she rushed through the house, trying to locate her hairspray that would keep her curls at least somewhat decent. She found it in Ado's room, as he was incapable of buying his own.

The two of them and Grandpa were on their own for the next few days. Dad had come back from Germany, and he and Mom, after years of refusing, finally went on a vacation. They would spend New Year's Eve in Istanbul, leaving Ado and Grandpa in charge of Mostarske Džidže.

"You can afford it now," Ado promised them as they all saw them off a few days ago. "I have increased your revenue by 20 percent!"

"It would be 30 percent if you stopped giving away things to cute girls," Mom reminded him. It was the truth. Ado was so much better at peddling džidže than Mirna could ever dream of. He would mostly help on the weekends, and if anything, his grades had slightly improved from the last year. For the first time, he was invested in his tourism studies. He'd finally found his calling. He also revived the social networks Mom got Mirna to make last year that had one post each, and he filled them with actual good content about the history of Mostar (and all the things available at Džidže) which was now pulling in pretty good numbers.

That's how he could afford all the food and drinks he bought for tonight.

"Well, your sister is a star," Mirna said, checking herself out in the hallway mirror. "Also, please, please, don't set the house on fire while I'm gone."

"I am sixteen, Mirna. I can take care of myself. Me and the boys will play FIFA and eat junk food," he said. He was in the kitchen in the process of cutting cheese and *sudžuka* dry sausage to make the perfect *meza*. She had never seen him this detail-oriented as he made sure all the bits of cheese and meat were of equal size and put them on the plate with surgical precision. "The ideal New Year's Eve." Sadly, Mirna had to agree with him, but she had already made plans and made herself look her best, so meza would have to wait for next year.

"Well, we are going to that club, and I'll spend the night at Franka's 'cause her mom is out of town with some friends," she repeated because he probably wasn't listening to her the first time.

"Ooh, more room for the two of you," he teased, pulling back to look at his cheese and meat board and make sure it was all in order, like it would survive for more than fifteen minutes.

"What are you talking about?" Mirna asked. He just rolled his eyes.

"You'll get it when you're older," he said. Mirna would have thrown something at him, but she was holding her black high-heel shoes that she would hate to mess up, and he knew that very well. "You will look like a tree in those shoes," he added, eyeing her carefully like he only now realized she was a full head taller than him.

"I know. That is the point. I have bonus intimidation points that way," Mirna said.

"You shine, Mirna," Grandpa said. He was also getting ready for an exciting night of chess with his buddies. Apparently, Safet got the good plum *rakija* from his brother in Semberija, so they would probably play as much chess as Mirna and Franka. "Like a star."

Mirna left the house feeling like a million dollars.

Franka was, as usual, late, but Mirna had worked around this by telling her they were meeting earlier than they actually were. The night was clear, a bit cold, but not too much. An almost perfect winter night. In theory, Mirna missed the snow, as it so rarely fell in these areas, but in practice, those few times she had experienced it in northern parts of the country, she actually hated it. This was better. Snow could stay in Christmas movies and screensaver photos.

Franka came out of her house, wrapped up in her coat, her hair perfectly sleek and shiny. The makeup around her eyes wasn't her usual slightly messy eyeliner. This was a lot more precise, with dark-green shadow and absolutely perfect wings that someone could cut themselves on. Goddamn it, did it look good.

"Ready?" she asked. Mirna smiled.

"More than ready," she answered. "Come on, we'll meet them there."

The club wasn't that far from them, so they decided to walk.

Even so, they were there before any of their friends because even the thought of being late made Mirna shudder in fear, so they made their way through the still half-empty club to the booth booked for them and their friends. Mirna took off her coat immediately because it was way too warm and revealed her outfit for tonight, which got the exact reaction she was hoping for.

Franka stared at her like she had seen the mythical vila, blinking with her mouth slightly open, like she didn't even realize it. Despite her better judgment, Mirna liked that look. Not on men, but Franka was different. She could drink her in as much as she liked.

"You look stunning," she said after her eyes returned to her head. Mirna brushed her off.

"Oh, I just threw something on," she said, so grateful Ado wasn't there to add one of his jokey jokes.

And then Franka took off her coat, and Mirna was the stunned one. She wore a simple, two-piece suit, dark blue pants and a jacket that fit her frame like a glove and a winter-themed bow tie over her white shirt.

"I don't like dresses very much," she admitted, probably thinking Mirna was surprised by her choice of clothing, even if it was so Franka. "This is my version of festive."

"It suits you well," Mirna finally managed to say before she had to call the waiter and order her first drink.

And drink they all did. Their friends came soon, one by one, and they were all in fully festive spirits, some probably already tipsy. They hugged and sang before it was even 9:00 p.m., all dressed in their best dresses and having an absolutely awesome time.

Music started off with generic American pop, but with every song, it got gaudier and gaudier. Balkan rap folk pop with too much autotune and lyrics that suddenly became fully comprehensible, now that an obscene amount of alcohol was flowing through her veins. The wine and shots were already paid for, and who were they to resist them?

"For our Mexican girl!" Ivona exclaimed, carrying a tray of little glasses of tequila and lemon slices, already drunk out of her mind, even if it was only 11:20.

"Colombian!" Franka corrected her, her speech already slurry, but she grabbed the shot glass anyway.

"For Pablo Escobar then!" Ivona continued. Franka and Mirna exchanged meaningful looks to make it obvious this wasn't okay, even if it was kinda funny.

Mirna, a proud daughter of Herzegovina, was a good drinker, but this was something else. Who would drink this? It tasted like a window cleaner.

Naturally, she had two more before midnight.

Franka was, apparently, deep-down, a party girl. She spent most of the night dancing with Mirna, her body moving to the rhythm of the music. Even if she didn't know the songs, she let the sea of people moving in sync carry her. The music was loud, probably too loud, but the beat carried them on its own.

The more alcohol they consumed, the closer they danced to each other and the more relaxed they became until they were so close it was hard to tell where one's body began and the other's ended.

As the DJ counted down to midnight, Franka approached her and put her arms around her, pulling her down.

"You have to kiss someone at midnight," she whispered, her words slurring, but the smile on her face, wicked and naughty, was as real as it ever was.

"It's a tradition."

"You can kiss me," Mirna said, letting the emotions that had built up inside her for months finally come out in one sentence. And, as the clock struck midnight, Franka did just that.

Her lips were very sweet and her breath smelled of alcohol, but as the club around them erupted into dance and screams of joy, Mirna's world grew quiet, as only Franka's face mattered. Her heart was beating very fast, but her brain forgot how to think. All she could do was enjoy this perfect moment.

It was far from her first kiss. She was known in her old high school as the one who turned girls gay (a stupid concept, she never kissed anyone who didn't make it perfectly clear they wanted to be kissed), but this felt different, like that mythical first time they described in songs. Franka pulled her down even closer, biting her lower lip, as the surge of pleasure and pain filled her entire body.

"Amazing!" she whispered in her ear as they continued to dance to a rhythm only they could hear.

"People are watching," the last rational part of Mirna said. No matter how open she was, she still knew where she lived. This was a small town filled with hate and fear and those things were as far from fertile ground for an LGBT movement as it could get. Maybe in Sarajevo, they could get away with it, but even then, their closeness was a risk. If the wrong person saw them, Allah only knew what would happen. But the adrenaline in her blood made it too difficult to really care about the future. Only *now* mattered.

"Let them," Franka said, too drunk to think straight. "*Jebaćemo im majku*," she swore, making Mirna smile against her lips.

Maybe the vila, the fairy spirit, saved them that night, as no one even batted an eye at the two of them, dancing closer and closer to each other, ignoring their friends and the rest of the world. They were alone in this club, as the music made their bodies move and their hearts beat in sync.

It could have been ten hours or ten minutes, but Mirna didn't want Franka to move an inch away from her. For all she cared, her entire existence depended on being close to Franka. She wanted their bodies to become one in this club, where the air was too moist to breathe and music too loud to think.

"Let's go!" Franka finally whispered in her ear. It was two in the morning and Mirna had been waiting for her to say those words for a long time. She kissed her again and went to pick up their things. They snuck out of the club without even saying goodbye to their friends. Tonight, only the two of them existed in this world.

The night outside was cold but dry. They weren't the only ones out. A few other groups of people were equally as drunk and as ecstatic as they were.

"Happy New Year!" a teenager yelled, still nursing his bottle of Ožujsko beer.

"Happy New Year!" Franka yelled back.

Franka held her hand as they walked through the Zrinjski park. The sight of a Santa hat on Bruce Lee's head made them both burst out into hysterical laughter. Maybe they didn't want him to get sick. It was dark in the park, in the middle of a cold and moonless night, and for a few moments, Mirna did consider someone mugging them at knifepoint, but she figured that the guild of muggers took a night off too, so they reached Franka's house safely.

Before the doors even properly closed behind them, they were already making out. As Franka led her upstairs to her room, she tripped and almost fell at least three times, giggling like she didn't understand the possible ramifications of a fall. Mirna wasn't much better either. Too much alcohol did its thing, and risks became a secondary concern.

Oh, dear Allah, she was so beautiful! Those eyes and that smile! That perfect body! Everything about her was amazing! It should be illegal!

Mirna fell for those eyes the moment she first saw them. They were the same color as Neretva. Why did it take her so long to accept this? She could have been kissing Franka for months already if she wasn't so goddamn stubborn.

"Ever since we met, I thought you were the hottest woman alive!" Franka switched back to English, probably too drunk to deal with Bosnian, and Mirna couldn't blame her. She could barely deal with words either. Only emotions, only instincts telling her she needed Franka more than she needed anyone else before.

Without thinking about it, Mirna unzipped her dress and let it fall on the floor of Franka's bedroom. Franka smiled like she had seen a falling star as she stared at her body, taking it all in. Any sense of shame in Mirna for being seen in her underwear was gone, and she didn't care. Franka had seen her in a bikini, but this was different. And so much better, intimate, to be shared only between the two of them.

"I have wanted to kiss you for a long time," Mirna said as Franka pulled her down into another kiss.

How sweet she tasted. How amazing was the touch of her hand against her bare skin. She wanted it. Her mind was hazy, but her heart knew the truth.

But something was off. Franka, beautiful, sweet Franka, who removed her bowtie, was unbuttoning her shirt so clumsily, her fingers no longer under her control. She giggled uncontrollably, looking at her shirt and at Mirna.

Would she be so up for this if it wasn't for the Neretva worth of alcohol they consumed? Would Mirna be either?

She wasn't sure. So she had to stop them.

"We are both way too drunk for this," Mirna said, shocking herself at voicing her thoughts out loud. She wanted to shush it up, but her own eyes were closing with exhaustion. That little bit of cold winter air brought back some of her rational thinking. Franka stared at her, her shirt halfway unbuttoned, and Mirna had to look away. They would both regret this in the morning. Heck, they might regret what they had already done. She valued this friendship more than a hookup.

"Too drunk," Franka repeated. She didn't argue, thankfully. Mirna would have cracked under even the tiniest of pressure. "Maybe when we're both sober, you lovely creature," she added.

Mirna did the right thing as Franka curled up on the bed and fell asleep almost instantly. Mirna followed her advice as she spooned next to her and drifted off into peaceful sleep.

Chapter Nine

Srećan ti rođendan, Sunce moje drago

When Franka woke up on that first morning of the new year, she felt like someone was doing construction work directly inside her brain. The sound of birds chirping outside scraped at her neurons, and her mouth felt like she swallowed a handful of sand. Within seconds of regaining her consciousness, she made a silent vow to never drink again—one that she knew she would break.

But, most importantly, Mirna's hands were wrapped around her, tenderly touching her midriff, Mirna dressed in nothing but her matching bra and panties. Franka stared at her, heart beating against her rib cage like a trapped animal, trying to remember how they got here in a blur of alcohol, loud music, and passionate kisses.

Mirna finally opened her eyes and stared for a few moments, breathing heavily, obviously on the edge of panic as she realized her hands were still around Franka. She let go in an instant and moved away as if Franka were suddenly radioactive.

"Did we...?" Franka began to form a question she wasn't sure how to finish. She remembered most of the night, even if she didn't want to. Or at least, she wanted to not want to remember Mirna's lips against hers, the feel of her body as they danced together like the world belonged to them. For a few hours, every single doubt that had made its home in Franka's mind was gone, along with all her inhibitions.

They were there for a reason!

"No, don't worry," Mirna assured her, her eyes wide, almost in horror, as she pulled up Franka's sheet to cover her half-naked body. "We both agreed we were too drunk."

"Oh, good," Franka said, even if a part of her didn't agree with that assessment. "I would really hate not to be able to remember my first time." Virginity was a social concept that no one should care about, but the idea of being so close with another person still mattered to Franka. She wanted to be fully present for it.

"Was that your first kiss?" Mirna asked, making her chuckle, despite that simple gesture causing another painful ruckus in her brain.

"Do I have that vibe?" Franka asked. "I mean, I can't blame you. But I have kissed other people. I was a different person in Atlanta." She also wasn't a person to drink at all, let alone as much as she did. She would pay for her choices dearly, but she would live with them.

"Boys?" Mirna continued to dig for info, her eyes narrowed in suspicion.

"And girls," Franka admitted. "Did you really think I was straight?" she asked—a direct and sassy question that the Franka in Atlanta might have asked. She smiled at the mere thought of that open and fearless response of a person who no longer existed.

"I mean, whenever I tried to get you to talk about it, you kinda ignored me." She shrugged her shoulders. "For the record, I am a lesbian. I love girls in all shapes and sizes."

"In Mostar?" Franka asked the stupid question without a shred of self-awareness until it was too late, and Mirna had interpreted it in the worst way possible.

"Yes, Franka. Despite being a third-world, undeveloped country, we have running water, internet, and even gay people," she snapped, probably back to thinking of her as a judgmental American.

"No, I didn't mean it like that," Franka said, trying to extinguish the flame that was likely forming in Mirna's mind. "It's just... Like, in Georgia, I came out when I was thirteen and everyone was cool with it. I mean, I remembered when Isabella started transitioning. We were always an accepting family. Dad took me to my first Pride when I was fourteen and told me that he and Mom briefly dated the same guy in college. But when I came to Mostar, the first day, and I mean the *first* day, some guy ripped the pride pin off my backpack and told me he hated the F slur. Thank God that was one of the Croatian words I knew. And, for the sake of my safety, for the sake of my mom, I went back into the closet. I didn't have any friends, let alone date anyone, so I buried it all. It was easier."

She took a deep breath, as a burden she didn't even know weighed her down so much finally began to dissipate. Mom never asked, probably not wanting to pick at it any more than she needed to. Franka was always closer to her dad, so she never learned how to communicate with her mom and talk to her as her equal. She didn't want to burden Isabella with it either, because she knew her aunt would leave everything to come and help if only she knew how much Franka hated her life in Mostar, so the only solution was to keep it all to herself.

"How come you're so open? Or is it just with me?" she asked.

Since she moved here, she had mostly heard locals refer to queer people as a joke or an insult. Only a few celebrities and one prime minister were out of the closet, seemingly in the whole of ex-Yu. Franka couldn't even wrap her head around a regular teenager like Mirna being so open in this society that demanded silence.

"I'm really bad at hiding it," Mirna replied with a smile that tried to cover the sadness in her voice, "plain and simple. So I never bothered. I've been harassed and yelled at a few times, but I'm a big, tough girl. And for all they know, I have every diver in this city watching my back," she said, suddenly looking away from Franka, staring at the floor instead.

"Do you?" Franka asked. A part of her doubted that a macho club so against girls diving would be much more open to them kissing other girls unless it was for their entertainment.

"That's part of the reason I broke Izmir's nose," she said. "You know how guys are supposed to jump from the bridge to prove they are worthy of dating a girl?" Franka nodded for her to continue. Classic macho posturing. "Well, he was being an asshole that whole day. The girl he liked, Sara, liked me, and she told him that for some stupid reason. Probably because he was being really pushy and a creep. So he decided to take it out on me. He told me I would never dive off the bridge, no matter how hard I tried, then insulted me for being gay, even if I wasn't even sure of my sexuality then, and I snapped and punched him in his stupid face and broke his nose. Everyone backed me up and said he was provoking me, but it still went into my permanent record. When I applied to transfer to Unbounded High School in my second year, they took one look at it, ignored my perfect grades and extracurriculars, and rejected me. Since then, everyone has kept their complaints to themselves," Mirna revealed her brutal but efficient approach, still looking at the floor like she was ashamed of what she did.

Franka would like to think she would have done the same thing.

"That's why no one bothers me about it. They know I will punch them if they deserve it. But Ado told me about the bet they all have. The first one to successfully seduce me and stop me from "being a lesbian" will get the bragging rights akin to winning the gold medal."

"Assholes," Franka said, her stomach turning at the mere thought of such a misogynistic line of thinking. "And your folks?"

"They know, but they pretend they don't. Like, they love me no matter what, and that is what matters. They don't know how to talk about it. I don't push them. They will accept me fully, sooner or later," she explained with a small smile.

Franka took a deep breath, as her insides filled with warmth and love for her mom and dad, not just for being so supportive, but for knowing how and being willing to talk about these things.

Mirna's parents loved her. That much was obvious, but, unlike Franka's college-educated folks from a big metropolis, who were surrounded with opportunities to see and meet people from all walks of life and learn about them, Mirna's parents didn't have that privilege. But they still had love.

They didn't say anything for a little while and avoided looking at each other. Did they mess up this friendship for a few hours of making out, Franka wondered as Mirna stared at her neck. Franka raised her fingers to it, catching a glimpse of herself on a mirror hanging from the door. A hickey. She'd never had one of those.

She didn't mind it at all, but did Mirna mind making it?

"And what now?" she asked as she gave Mirna one of her oversized shirts, so she wouldn't have to walk around in her underwear or in a dress. "Where do we go from here?"

"We continue like nothing happened?" Mirna suggested. Something in Franka wanted to fight her, to tell her she didn't want to go back to how things were only yesterday. She wanted those lips on hers again. She wanted them to do what they didn't last night, but sober and prepared this time.

But she didn't. The last trace of alcohol was talking. Mirna seemed content with being friends again, so who was Franka to complain?

That conversation should have brought them back to stage one, to how they were before that first kiss, but human minds are rarely so simple. When Mirna left her house not even half an hour later, everything had changed.

"Yeah, a bit of experimentation, teasing," Franka assured Ivona and the rest of the girls when they returned to classes a few days later. "Haven't you ever kissed your best friend? It's all the rage in America. Guys think it's like the hottest thing."

As she told them that, trying to look as casual as possible, like it didn't bother her at all, Franka had never felt dirtier in her life. Fetishizing her own sexuality broke her heart, but it was the safest option. Safety was the most important thing in this country.

Franka: Heey, gym tonight? Around 8?

It was a few days after New Year's Eve.

> **Mirna**: Ooooh, I would love to, but I got my period. Cramps are killing me more than usual.

She had texted back three hours later, which in Mirna time was a century.

> **Mirna**: Sorry about that. But you go yourself. I'll meet you in a few days when my uterus stops waging war against me.

Mirna did not meet her in a few days. In the next month and a half, they met three times, and only at the gym. Mirna barely spoke the whole time she was there. She ran and did her exercise and left quicker than ever before. But she went to the gym on her own. One of the guys working there told Franka. Obviously, she just didn't want to go with Franka.

But Franka couldn't spend too much time wondering about how a few kisses had ruined the best friendship she had in this city. Classes were soon done and exams arrived in full force. She had to focus on studying.

Growing up and preparing to attend a university in the US her whole life, Franka was still trying to wrap her head around the way Bosnian schools did things. The entire semester was moved a month back from what she expected, with classes only ending in early January. Like most others in this whole region, after the fall semester, Franka's college had two examination periods, but only after the New Year and Christmas, in January and February.

This school was no joke, and she had worked too hard to mess it up now by wasting her time thinking about people who didn't want her in their life. So after New Year's Eve, as the classes came to an end and the exams drew closer, she did nothing but study. The dark circles under her eyes made a triumphant comeback, and coffee and Blue Stallion energy drinks became her new best friends.

"Where is your buddy?" Mom asked her as she watched her in her room, drowning in books like it was last June again. But this was June on steroids, even if Franka was now more confident in her ability to beat it.

"She's also studying, I guess," Franka concluded, fidgeting with her glasses, convincing neither herself nor her mom.

Her efforts worked out in the end, which was the most important part. Even without Mirna, she was capable of learning.

In the first exam period in late January, she passed everything except math. But since she didn't practice at all, going to the exam just to see the questions, she didn't care. She had more time to prepare for second period.

She did, passing with ease in early February and scoring a solid B. As far as she could gather from her fellow students, she was near the top of the class.

"I am so proud of you, sweetie!" her mom gushed like she hadn't had the chance to in a long time. She took her out to a fancy dinner as a celebration, and Franka wasn't about to reject such an offer.

"That's our girl! Your dad would be so proud of you!" Isabella wrote in the letter she sent, along with a brand new laptop as an early birthday present.

"Auntie, aren't you broke? You really shouldn't have spent so much on me," Franka asked her when they hopped on a video call. Bella gave her a cryptic smile.

"Not for much longer," she promised her. "But I don't want to jinx it by talking about it."

Still, despite everything being so good, Franka found herself falling. She would hang out with her friends less than usual. Without Mirna, the gym wasn't as much fun, so she slowly stopped going. She needed the extra time to study anyway. Wasn't the whole point of the gym to get her ready to dive off the bridge again? Who would teach her that now? Not Emir Kapo, that's for sure. It was either Mirna and Grandpa Džemal, or no one. For now, Franka would have to stay on dry land.

Franka's heart yearned for the freedom diving brought with it. She wanted to do it again, to fly like Mirna did. But maybe it wasn't in the cards.

What *was* in the cards was ten days of uninterrupted rest, filled with anime, snacks, and walking around the house in her pajamas from dusk till dawn before the second semester started.

"What're your plans for your birthday?" Mom asked her a few days before February 14th.

"You will bake me a nice chocolate cake?" Franka suggested with what Mom once described as the "little brat" smile.

She was in the middle of the second season of a "pretty boys do sports things" kind of anime, this one about swimming. Thank God their house was old and creaky because the noises gave Franka enough time to wipe the tears caused by a scene she would have probably called generic and lame before, but "they were friends, Goddamn it!" So it hit right in the solar plexus as if it were high art.

"How about you call Mirna over, and I'll order us a cake? Maybe chocolate? Or a cheesecake with strawberries? I haven't seen Mirna in a long time," Mom said. Her excavation of information would have been more subtle if she brought a backhoe.

"Exams," Franka reminded her like she wasn't 100 percent sure Mirna had aced every single one a long time ago.

"You know you can talk to me, Franka, about anything and everything," Mom reminded her as she sat on the bed next to her, pretending she didn't notice the potato chip crumbs on her sheet that were bound to attract ants sooner or later.

"I'm... I'm a bit homesick," Franka said. It was at least one of the things that was on her mind, and a true one at that.

In the years she'd been in Mostar, birthdays had always been the worst. Ever since she could remember, on February 14th, Dad would take her to the zoo or to the aquarium or whatever they came up with for that year, and they would spend the day together, rewarding themselves with some good food of Franka's choice (Burger Man in her younger days, but later she would ask for something slightly more refined).

Her birthday was one of the last full days they had together before his accident. Soon after, he was gone. For the last two years, Mom suggested different activities, but all Franka wanted to do was be alone with his records.

"I'm sorry, love." Mom was sympathetic, but, like usual, didn't know how to help. "Maybe calling Aunt Bella will cheer you up?"

Hearing her voice and seeing how Bella's fifth ferret was fitting in with the rest of the crew did help, but at the end of the day, Franka was left with the third season of her swimming anime and a hole in her soul she tried her hardest to fill with potato chips.

She thought about calling her college friends over for drinks, but her birthday was on Valentine's Day. Even if it wasn't as big a deal here as in the US, most of them still wanted to go out with their boyfriends. The only one free was supposedly Ivona, who suddenly had to study that night the moment she realized she and Franka would be alone on Valentine's Day.

But it didn't matter. She would still have a well-deserved lazy day. Even if her diving girl ignored her, Franka still had her swimming boys to keep her company.

Except, on the night before her birthday, she got an unexpected message.

> **Mirna**: Heey, as far as I remember, it's your birthday tomorrow. Do you want to hang out? I have a plan you might like.

> **Franka**: You have been ignoring me ever since the New Year, you asshole! Now you have the decency to text, you stubborn, holier-than-thou jerk…

Franka began to type in a fury that subsided before she could finish. But it was Mirna. She couldn't say no to her.

> **Franka**: Yep, big 19. What do you have in mind?

> **Mirna**: Meet me at the Spanish Square tomorrow. Does 5:30 p.m. work for you?

Franka ended the texting with a thumbs-up emoji.

The next day, with nothing better to do, filled with the desire to see that stupid beautiful smile again, Franka got dressed in her favorite black sweater and ripped jeans and made her way to their meeting location.

For once, she was the one waiting for Mirna. She sat in the small park next to their high school. It looked more Greek than Spanish, in her humble opinion. She only realized she'd bitten her nails to the bone when her middle finger began to pulsate with dull but annoying pain. Weird. She hadn't done that in years.

Mirna showed up a few minutes late, sticking out like she usually did on a cold winter day in her bright yellow coat, her hair styled in an intricate braid around her head like she was trying to look extra Slavic today.

"I'm sorry" was the first thing she said as she pulled Franka into a hug that she was powerless to resist, if she wanted to resist it in the first place. "I have been a terrible friend."

"Oh, you absolutely have," Franka confirmed, even if she kept hugging her. Her body was warm and soft in all the right places, and Franka never wanted to let go.

"I know, I know. It was... I don't know... I was just an idiot," she said as they finally separated after what felt like too little time.

"Once again, correct," Franka said. Mirna looked at her, eyes filled with tears. Her face looked slimmer and her cheeks more hollow than usual, like she hadn't been eating properly. A part of Franka gloated at the fact Mirna wasn't doing much better than she was. "So why now?"

"Ado called your mom, and she told him you have been sulking," she admitted. "I may have been sulking too. And I couldn't let you be alone on your birthday."

"I missed you," Franka admitted. She wanted to bury this emotion too like she had buried so many before and replace it with apathy, the only safe option, but it burst out of her in an instant.

"I know. I missed you too. I'm sorry I was a terrible friend. You really deserved better," Mirna said, looking her in the eyes. "But after that night, I don't know...I froze. I didn't know how to talk to you. I thought it would be awkward."

"So you cut me out," Franka said. "I thought that would be *my* move," she added with a smile.

"Maybe we are more similar than you think," she said, her cheeks already red. "Will you give me another chance? At least to treat you to some food?"

"What do you have in mind?" Franka asked as her stomach growled in anticipation. "It all depends on that answer."

"Come on, let's walk to this fine establishment," Mirna said with a smile that lit up the whole square. When she grabbed her hand, Franka's body caught on fire, but she still followed her to the local mall.

"Are you taking me where I think you're taking me?" Franka asked as the sight of the familiar red and orange logo gave away Mirna's secret plan.

"A prestigious and premium location, worthy of my favorite American," Mirna said with a goofy smile on her face.

"Still, Burger Man?" Franka asked, but she wasn't complaining. Chicken nuggets from the stupid American fast-food franchise were her most faithful lover.

"I can't get any Colombian food, probably anywhere in the Balkans. I can't take you to a proper American restaurant. But what is more American than Burger Man?" she asked. Usually, Franka hated the assumption Americans only ever ate fast food. The whole country was a melting pot of different cultures and ethnicities bringing a piece of their homeland in food and in customs. But she never said she was too good for fries. "Come on, it's all on me."

"Okay, I can't say no to free food." Franka tried to play it cool, so Mirna wouldn't know she made her redemption so much easier now that she guessed the exact, correct thing her heart was craving—and her stomach.

Franka ordered a ton of chicken nuggets, French fries, and diet cola, to save room for an apple pie, while Mirna chose a chicken wrap as her main dish, an equally large mountain of fries, and an ice cream as a dessert.

God bless the amazing fast food that was so salty and fatty and so delicious. They sat at the far end of the restaurant, at first focused on the food, but as the hill of fries between them grew smaller, they couldn't hide behind it anymore.

"What happens now?" Franka asked, dipping her nugget into the sweet and sour sauce. For the record, this was considered exotic in Bosnia!

"We start over?" Mirna suggested. "I... I am very confused about my own feelings, but I know that I want you in my life, so we can take it from there. We'll see where it will lead us."

"Okay," Franka agreed. "But we won't distance ourselves from each other like we did." Now that she was by her side again, Franka didn't want to let go.

"No, I promise you we won't. I have missed you too much to do that ever again," Mirna said. "Also, I needed my study buddy this semester."

"How did it go?" Franka asked, chewing on her fry, trying to keep cool.

"I got a C in chemistry! Can you believe it?" Mirna asked, raising her fist up to the sky.

Franka took a sip of her drink.

"What a tragedy," she teased, with her flat voice, trying to hide her smile. "How can you even live with yourself?"

"Hey, good grades are like half of my personality; cut me some slack," Mirna joked, obviously not that upset that she wouldn't have the perfect grade average when she graduated.

"That's because you didn't have me to study with you," Franka concluded, still with her cool voice, making Mirna smile.

"On a related note, they are predicting a warm spring ahead," she said with a conspiratorial look on her face. "Which means we will be able to swim and dive pretty soon."

"That's good to hear," Franka said as her heart began to beat faster at the thought of Neretva, her second favorite Mostarlija. "We need to be ready for summer. I need to dive off that Bridge again. But, like, for real. Prepared."

"And you will," Mirna promised. "Even if I have to assassinate Emir Kapo myself."

"You are not using your freshman knowledge of pharmacology to poison a man," Franka warned her. Mirna frowned, rolling her eyes like she had the whole thing planned out.

"Okay, okay, I'll find an alternative," she said, stealing a nugget from Franka. "I got you something," she added. "I hope you don't mind. I scouted all the stores in the city, but I think it's perfect for you."

The bright yellow paper bag Mirna gave her contained three things: the biggest chocolate on the market ("I know you like strawberries"); a tiny replica of the Old Bridge ("To remind you of our first meeting. Also, can you believe Adnan made me pay for it?"); and a small, dark-green paper parcel, perfectly wrapped, with a yellow bow on it, matching the bag.

The parcel hid a one-piece swimsuit, white, elegant, but simple and sporty, with shorts instead of regular bottoms. It was perfect.

"I think it will fit you," Mirna said, her cheeks already pink. "I wanted you to have a new one—one perfect for you." She took Franka's hands in hers and stared into her eyes. "We are going to dive, Franka," she promised, and Franka believed her like she'd never believed anything else. "We are going to be free."

Franka squealed in excitement and pulled her into a hug right over the table.

"It's good to have you back," she simply said.

NEIRA FAZLOVIC

Chapter Ten

Klizim po mahali, skrolam Quckgram

Maybe the day would come when Mirna would look at Franka's dive with anything but complete awe, but today wasn't it. Franka flew off that board like gravity wasn't something her body was familiar with as she contoured herself in a way Mirna might have thought was impossible if she hadn't seen it with her own two eyes. And if she didn't have video evidence to prove it to the skeptics.

This year, as predicted, spring was a lot warmer than usual. The last cold front hit the country in January, and by February, daisies were already in full bloom. Thank you, global warming. Even their moms agreed they could go back to practice in March.

Yeah, Neretva was, as Franka put it, terrifyingly cold, but she was equally icy in August. The problem was in leaving the water and the frigid wind that welcomed them when they dared to do so. But they would survive, even if they had to carry around tons of tissues all the time to deal with the near-constant runny noses. They didn't have time to waste. Classes, study, and practice were all they had time for. And Mirna loved it.

"I can't believe you want to jump off the bridge," Selma said as they sat in a coffee shop between classes. She just finished watching a video of Mirna's dive from yesterday that she had posted on the @thick.pharma Quickgram. A near-perfect swallow she had to share with the world. "Like, aren't you scared?"

"A bit," Mirna said with a shrug, trying to find the right words to explain an unexplainable feeling. "A healthy dose of fear guarantees you won't do something stupid. But nothing beats the feeling of flying! You feel alive. That trumps the fear!" Her heart began to beat faster at the thought of a dive. "You are from Mostar too. You never thought about diving?"

Selma frowned. "When I first saw my uncle jump, I really wanted to do it too, but my dad told me it was for boys only. I've only seen that one woman dive. I mean, from the locals. And you, I guess. But it does look really fun," she admitted with a smile.

Mirna smiled back but didn't say anything as Selma looked away and pretended to check her phone again.

Most guys in the city never jumped either. It was an extreme sport and not for everyone. But an equal number of crazy girls would love to try it too; they were never allowed to even consider it.

Every now and then, a young girl would show up at the diving club and try to join. Usually, one of the older guys, like Emir, would come down from his ivory tower and have a little chat with her.

"It's a boys' sport," he would remind her like she didn't know that already. "It's really not for fragile little girls like you. Have you tried swimming?"

Most of the time, that conversation would be enough to spook any potential female members away. However, once or twice, the girl in question would still insist on joining. And being the egalitarian and woke person he was, Mr. Kapo would, of course, agree, and she would be allowed to practice.

That is where the real challenge began. Not because cliff diving was more dangerous for a woman in some way—Mirna's favorite was being told that her uterus would shake too much, making her unable to have babies—but because everything about the system was designed to make her regret ever trying to be a part of it or, Allah forbid, change it. For the most part, guys weren't violent or outright cartoonish misogynistic, but boy were they so good at low-key shittiness. The toxicity of the environment, the constant bullying disguised as boys being boys, and pushing each other into riskier and riskier behavior caused most of the guys to quit after a while too. A lot of them got injured trying to do stunts they weren't ready for. Only those who managed to fit in and didn't see anything wrong with how things were done stayed long-term. But out of all the girls who began training, only one remained, and her name was Mirela Lakić.

It wasn't because she was somehow better or unlike other girls. She had the stubbornness that would make any local donkey proud and focused all of it on this one activity. Her grandpa being a local legend helped. They subconsciously or consciously knew not to mess with her as they might mess with a complete outsider. Her height and strength kept them in check too. Franka would have been eaten alive by the end of the first week.

It should not have been that hard. That was the worst part. Maybe it really would be too scary for Selma and she would quit after a while, but maybe she would have been a natural like Franka. It was impossible to tell.

Mirna and Franka went back to practicing as soon as the weather improved and this time, Grandpa was even more involved, shouting advice from the coast. He would also occasionally recruit some of his old friends, other guys who made the most jumps off the bridge, some of whom were more than happy to help if for no other reason than the novelty of seeing women dive. Others still thought this "experiment" of his was total and complete bullshit, and they were not too shy to say that to his face while pretending the two of them weren't even there and perfectly capable of hearing them.

"Safet, my Mirna is still training while your Izmir suddenly quit when it was actually time to jump. Don't tell me girls can't do this when they so clearly can," Grandpa snapped at his friend when he got too annoying one time. Safet scoffed and walked away, but after that, he kept most of his complaints to himself.

To be perfectly honest, as it turned out, Grandpa was not the best of coaches, maybe because he was old or because he hadn't jumped in decades. He was great at the little touches that distinguished a good jump from a great one, but he didn't give clear and precise instructions about what exactly to do with one's body. They mostly taught themselves, even if his backup was immensely valuable every step of the way.

Franka's hard work paid off and her swimming improved so much that she wasn't in immediate danger of drowning. Mirna's landings were so much better than they were in August. If they let her jump now, no way she would have messed up her shoulder.

Franka taught her how to do a great somersault Mirna would never be a natural at it like Franka was, but she was getting better with every practice. Franka even helped her with Spanish whenever either of them remembered Mirna's vow. It was going slowly, but it wasn't stopping so that must have counted for something.

The near-constant filming of the dives was a great tool to spot little mistakes and make sure they were at their best. From time to time, they would publish the videos on their social networks.

"Give the people what they want!" Franka said as they watched the number of likes and comments on her video rise. Mirna had to agree. Praise was a powerful drug.

Franka texted her sometime in April.

> *Franka (sometime in April)*: Isabella is sending me an old sports action camera. One of her colleagues, Jonson, a mountain biker, got a new one. When Bella showed him some of our videos, he really wanted to pitch in! She says it's better we have it instead of her using it to film her ferrets.

Mirna had to agree, even if those ferrets were so damn cute.

"Tell that civil engineer I love him!" she wrote back. "And that he also gets a free tour of the bridge if he ever comes to Mostar!"

For the first time since she started training, Mirna wasn't obsessed with whether she would ever actually get to dive off the bridge itself. She was enjoying the moment too much.

From time to time, the guys from the club also came by to congratulate them on their hard work, or they commented on their videos with encouraging messages. The good sign was that most of the comments on the @Columbian_bowtie Quickgram account were of the "good technique" variety instead of the "you are so hot" type. It was probably because the first (and the last) guy who commented: "My Mexican goddess, how I wish to see what is under that swimsuit *eggplant emoji* *peach emoji* *drooling emoji*" was hit with a block and relentlessly mocked to Franka's growing online following.

Only one voice mattered, but Mirna had burned that bridge in August and then gone back to scorch it a few times, for good measure.

It was late April. Maybe Grandpa could do something by July. Or maybe Emir would decide to retire from his retirement and leave the diving decisions to someone who didn't hold a grudge against her. Maybe Aca—he was always a good one. But that was the future. For once, she liked the present as it was.

After their little break caused by Mirna's inability to deal with her feelings, they went back to cleaning the Partisan Cemetery every second weekend. *Kreteni* still left trash, but at least those people who died had some dignity in their final resting place. To be honest, it was a good excuse to spend time with Franka, all alone in nature. While they cleaned the trash, she wasn't thinking about New Year's Eve and the feel of Franka's lips against her own. Not at all. Nope. *Jok.* They were there doing a good thing.

I just freaked out for a month and a half, okay!? It happens to everyone! She had thought they could go back to what they had before, but the moment she remembered it, an avalanche of emotions buried her mind, and instead of digging herself out, she made an igloo in her head and lived there for a month, pretending she didn't feel the cold. But thank Allah for Ado (a sentence she never thought she would say). He even started doing the dishes occasionally. A miracle indeed.

On that particular Saturday practice, Grandpa wasn't with them. Ado had some schoolwork and Emira really needed Mom's services with her apartment, so Grandpa was selling džidže, leaving Mirna and Franka on their own.

Midterms were rapidly approaching, so they had to focus on schoolwork for the next few weeks if they wanted to pass. This was mostly a relaxing practice, where Franka tried to improve her swallow but kept chickening out and landing perfectly headfirst like she was ready for the Olympics.

They were so focused on their own diving that they didn't even notice the crowd gathered at the top of the bridge and a man getting ready to dive.

"Is that...?" Franka began to ask as the man cheered the crowd on as much as they cheered him.

"Emir Kapo?" Mirna asked as they slowly got out of the water, realizing their practice was now over. "Yep, no one else is that much of a showman."

And a showman he was. Before he ever got to the top of the bridge, the crowd turned wild, like he was attempting an impossible feat never done before by a mere human.

Only one person didn't seem that impressed. A small boy sat on one of the large stones under the bridge, moving pebbles with his foot that drew his attention instead of his dad.

"Hey, Emil," Mirna said in her nicest voice. He looked up and smiled as a hello. Every diver had known Emil since he was a little baby, as his dad liked to parade him and hail him as the future of the sport before he could even walk. In fact, the ever-present choir of city gossip even suspected that was one of the reasons Maja Kapo filed for divorce. "Franka, this is Emil, Emir's son," she added as the boy politely shook Franka's hand.

"What are you two doing here?" Franka asked. The way she held herself in the presence of a child—like it was a tiny, dangerous alien—gave away that she never had kids in her family.

"*Babo* wanted me to see him dive again. He said I wasn't taking my practice seriously enough, so he wants to show me how awesome it can look."

"He does dive very well," Mirna said. Emil nodded, looking up at them, his eyes full of wonder.

"He's the best!" he said. "But he said he would take me to the movies today," he added, pouting his lips.

"And do you want to be a diver?" Mirna asked, kneeling next to him.

"Of course," he said with a smile that never reached his eyes, as if Mirna were looking at a twisted mirror of herself.

By that time, Emir had worked the crowd into a frenzy, so he finally poured cold water on himself so his heart wouldn't give out and dove off the bridge.

He was the most famous diver in this city, a future legend of this generation, for a good reason. He was powerful, yet graceful, not like the most common brutes who too often jumped and hoped for the best. He appeared to command the air around him to give him a bit of that extra kick and make his dive spectacular. He did a somersault and landed perfectly in the water.

"Wow," Franka simply said, her mouth slightly open in shock. Their wetsuits were a good protection against the spring wind, but it was like the sight of that man lowered the temperature of the city.

"Thank you, everyone!" Emir yelled to the crowd that was going apeshit above them. He swam out slowly, like he was taking his time in the ice-cold river.

"I haven't done that in a long time," he said as he approached them. "It really is the best feeling in the world."

"Isn't it?" Mirna said, despite her better judgment. She shouldn't give him a bit of satisfaction of knowing how much her heart yearned for it.

"See, kid, don't you want to do that too? Be like your old man? You don't have to fight as hard as I did. I paved the way for you. You only have to follow in my footsteps," he said, tossing Emil's hair with his wet hand. The kid nodded and smiled but didn't say anything.

"Quite impressive," Franka said in her most polite voice, and Mirna breathed a sigh of relief. Maybe Mirna had messed up her chances for a civil conversation with Emir, but Franka did not. She was "exotic" and new and maybe she could get on his good side. What could help the profile of the sport more than a face like Franka's?

"I know," he simply said. "Some people are just born with it, I guess. Aren't they, Mirna?" he asked.

"Thank Allah for that," Mirna said, not even annoyed this time. She knew his game by now. "Those people should be given a chance to show their talents," she added with her most polite smile.

Emir looked at Franka. Not in the lustful way of a creepy man looking at a young woman, but meticulously, like a businessman, examining his investment before he sank money into it. Franka did not back down from his gaze, looking him in the eye, until he finally smiled.

"Franka, you really are something else," he finally admitted.

"Then let me compete if you're so sure of your assessment." She seemed so tiny next to him, but she didn't back down. He shook his head no.

"That is not going to happen and you know it," he said, his eyes cold, almost robotic. "You can practice all you want, girls, but it's not about how good you are anymore. In the end, the choice is mine. And I chose a long time ago that Mirna will never, ever jump off that bridge again. Simple as that. We made a deal," he said.

Mirna swallowed whatever she had to say, trying to keep the orb of anger inside her stomach from exploding and enclosing her whole. Whatever she said now, she would only make the situation worse.

"This sport is our legacy. They destroyed our bridge, but we rebuilt it, and I will rebuild this piece of our history on my own, if that's what it takes, to how it used to be, or better. When I'm gone, Emil will continue on my path. We are making history. It's about longevity, not gimmicks. We don't need female competitors. Our elders didn't have them either," he said. Emil now hid behind him, like he didn't want his dad to even see him, but Emir had a new target. "I was good to you, Mirna. I allowed you to train with us, to live out your little fantasy, but you made your choice when you did that swallow. Now you're in the real world, and you have to suffer the consequences." He turned to Franka next, like Mirna's existence didn't even bother him anymore. "As for you, little one, it's a different story. I can see what Džemal saw in you that day. Maybe, if we need another act to show off, you could work as well as Mirna did last year if you are smarter than her. You are a natural at this. We could show you off if you let us."

"I'm not doing it without Mirna," Franka said, staring him down, ready to fight. He shrugged.

"Suit yourself," he said. "I can ask the firefighter again. She at least knows how to follow commands."

He left them alone under the bridge that they wouldn't ever have the chance to conquer again, two girls too insignificant for him to even bother. Emil turned around and waved goodbye. Poor kid.

"Mirna, he really isn't going to let us compete," Franka said. She sat on the white rock, wrapped up in her towel, gazing at the river ahead.

"No." Mirna finally accepted what she had been trying for so long to ignore. No matter how many times she said it, as a joke or seriously, a part of her still hoped things would change.

He had to let them compete. He wasn't a bad man, just a stubborn one and obsessed with traditional ways of doing things.

But he was more than that. This man was a businessman, not a brute stuck in the eighteenth century who thought women should be in the kitchen. He just wouldn't allow these two women to do this one thing.

"What do we do now?" Franka asked.

"We focus on our midterms for the next few weeks, like we agreed we would," Mirna said, trying to give the reins of her brain back to its most rational part. "And then, I don't know, Franka. I really don't know."

For the next few days, Mirna came to terms with the fact that she would probably never get to dive off the Old Bridge again. She could dive off a million other places, some of them even in Bosnia, but maybe Mostar was simply not in the cards anymore.

Exams kept her too busy to fall down the rabbit hole of bad thoughts. She had to nail this semester, even more than the last one, so she and Franka increased their study time at the expense of everything else.

Mirna adored academia. She loved to learn new things, understand new concepts, and see how the world around her worked on a fundamental level. No one could stop her from using her brain and studying. She didn't only study with Franka anymore.

People in her year figured out pretty quickly she was not only the best student there, but also loved helping others, so they kept asking her for help, which she loved providing.

For the next few weeks, she studied, ate, and slept. But in the end, when the midterms were behind them, it was worth it.

Since she didn't have time to dive, she also didn't have time to think, which suited her well. But every night, no matter how tired she was or how much she thought she would fall asleep the moment her head collided with her pillow, the pair of eyes that reminded her of Neretva crept back into her mind and kept her awake.

Okay, maybe she wasn't totally over the whole New Year's Eve thing!

So one night before the exam she feared the most, at 2:00 a.m., she broke down and did what she did best: made a list.

Pros:

- Franka was amazing.

- She was gorgeous.

- She was really smart in three different languages.

- She was an amazing diver.

- She liked her back.

Cons:

- One day, sooner rather than later, she would probably disappear when the call of Atlanta became too great, and Mirna would be alone again.

The choice was clear to Mirna, so she ignored those weird feelings in her tummy whenever she saw Franka or, Allah forbid, if they accidentally touched. They would pass. She would kill the butterflies with an insecticide called "*inat*," if that's what it took.

Mirna had just finished her last midterm exam until June and she was more than happy with herself. Maybe her past practice of thinking she would flunk everything wasn't actually the best choice for her mental health.

As Selma checked the answer to the third question (Mirna said it was B, while Selma swore, wrongly, it was D) Mirna took out her phone to find a single new notification.

Franka had sent her a screenshot.

Blue Stallion's official account liked a video of Mirna's dive Franka had posted a few weeks back. It was one of her best. She did a backward somersault and landed perfectly.

A vision came over Mirna, like a prophet receiving revelation from heaven. For the first time, the only possible plan for the future was right in front of her.

Emir Kapo did not own the bridge. He did not own the concept of cliff diving. Neither did Blue Stallion, but Emir was a small fish in their big pond. If he was a businessman, he knew he had to play nice with them.

If he wasn't going to listen to Franka and Mirna, maybe he would listen to Blue Stallion.

Mirna: "Frana, we hav to g viral!"

In such a rush, Mirna misspelled the message.

They met at the Burger Man about an hour later. Mirna was already wolfing down her fish sandwich because she needed all the energy she could get for plotting and scheming.

Franka ran in, straight from an exam herself, her glasses wonky, because Mirna might have sounded like it was a life-or-death situation in her text.

"Look, if we get their attention, gather enough followers, and then make a big fuss about it, do you think Blue Stallion will risk being seen as sexist and misogynistic for the sake of one guy who won't let girls compete?" she presented her idea to Franka once she caught her breath again and was done scolding her for being overdramatic.

"And how do we do that?" Franka asked, stealing one of her curly fries as compensation for her mental anguish.

"I told you already," Mirna said. "We go viral. We make a bunch of videos showcasing our talents and then make a big deal about them not letting us compete. I know Blue Stallion isn't in charge of the competition we want to participate in, but it's still potential bad press they can get rid of by letting us jump off the damn thing. I know it's not a perfect solution, especially the whole 'going viral' thing, but we have nothing to lose!" she insisted as she took another big bite of her divinely generic sandwich.

Franka stared at her for a few moments, wordless, her gorgeous head tilted in confusion as the wheels in her brain spun. It was all so crazy, and it relied on chance way too much for Mirna's comfort. But if they really wanted to do this, they had to think outside the box.

"Mirna Lakić, you're a genius!" she finally exclaimed.

By the end of that evening "Swallows of Mostar" officially flew into the world.

Chapter Eleven

Mirna i Franka ustale malo ranije da nešto završe

Okay, this was really stupid, and it might result in their own deaths. Both Franka and Mirna were perfectly aware of that, but their choices were limited, so it was either this or giving up. They were way too stubborn to settle for that second option.

"We have to land perfectly, dry ourselves, and run." Mirna repeated their plan last night for the millionth time, now visibly shaking with excitement. "I know it's early and a tight schedule, but this is our best chance."

And early they were: 4:10 a.m., to be exact, when Franka sneaked out of her house, her swimsuit already on, carrying a large backpack with spare clothes and something else she had never worn in her life. She would finally do it. She would dive off the Old Bridge. On purpose!

Her mom would kill her. So would Mirna's mom. And Emir. And Grandpa Džemal. And possibly half of Mostar if this went too far and they lost an important source of tourists. The Lakić family was far from the only one who lived off tourism. Mirna and Franka probably weren't nearly influential enough to mess this whole thing up, but the possibility still lingered in their minds, no matter how insignificant it actually was.

***

"They should kill Emir Kapo, not us," Ado had said when Franka had first pointed out a similar observation. They were in Franka's room. Her mom was out, leading the Shakespeare drama club with her students, so the three of them could scheme all they wanted without being interrupted. "He is the one who made you go to this extreme."

"Hit him in his wallet, that works the best," Mirna assured her. "If Blue Stallion says anything, he will have to let us compete if he doesn't want to risk a PR disaster."

"The Swallows of Mostar will conquer this!" Ado assured them like a proud general leading his people into a deadly battle. "I will make sure of that."

Franka believed him. Over the last month or so, he became a vital ally in their fight against the forces that kept them grounded.

Mirna's and Franka's scheme to take over the internet with their social networking skills had one fatal flaw: neither of them had any social networking skills.

@Colombian_bowtie had gathered a few hundred followers on her different accounts over the last few months, mostly by sheer dumb luck, but @thicc.pharma was somehow even worse. In a stunning turn of events, while Franka used her social networks to look at cute animal videos, Mirna used them to follow every fan account for Lyfe 3 Pynk, a K-pop band known to only her and, like, twelve other people.

"You could've at least gone with one of the mainstream ones," Franka said, shaking her head, as Mirna blushed into oblivion. "Not that I know any of them," she added quickly, to cover up the fact that her playlists did not consist of only 90s grunge like she would like to pretend.

"They will be big soon!" Mirna promised, shaking her fist to the sky. "But you are not much better than me either," she noted, pointing to what the last few months of posting videos and photos of their jumps had gotten them. It had a lot of potential, but it wasn't nearly enough. Not if they wanted the attention of the people in charge.

"We need an expert," Franka had said, making Mirna look her in the eyes so she knew she understood this was the only way. "I think you know who I'm talking about." Mirna nodded in agreement, but still pouted her lips in protest.

"My pride might never recover from this," she'd said, even if they both knew they had no other choice.

So on a Saturday morning, Franka and Mirna had made their way to the Mostarske Džidže to find their target. They had gotten there early, before the train from Sarajevo carrying one-day visitors arrived, so the Old Town was mostly empty as vendors set up their stalls, including Ado.

He must have noticed them, even if he was so perfectly focused on making sure his džidže were the best-looking ones in the whole Old Town, but he continued to center his "*We accept marks, euros, credit cards, and you*" sign until he was happy with it and they were breathing down his neck.

"Oh, who do we have here? The infamous Swallows of Mostar came to ask for my help!" he said, finally turning to face them. He wore black, loose *čakšire* pants, with a thick red cloth belt around his waist, perfectly matching his red fez, like he'd dropped straight out of one of the Turkish period dramas that were constantly on every TV station in the country.

"How did you know we were here to ask for help?" Franka inquired with her most polite smile.

"Because Mirna bought my favorite chips last night: sour cream and onions. The chips she hates," he said with a smirk, pointing at his sister. "Hand it over." Mirna gave him a bag from her backpack as if it were a very stinky diaper. "Oh, the food of gods," he said, opening the bag to Mirna's visible disgust. "Quickgram algorithm suggested a new account to me this morning. 'Swallows of Mostar,' a great name. For now it only has one video of Franka's dive. I think I know where this is going. Now, how can I help you with your little start-up?" he asked, nibbling a chip like it was a filet mignon.

"Oh, magnificent Adnan sensei, help us go viral," Franka said, making both Mirna and Ado smile.

"You know how to dazzle a man," he said, putting down his bribe so he could give them his undivided attention. "How viral are we talking about?" he asked.

"Enough that Blue Stallion notices us," Mirna clarified. "You have made Džidže go viral since you took over the social networks…"

"Correction, since I made the social networks," he said, and Mirna nodded to confirm his assessment. "I think I could do the same thing for you. You two are selling something even better than kitschy souvenirs: a story! A brand! I like that!" His eyes were full of ambition, ready to take on a new and exciting challenge. "And I get to stick it to Emir Kapo, Count of Monte Cristo style! What else can a man want?"

"What has he done to you that you want revenge?" Franka asked. Ado turned away from them, fixing knick-knacks on the shelves that already looked nearly perfect, avoiding Mirna's intense stare as she stood, frozen in place like she knew she wasn't going to like whatever she would hear.

"He dared me to do a swallow to prove I was 'a real man,' called me a coward and a pussy until I did it, and I ended up in the emergency room," he said in a cold voice, finally turning to face them.

"I did not know that!" Mirna said, her eyes flaming with a fresh dose of fury as her ever-present hatred for Emir Kapo found a new reason for its existence. "I'm going to kill him! You were a child!"

Ado brushed her off with a stance and acceptance of someone who had made his decisions a long time ago and learned to live with them.

109

"Well, I didn't want to tell you because you or Grandpa would have punched him, and that would have ruined your chances to dive," he admitted, shrugging his shoulders. "This is more me: a trickery revenge like Loki, like Veleš!" he added in a grandiose voice that barely masked the anger in his eyes. Likely, the anger was at himself as much as at Emir.

"Okay, supervillain, how will you help us now?" Franka asked to cheer up the atmosphere before it turned too glum, because Mirna still looked like she was about to throw Emir off a bridge and into hell where he belonged. Franka would help her in that effort, but now was not the time.

"Give me the password to that account and send me videos and photos of you diving. I'll do the rest. I promise," Ado said as they shook hands in this business deal of the century.

He did not disappoint. After every practice, Mirna and Franka had sent him some material to work with, and he had always spun it into pure gold. Franka had translated the posts to English and Mirna made sure his Bosnian grammar was correct, but he did most of the work.

Thank Allah he had because, with the classes and the exams and practice, Mirna and Franka couldn't have done it on their own. Luckily, Ado enjoyed every minute of his new job. As the number of followers and likes rose, their excitement followed. People from all over the world left them nice and positive comments, telling them to keep up the good work and post more often. They weren't the only ones, of course. Numerous breeds of jerks and creeps were also always there with an insult or something wildly inappropriate, but they were in the minority.

"I have pulled off a miracle," Ado told them after a few weeks. "But that's because I'm just that good. Swallows of Mostar is on constant growth on every major social network. We have been especially popular on Quickgram ever since that GoPro arrived," he'd explained, like this was a Fortune 500 company and he was the CEO.

"Everyone loves us at Isabella's new job!" Franka said with a smile, showing them a photo of five people, Bella in the middle, holding five unruly-looking ferrets and smiling at the camera. Finally, after so long, Bella had a full-time job she loved. Franka couldn't have been any happier for her.

"If everything else fails, you can be social network influencers in a few years," Ado suggested. "It's not a bad gig, just saying."

"That is not what we want, but thank you," Mirna said, handing him another bag of his well-deserved chipsy bribe that became at least one third of his daily caloric intake.

"I know, I know, but keep all your options open," he said, shrugging his shoulders. "Blue Stallion's official account liked numerous posts of ours, and they have even commented once. They are beginning to notice us, just like we planned. Also, Mirna, your New Zealand wife followed us last night," he added in a casual voice like he didn't know how his sister would react.

"She did!?" Mirna squealed, her eyes giant with excitement, like the woman asked her to marry her, not followed their account. "Oh my god, oh my god!!!! That is amazing!!! She is amazing!! All of this is amazing!!"

For whatever reason, a tiny pit of jealousy opened up in Franka's stomach, threatening to swallow her whole. Maybe she wasn't as over that New Year's Eve as much as she thought she was. That would explain why she found herself staring at Mirna when they studied together and had the desire to tuck a loose strand of her golden hair just for a chance to touch her, even for a few moments. To say nothing of the occasional dreams of Mirna coming out of the water—sans her swimsuit.

"But we are still not getting our message across!" Ado said, thankfully dragging Franka from her thoughts before they could go too far. "They see you dive and think you are regular enthusiasts showing off their skills and nothing more. We are missing our core story: Why are you two, as great as you are, not allowed to compete?" he asked.

"What do you have in mind?" Franka asked.

"One video," Ado said. "One video of you diving off the Old Bridge, to show the Blue Stallion people and the rest of the world that you are not allowed to compete even if you are good enough. That is what we need!" he revealed his pitch.

"You want us to jump off the bridge without permission?" Franka asked as the "Danger!" alarm blared in her brain, even if she tried to silence it. Mirna was the one to answer.

"No, that is what I want, plain and simple," she said, her face emotionless, refusing to look at any of them. "Emir won't give us his blessing. This is the next best thing, a guerilla action. And we get to dive again." Without a warning, she took both of Franka's hands into her own. Franka could only hope she couldn't feel that her heart was already beating like crazy. "Do you feel ready? Because I know you are. It's up to you if you want us to take this chance."

Franka didn't hesitate at all. This is what she was born to do.

"Hell yeah!" she yelled in English. "Count me in!"

Mirna picked her up and pulled her into a hug, setting every single nerve ending in Franka's body on fire in the best way possible. If the actual jump was as good as this, Franka was in for a treat.

"I can't wait!" Mirna said. "We can do this, Franka! And it's going to be amazing!"

So, they had started planning.

Time: Second week of May, very early Tuesday morning. Old Town should be basically empty then.

Place: Old Bridge.

Equipment: Franka's phone, as it was the newest one; the video equipment from Mr. Jameson and a drone that Ado had borrowed from a friend of a cousin who knew a guy.

Editor: Adnan Lakić, as long as he was bribed by Mirna doing all his chores and Franka doing his math homework for the next three weeks (which they had both agreed to, even if Emina would kill them if she had any idea).

Jump: a simple somersault with a feetfirst landing, nothing too spectacular. They filmed the more impressive stunts on the diving board, where they could practice and make sure it was perfect. It was Franka's first real jump, and they had one chance to make it work. It wasn't worth the risk to try to overcomplicate it.

Costume: Well, that wasn't going to be so easy.

"I think, and Mirna might kill me, that you two in traditional costumes might make it so much cooler," Ado said a few nights before the planned jump.

They were in Mirna's room. Even if it was much neater than Franka's, with not a speck of dust on any of the shelves and all her textbooks sorted in order of importance, it still felt so much more like a place where someone had lived for almost nineteen years. It had red ćilim carpet with traditional geometric patterns, and an ancient wooden chest Mirna said was over a century old, filled with all the things Mirna didn't want people to see (mostly diving and Lyfe 3 Pynk merchandise).

"I know you don't want to wear it, but you don't have to jump in it. A few shots on the bridge; that's all we need. A traditional Balkan woman takes charge! It would really sell our story," Ado had explained his pitch.

"I think Mom has some Croatian costumes I could borrow," Franka said, avoiding Mirna's eyes, as she'd had the same idea as Ado, but hadn't wanted to say it.

Mom had been practicing traditional dances with her friends for the past few weeks, to Franka's great delight. She was out of the house more often, just like Franka, enjoying her life in Mostar for the first time since they got here, and Franka couldn't be happier for her. She even spoke more Croatian at home, which was a lovely surprise.

Mirna didn't say anything for a little while. She stared at the two of them, trying to find a way to contradict them and tell them exactly why they were both stupid.

"You might be right," she finally said after a while, like those words caused her physical pain. "Especially since we want to compete in the traditional competition, not the Blue Stallion one. It completes the whole story."

"And, despite your objections, you look very cute in your costume," Franka had added, making Mirna turn the color of a very ripe tomato, just as intended.

***

So here they were, bright and early. The sun was barely out, and the river would be even colder than usual, but this is what they had to do, and by gosh, they would do it.

Mostar was gorgeous this morning, the perfect day. They were alone except for a pair of cats that tried to get Franka's attention as she walked to the bridge. She was, of course, the last one to arrive, as Mirna and Ado were already setting up the equipment on the bridge itself.

"You can change at the store," Mirna said when Franka arrived. She was already in the costume, with a long bright red dimije and white shirt with *jeleče* and a fez.

"You look gorgeous," Franka couldn't help but say. Something about the sight of Mirna in that costume made her heartbeat just a bit faster. Maybe it was the quintessential Bosnian feel of it all.

"I feel like a novelty Barbie doll," Mirna answered, fidgeting with the golden braid of her hair. "Come on, let's see what they wore on the other side of the river," she teased.

It took Franka a while to figure out how to put this thing on, especially in the tight space of the Lakić family store. The fact she wore one dress, once, when she was seven, didn't help either.

Still, the final product wasn't half bad. Franka wasn't sure how authentic the dress was, but it looked good enough to trick someone who knew only the basics about this country (such as herself). It was a long white dress, with long sleeves embroidered with red, just like the area around the neckline. Over it, she wore a matching red belt, as well as a *jeleče*, not that much different from Mirna's. She would feel much more at home in Ado's *chakšire* pants made for guys, but for a one-time stunt, this would work perfectly.

"Wow," was all Mirna said when she finally walked out into the warm, spring sun.

"I'm kinda rocking it," Franka said as she twirled around in her dress. She was never going to be a dress person, but twirling was a universal need of all humans.

"Ladies, we are wasting valuable filming time here," Ado said, but Franka couldn't help but notice his gaze also lingered on her longer than usual. "I have to be in school in two hours."

No one told Franka filming a video could be so, for the lack of a better word, cringe-worthy. She felt so dumb, even if they didn't do much more than walk to the middle of the bridge, each from her own side, then meet in the middle, where they would high-five each other and take off their costumes to dive.

For half an hour, they filmed the intro part of the video, walking up and down the bridge. Ado assured them it would all work out well in the end.

"I have followed numerous video channel tutorials on editing. I will make this work," he promised. "And now, let's do the really big thing. You go and change while I set up the drone."

As she took off her dress, Franka's hands ceased to be under her control as the sudden realization she was about to really do it finally made its home in her mind. Her hands shook too much for her to unbutton her dress. She would jump off that damn bridge, not by accident, but because she wanted to.

Mirna grabbed her hand in the dark of the store.

"We can do this," she said, and Franka could almost see her smile through the darkness. The softness in her voice didn't dissipate Franka's fears, but they didn't overwhelm her anymore. She had Mirna by her side.

In the warm morning sun, Franka stood at the wall of the bridge. The river seemed to be miles below her, but calmer than usual, ready to accept her daughters.

She and Mirna agreed on matching black swimsuits to look more uniform and aesthetically pleasing.

"Are you ready?" Mirna asked.

"I can't do much worse than the first time," Franka said with a smile, even if they all knew that was far from the truth. "Now I know what I'm doing."

"Same rules apply," Mirna repeated what she had said a million times before, her voice almost cold to make up for the anxiety that made the rest of her shake in fear. "There is nothing to be afraid of," she added, to herself as much as to Franka.

"But still, please be careful."

"I will," Franka promised with a smile. "Are you okay?" she asked Mirna who was still slightly vibrating. "I mean, you're the one who got injured the last time."

"Last time, I was diving angry," Mirna said. "Now I'm happy." Her grin engulfed the whole city again and made the world seem like a better place.

"Come on, girls, we are wasting good lighting here!" Ado yelled. He was under the bridge already, ready to make the best video possible.

"Okay, it's time," Mirna said, even though her face was white as a sheet. Franka understood her well enough by now. She wasn't afraid of the dive, but of being caught before they could do it.

But Franka forgot how to be scared. Why should she be scared when she could be excited? Her heart threatened to beat its way out of her chest, but that adrenaline was her drug of choice, and she wouldn't have it any other way.

They climbed over the fence, separated a few meters from each other, so they could both land safely.

"Three! Two! One!" Franka yelled as they agreed and made that leap forward.

Adrenaline took over her body, and it knew exactly what it was doing, far better than Franka herself. The water wasn't her enemy anymore. Neretva would welcome them, to break their fall and help them relax after an amazing feat.

Franka's body contracted like she demanded it to without much of a fight. A somersault was now child's play for both of them. She straightened her body again just as the river took her.

The blue world around her was mesmerizing as she opened her eyes in the water. Freezing cold threatened to paralyze her as the currents began to drag her farther away, but this time Franka was ready for them, so she fought them off and swam back to the real world.

"*Jebeno predobro!*" Mirna yelled when Franka finally surfaced. It really was effing amazing, unlike anything she had felt before, her body filled with energy and power. She could take on the world right now!

115

Mirna pulled Franka into a hug and Franka hugged her back, even though they were still in the water. In Mirna's arms, she was safe, no matter where Neretva's currents took them.

"We really need to talk about your language!" Ado yelled from the shore, but his mouth opened in shock to let them know he was equally impressed. "That was amazing! We have something special on our hands."

Chapter Twelve

Dok čekaš sabah sa šejtanom

Cliff diving would never pay Mirna's bills. Pharmacology would. When exam season reared its ugly and dangerous head, Mirna and Franka focused on nailing them.

"We can jump off the moon if you want to when we're officially sophomores!" Mirna promised Franka, calculating how many hours of sleep were enough to keep her sane, so the rest of the time could be dedicated to studying.

Pharmacology was no joke, which is why Mirna fell in love with it. She made a simple decision: she would crush it this semester. Every day, she learned something new, enjoying every minute of it. Statistics, chemistry, biology: she had to master it all.

Her school was relatively new, so she couldn't rely on notes and questions left behind by previous generations or professors who got too lazy to come up with new challenges. This was a whole new territory for all of them. Mirna was living for it. Most of the professors and TAs noticed her efforts, and they were more than happy to help her gain even more knowledge and prove her worth as a future colleague.

"Keep it up and you'll have a great future ahead, young lady," the professor told her when she got an A in her oral exam. "I can't wait to see you dive off the bridge soon," she added with a smile. Mirna rode that high for days.

Her hard work was paying off. So was Franka's. Mirna got A after A, while Franka had a slightly less impressive, but equally awesome spread of As, Bs, and Cs, which were all she wanted. She wasn't as much of a perfectionist in academia as Mirna was, which was probably for the best. That's why Mirna didn't try to redo that C from the first semester. That way, she wouldn't be tempted to chase the perfect grade average that would probably cost her health in the long run.

Amidst all those exams, they almost forgot about the video they filmed until Ado published it one day without even saying anything. Mirna's head had been stuck in a book so she didn't even notice.

The video went live in the first week of June, and neither Mirna nor Franka had the time or space in their mind to deal with it. It was probably for the best, so they weren't tempted to obsess over the stats it was generating. Exams fell upon them like the biblical flood, and they were both determined to get on that boat and be free.

It really was a fantastic video, as good as could be expected from three people new at this. It opened with a few drone shots of Mostar, early in the morning, before zooming in first on Franka, and then Mirna, walking to the middle of the bridge in their ridiculous costumes. They met halfway and high-fived before a cut to them, in the same pose, in their matching swimsuits.

Then came their jumps, where Ado really outdid himself with the choice of shots and dramatic music to complement them. Mirna and Franka looked great, almost perfectly in sync as they dived off the Old Bridge, true Swallows of Mostar.

After they landed, the video cut to a few more shorts of their most impressive dives and text saying, "Why aren't we allowed to compete?"

Mirna and Franka would never be famous social media influencers. And that was okay. That wasn't what this was all about. They wanted to make a splash, pun intended, and that was exactly what they did. Despite the exams, the ripple effect still reached them, even if it took a few days. Mostar was a small city, and they were doing something that no one had done before. The ever-present choir of city gossip hadn't had something this juicy since Emir and his wife divorced.

For all they knew, never before did two women dive off the bridge at the same time. Mirna liked to think that some five times great aunt and her friend did the same thing but were never remembered for it. She had to have gotten the genes from somewhere.

Most people called them brave and cool. Even Mom didn't freak out as much as Mirna was afraid she would when she saw the video. Instead, she congratulated her.

"You really love this," she simply said and pulled Mirna into a hug.

"Your dive was good," Grandpa said. "I'm proud of you. I knew you had it in you, and I can't wait to see you compete." Mirna's heart grew three sizes. If an expert like Grandpa approved, she must have been doing something right.

Aca and a few other guys approached her the day after the video went up to share their two cents with her.

"I look forward to competing against you," Aca said with a bright smile on his face as he shook her hand. Most of the guys were more accepting of two girls diving alongside them than they were even a few months ago. Franka and Mirna proved they weren't going to back down and that they were good enough. The guys could do nothing more than accept them.

"*Glupo žensko,*" was also something she heard more than once. But she'd heard it before, so it was nothing new. She was a woman in space occupied by men for centuries. Those who didn't want her there did everything they could to keep her away. When they ran out of arguments, they settled on insults. If it didn't work when she was a kid, it wouldn't work now.

The weirdest and most unexpected was the message she got from Bisera, the TV hostess.

> Very proud of you two. I would be very interested in doing a follow-up story with you if you are up for it. And a little birdie told me about your cleaning efforts in the Partisan Cemetery. You girls are a gift that keeps on giving. Loads of love and kisses. Bisera.

"If Emir Kapo doesn't call soon, I think we might take her up on her offer," Franka said when Mirna showed her the message.

As the number of exams they had left went down, the number of comments and views went up, which meant they could spend more time appreciating it.

"Mirna's New Zealand wife" only wrote "<3" in the comments of the video, but it was more than enough to make Mirna wake up the whole house with the sounds of her screams of joy.

Almost a week after the video went up, when she was studying in her room, Ado ran in, smiling like he won the lottery.

"Who is the best brother and PR manager on this planet?!" he asked, grinning as he showed her his phone.

The official Blue Stallion account liked the video, followed them back, and commented: "We support equality in sports #forwomen □□□"

"They saw it!" Ado said. "And since they commented, they must be planning to do something about it! You are going to dive off that bridge, Mirela Lakić! And you are going to win!"

"Amazing!" Mirna said. "Now, get out of my room. I have an exam tomorrow!"

It was during that exact exam that Mirna got a phone call. She, of course, missed it, as her phone was off and in her backpack, but the sight of the caller brought a devilish smile to her face when she finally saw it. She won. Game over for Emir Kapo.

Mirna sent her a screenshot of Emir's missed call.

Franka: He's going to freak out.

Franka was right, because the moment Mirna called him back, he made it obvious that he was on the verge of making her participate in involuntary cliff diving by throwing her off the nearest mosque minaret.

"Mirna, *šejtane*, we need to talk," he said without a word of hello. Cool. He had never called her Satan before, so she must have struck a nerve. "Me, you, and your girlfriend."

Mirna had to take a break from studying to meet him. Franka would, of course, be with her to keep her sane and provide safety in numbers. Even if Emir blamed it all on her because she had been a consistent source of stress in his life for years—she was one stubborn twelve-year-old—Franka was equally as "at fault" as she was.

They met that same evening, in a public space, because Mirna wasn't going to risk being quietly disposed of.

"It's cliff diving," Franka reminded her. "He won't resort to murder. It's not that big of a deal."

But it was. Both to Mirna and to Emir, who was already waiting for them at a local coffee shop, his brows furrowed, his mouth a barely visible line, looking like he was more than happy to feed them both to the Neretva demons if only they would listen to him. Of course, he wouldn't resort to murder. The last rational part of Mirna knew that, but not for the lack of motivation.

Mirna wanted to laugh, but she kept her emotions in check, to be polite and not rub salt in his wounds.

"I got an email last night," he said when the two of them sat opposite him. "From Blue Stallion people. They asked me if what they saw in that video was true and what I planned to do about it. It's very important for them to look like they support women. Very, very important."

"And what did you tell them?" Mirna asked.

"You really have a lot of guts doing this, Mirna," he said, his eyes cold and full of hatred.

"You left us no choice," she simply said. It was the truth. What else was she supposed to do?

Franka grabbed her hand under the table and kept her calm and collected as she took a deep breath and tethered herself to the moment.

"More importantly, my aunt called me to yell at me for not letting you compete," he said, sounding so much more hurt by that fact than anything the Blue Stallion people could tell him. The plastic spoon he used to stir sugar in his coffee snapped in half from the pressure, but he didn't seem to notice.

"Your aunt?" Franka asked, her eyes wide with shock. Mirna could only hope she looked even slightly less baffled.

"Bisera Bošnjak, you met her already," he said, his voice as bitter as the Bosnian coffee in front of him. "Coming after my family; that is a bitch move and you know it."

"What about it?" Mirna asked, even if neither of them had any idea they were related, but Allah bless small towns and Bisera Bošnjak for calling out her nephew on his sexist ways. "You made us go this far; you know that."

"So, will you listen to your auntie and let us compete?" Franka asked, now the one who was taunting him. "You wouldn't want to make her sad, would you?"

"My hands are tied," he said simply, his voice ice. Most of the common brutes would have started yelling by now, but he kept his cool. "Blue Stallion doesn't want bad press, and they are putting pressure on me. You can compete this year," he said, but the wave of relief Mirna expected to wash over her the moment she heard those words was destroyed with one simple question. "When the hype dies down and my aunt moves on from your story, and Blue Stallion has better things to care about when it's only me again, will you be able to pull the same stunt next year?" he asked.

For a moment, she froze. She wasn't really thinking that far ahead, even if she maybe should have. People of Herzegovina were a stubborn bunch and forgiveness didn't come easy to them. Was this that one step too far that they could never recover from?

"Maybe," Mirna admitted, trying to hide the monstrous beating of her own heart as it tried to pump enough blood for her brain to think its way out of this mess.

"Maybe not. Maybe we won't need it," she tried to argue more with herself because Emir wasn't listening.

"Prove it to me," he said. He stood, towering over them as he looked her in the eyes. "Prove to me that you really are good enough to compete."

"We already did!" Franka said, also standing, her voice high-pitched and angrier than Mirna had ever seen her, a wild cat about to maul him.

"You didn't!" he snapped. "The last time I let Mirna dive, she almost killed herself. People didn't notice, but I did. You really don't know how terrible that dive was!" Mirna's heart skipped a beat. Yes, it was bad, but she saw the footage. To her, it didn't seem that terrible, despite the consequences. But maybe she couldn't see the truth Emir saw. "That proves she wasn't ready!"

Her face instantly turned hot. Only Franka's presence next to her stopped her from punching him in the face and ruining her life for the second time. She wasn't the first or the last one to injure herself. It was an extreme sport; people made mistakes and ended up in the ER. That didn't mean they could never dive again. Instead, she stared at him, stunned by just how low he was willing to sink. But he wasn't even done.

"And you, Franka, you couldn't even swim last year. You fell off the bridge! How do I know you won't die if I let you dive? So, prove to me you are ready!"

"No one else had to do this much!" Franka said, shaking her head in shock.

"Well, you have to," he said, sitting back down, returning to his cool self. "I'm not going to let you make a mockery of this sport! Not while I'm in charge. You have to be amazing if you want to compete. If you win a place on the podium at any other local competition, not only will I let you two compete, I will let every other girl compete. I will let them train if they want to. For as long as I'm in charge; and I plan to stay in charge for quite a long time."

Mirna froze before the barrage of insults aimed at Emir could surface. She wanted to fight him, to call him a sexist asshole who couldn't even do this, who couldn't stop them from competing or from training. He didn't own the damn bridge. They would compete this year, and they would win.

But years of living in this country had taught her she couldn't let her temper get the better of her, not if she wanted to be taken seriously. It was a sexist world, a small city that sometimes seemed stuck in the last century. She had to take the long way to the top if she ever wanted to reach it.

"If that is how you want us to do this, then it shall be done," she said. As those words left her mouth, her heart began to ache, but she shouldn't say anything else. Franka grabbed her hand again, as if trying to stop her from saying another word. Mirna knew what she had to do. "As long as you make sure those events let us compete. If no one lets us compete, we automatically qualify for Mostar," she said, her voice as cold as Neretva. Anger subsided in an instant. All that remained was a deep sadness that would never leave her. She sold out everything they did for a chance at a future that might never come.

Emir smiled.

"Okay," he simply said, sitting back in his chair, with a crooked smile on his punchable face, like he would win in the end.

"Mirna, you're making a mistake," Franka said, turning to face her, her breathing shallow and her eyes wide. "Screw him and his made-up rules. Let's just compete."

Those eyes that looked so much like Neretva made Mirna shudder. She would have done anything Franka asked of her, but not this time. One simple reason: Franka was the present, but she would not be the future.

"I am not leaving this country until I'm legally allowed to jump off that bridge," she said once when Mirna asked her about her plans. But Mirna never fully believed her.

Franka had a way to leave and she could use it: American citizenship and a diploma from a world-renowned private high school. It was just a matter of time before she realized that. Mirna had nothing but Mostar. If she could make a future here, even if it meant playing Emir's game, Mirna had to take it.

Why did this all feel like it could be so easily lost, like Franka was here now, but wouldn't be by the morning? Why did all of this have to be so difficult?

"This year. We can compete this year," Mirna said, the calmness of her voice a surprise even to herself. "What about the next one? What about other women who want to dive?" she asked. Franka didn't answer her. Neither of them considered the future enough, but Mirna had to start now, even if Franka didn't want to.

"She is a smart one, Franka," Emir said. He smiled at her, but she didn't smile back. Maybe she just signed the deal with the devil and messed up everything they had worked for all this time, but what else was there to do? "Listen to her."

If he wanted to put another challenge in front of her, she would win, so no one, not a single person, could say she got into that competition because of anything other than her own skills.

Franka shook her head, the confusion on her face painfully obvious, but she didn't fight her anymore.

"Okay, Mirna, I trust you," she simply said. "And you, asshole, you better keep your word."

"I am a man of my word," he promised without a trace of worry on his face.

Mirna now knew she had no other choice but to be the best.

Chapter Thirteen

Ljeto nam se vratilo

In a flash, the exams were behind them. They could finally breathe freely again, relax and swim and dive and maybe occasionally stay up too late, drinking ciders, eating chips, and watching anime with Spanish dubs to help Mirna learn the language, a dream come true.

Summer was a magnificent season, and for the first time in a long while, Franka could truly appreciate it. Maybe Mostar wasn't so bad, especially now that she had someone to share it with.

Tourists occupied the city again, gawking at the beauty of the Old Bridge and enjoying the good food. They made the city feel alive, as they got to enjoy it for the first time. Even Mirna wasn't as hostile to them, since she didn't need to interact with them. Ado took that burden on himself as Emina had more work with the cleaning. He was, of course, loving it, as he had made Emina sign a deal with a few local artists to sell handmade souvenirs, too, something he was very proud of.

"That is going to set us apart from the competition! Not just generic souvenirs, but a true piece of Mostar they can bring home!" he described his effective strategy.

Mirna and Franka were free to enjoy the summer any way they deemed fit.

The Old Bridge diving competition was scheduled for Saturday, the twenty-third of July, Mirna's birthday, and it was looking like they would simply get to compete, despite Mirna's deal with the devil.

"Organizers of the cliff diving event in the city of Jajce said they are very honored by our desire to compete and that they thought it was very cute, but it was a no from them," Mirna said a few days after their talk with Emir. That day, she had written a million emails and called so many people, only to be met with nothing. "They were polite and very condescending as if I were twelve," she added, rolling her eyes. God only knew how they would have reacted to Franka and her higher-pitched little voice.

"I expected nothing less. Too bad, but it's their loss," Franka said, but she didn't sound as if she really meant it. In Jajce, a small historical city in the middle of Bosnia, she could dive off waterfalls in the middle of the town. It looked so damn stunning in the pictures. But if no one else allowed them to compete, they would qualify for Mostar automatically.

Maybe they could go to Jajce some other time. She had been in this country for three years and had barely left her neighborhood.

Franka still couldn't wrap her head around Mirna's decision to agree to Emir's stupid demands. He lost. Plain and simple. They had no reason to play this petty game. But she believed in Mirna enough to go along with it. If he wanted them to win, they would simply win. Spite had gotten them into this mess, and spite would get them out of it.

"And Sarajevo?" Franka asked. Bentbaša diving competition was held every year in the capital city, even if Franka couldn't figure out who would jump in the Miljacka River and come out alive. Unlike the wild and cold Neretva or the massive Pliva waterfalls in Jajce, Miljacka was more like a glorified creek, so shallow and tiny that any dive would be just tempting fate. But Mirna assured her it was all perfectly safe and that people had jumped off that cliffside overlooking the City Hall, which looked like a fancier version of their old high school, for a long time.

"Nothing," Mirna said and shrugged her shoulders. "They didn't even answer my email. It looks like we are competing in Mostar anyway."

Franka breathed a sigh of relief. She would get to compete next to Mirna and prove to her what she had learned. Mirna might have had slightly better grades, but Franka would win this battle. And even if she didn't, she was having too much fun to care. With Mirna by her side, even the brutal gym regimen she put them both on was actually fun. Summer sun warmed up the water, allowing them to swim and train again, and Franka was happy to say she was pretty sure she wouldn't drown anytime soon.

"We'll be cheering you on virtually, *Conejito*," Isabella promised her. "The whole office is following you and Mirna's crazy hobby, and we love it." Now that Franka didn't have to get up early to go to classes, they could talk more often. Thank God for social networks and modern technology.

"How is your work going?" Franka asked as it seemed like the greatest office ever.

"It's amazing! I love my coworkers and I love my paycheck even more," she said, her eyes full of childlike wonder. "I'm paying off my student loans, and I'm thinking about buying a place for me and my ferrets soon. It could have a room for you if you want to," she added with a smile that looked so much like Dad's. They had the same dark-brown skin, same black hair, and eyes, but her features were softer and younger. "Just saying. No pressure." She had mentioned it a few times already, but Franka had never answered her.

She missed Atlanta so much, all her friends, all the culture. And the food!

Her mom could not cook. That was why the only homemade meals they had eaten recently came from Mrs. Emina, who loved feeding others. Even if Franka were the greatest chef in the world, Bosnia just didn't have the ingredients for true Colombian food like her dad made. Isabella was a pretty decent cook, not nearly as good as Dad, but in Atlanta, Franka could eat everything she missed so much. Mirna's occasional trips to the Burger Man kept her going, but Franka's homesickness couldn't be healed so easily.

And Mirna must have noticed that.

"Your heart will always belong to America," she said once with a melancholic smile. At that moment, Franka finally understood why Mirna would always change the subject whenever she wanted to talk about what happened on New Year's Eve.

"I'm here for now. That is all that matters," she told her, but Mirna didn't answer her. "For now" didn't matter to Mirna. Not when the future was so blurry.

When Isabella asked her what she and Mirna were, Franka couldn't give her an answer so easily. She wanted to give it a shot, despite the risk of losing this amazing friendship they had, but Mirna wasn't ready for that step.

That was fine, of course. Franka wouldn't rush her into anything, but every time Mirna made her smile or taught her something new, or just got out of the water looking like she did, it all became clearer in her mind.

But she loved what she had already to complain too much.

June passed and July reared its gorgeous, sun-drenched head in full glory. They spent more time in the water than out of it. After the second exam period, Selma and Ivona joined them sometimes. Selma even dared to jump off the diving board, mostly so she could post the video on the internet. She would never be a pro at this, but they were all having too much fun to care about it.

Mostly, it was Mirna and Franka, their little world filled with adrenaline and the cold embrace of Neretva. Franka wouldn't have it any other way.

"Have you ever considered going pro with cliff diving?" Franka asked her that night. They had called it quits for the day and decided to treat themselves to slushies because Mirna considered them very American for some reason. Franka wasn't complaining, even though her teeth were starting to hurt from all the sugar and ice after a few bites.

"Of course not," she said like the mere idea made her laugh. They sat on a wooden bench in an old graveyard, because it was quiet and peaceful and not that far from Mirna's house. "It's not that I'm not good enough or that I couldn't be. I see myself in a lab coat, no matter what," she said with a proud smile like she was already that scientist she pictured in her head. "I think I could have gone pro with swimming. It's less dangerous and a smarter choice than cliff diving, but I like academia too much to ever let go of it. But you, Franka, I really could see you doing this professionally," she admitted, making Franka blush.

Franka hadn't been this passionate about anything ever before in her life. She loved pharmacology, almost as much as Mirna did, because of how amazing and fun and challenging it was. But a part of her knew she got into this college because her dad studied the same thing. If she couldn't have him next to her anymore, maybe this would keep them close.

When she was a kid, the little chemistry experiments they did around the house together made her fall in love with the world and the sciences that governed it.

The music she listened to was also mostly his. To Mom's great and utter surprise, baby Franka never listened to nursery rhymes or songs for kids. Ever since she could remember, Dad played her Nirvana and Black Sabbath and King Crimson. Mom would mostly shake her head in confusion, but she liked seeing the two of them scout thrift stores in search of old vinyl they then decorated their house with.

It was supposed to be a day like that, a rainy day where he would pick her up from school to go to their favorite record store. Then it all went to hell.

She had known something was wrong the minute he was late. She had said goodbye to her friends, left the practice early, but he wasn't in the parking lot where they had agreed to meet. He was never late. She and Mom were never on time for anything, but not her dad. As the rain poured all around her, she could only call his phone over and over again, getting no answer, until the call that she never wanted to hear came.

Slippery roads and fast speeds. That was all it took. He kept fighting for almost a month more before his body gave up, and Andrés Garcia was no more. Neither was that old version of Franka, who took risks, who dared to dream, who wasn't just an empty shell of a once-living person.

He would love her new hobby. But, like, really love, not just tolerate it like Mom did because she was happy to see Franka out of the house. He would love

Mirna because they were the same kind of nerd: passionate, sincere, and so smart. But they would never get to meet.

They'd had it all figured out. She would finish high school and go to college to study science like him. She would be happy and healthy, and he would be there for her every step of the way like he always was. Then he was gone, and he would never be there to help her ever again, to comfort her, to listen to music with her. She would have to face the future on her own. But how could she plan for the future when one bad decision, one rainy day, could change everything?

"I don't know what I'll do. Not even at this time next year," Franka confessed, looking away from Mirna, stuck again on that day that she could never escape. "Time is so fleeting. Everything can change quickly. Maybe I'll stay here. Maybe I'll be with Auntie Isabella. Who knows what the future will bring?" she said with a smile, hoping that the tears she felt pooling in her eyes weren't that obvious to Mirna. "All I know is that we are watching Bembaša dives on Saturday and laughing at the fails with a bag of popcorn."

They had been looking forward to that ever since they had ghosted them so rudely. But Mirna didn't return her smile. Instead, she turned quiet and somehow invisible, even if she was clearly right next to her, smaller than Franka had ever seen her.

"Any possibility of Auntie Bella dropping by Mostar this year?" she asked Franka after a while. In retrospect, everything about Mirna, from her slumped posture to the trembling in her voice, screamed that she didn't want to hear the answer, but Franka didn't realize that at that moment.

"Nah, she just started at her new job, and she can't take that much time off," she explained. "But she did invite me over. And maybe to even move back with her." Her voice was quiet and soft, like Mirna wouldn't be able to hear it if spoken that way, but of course, Mirna must have understood her perfectly clearly.

"Oh, how long has it been since you have last been in the USA?" she asked. Her voice was just a bit too high-pitched to sound completely sincere.

"Three years now, almost to the day," Franka said. They had lived in Bella's shitty, cramped apartment meant for one person for the last few weeks, after their house was gone and before the paperwork was done. After that, even Mostar seemed like a good choice.

"So, will you take her up on her offer?" Mirna asked, rubbing the back of her neck as she stared into the distance.

"I don't know," Franka admitted. "But I should get back to her soon. The clock is ticking."

"Indeed it is," Mirna noted.

They said goodbye soon after. Mirna said she had a date with a man named Spike, as Franka was trying to convert her into her little but ever-growing cult, while she would listen to Lyfe 3 Pynk's newest album like she had promised Mirna she would. To be perfectly honest, it sounded amazing, in that artificial but fun way only K-pop could. Yes, it was no Moody Blues, but few things in this world were.

The next practice, Mirna was a mess. From the first jump, she wasn't the sleek, yet powerful diver they were used to seeing. She was diving angry again, and it showed in every sloppy and dangerous move she made. Her splashes were huge, her form all off, like she was trying to drown herself.

"Are you okay?" Džemal asked after only ten minutes when it became obvious those first few bad dives weren't a fluke. "You don't have to push yourself. Take it easy. Nothing in this river is worth your health," he assured her.

"I am fine, Goddamn it!" she yelled to demonstrate how *not* fine she actually was. Before they could stop her, she climbed on that diving board and jumped like she forgot all the rules of the sport, like an amateur who knew nothing about safety, let alone grace.

Of course, it ended badly. The river must have sensed her anger. Mirna made a mistake, and Neretva would punish her for it. The moment her body hit the water, Franka knew it had gone wrong.

"*Jebem ti sve!*" Mirna yelled, surfacing again, her face red with anger despite the cold water.

"Are you okay?" Franka rushed to her as she got out of the water, swimming slower than Franka had ever seen her.

"I will be," she said. As she tried moving her shoulder, she bit her lip, probably to stop herself from yelping in pain. "It's okay. It wasn't nearly as bad as it was in August. This was a third of the height, but it still hurt like hell," she admitted, trying to fake a smile, but her eyes were filled with tears. "But I am done for today. I should be done forever for being such an idiot!"

"It happens to the best of us," Grandpa said, rushing to her side faster than Franka had ever seen him move. "Is your shoulder okay?"

Mirna didn't let them look at it.

"It will be okay with some rest and an ice pack. That's all I need," she promised. She dried herself quickly and put on her shorts and T-shirt, all while trying to keep the movements of her right arm to a minimum.

She tried to go on her own, but Franka was having none of that, so she picked up her things and ran after her. The Old Town was filled with people, and Franka had to squeeze through the crowd to keep up with Mirna. She ignored her mom greeting her in front of their store, where she was selling a trinket to an older pair of gentlemen.

Franka got to Mirna just as was entering her house. But she knew Mirna well enough by this time to know pressuring her to do anything would just make her clam up more until she became impenetrable like a diamond. Mirna was already much calmer, directing her anger inward, even if she had nothing to be angry about.

"You'll tell me if you need help, right?" Franka asked her. Mirna smiled, her eyes filled with tears, but she wouldn't cry. At least, not in front of Franka.

"I know, Franka. I just need some alone time," she said, taking a deep breath. "I don't want you to see me like this. You deserve a better version of me."

Franka smiled and shook her head.

"I like every version of you because they are all you," she said the truth. "But I get what you need. Keep me updated on your shoulder situation, and let me know if you need anything."

Mirna finally smiled back and pulled her into a one-armed hug.

"You really are amazing," she said.

"Funny, I was going to say the same thing about you."

With her training partner out of the equation, Franka also took the rest of the day off. She tried to cook lunch for herself and Mom. Mirna convinced her cooking wasn't that difficult, so she had to try. Miracle of all miracles, her pasta with chicken and cream turned out perfectly edible.

"Don't be like me, kiddo," Mom told her as stabbed her slightly overdone chicken with a fork. "I mean, be as cool as I am, but a better chef. I relied on your dad too much."

"I don't think he minded," Franka said as the mouthwatering smells of the kitchen and the memory of his loving smile as he presented his newest creation brought her back to the past for a few moments. "I do wish he taught me some things too."

"We both thought we had more time," she simply said.

Franka spent the rest of the afternoon watching anime and getting invested in the fascinating lives of these teenagers fighting magical alien cat people. But her peace was ruined by an unexpected phone call.

"What are you doing over the weekend?" Emir Kapo asked without a word of hello. Franka didn't know where he got her number or why he was calling her, but she was too confused to ask valid questions.

"Ignoring you," she said because snark came so naturally to her in this case. Mirna would at least try to be tactical.

"Very funny, Franka," he said like it was the least humorous thing he had heard all week. "I got a call from Sarajevo. Bentbaša cliff diving competition is this weekend, did you know that?"

"Of course," she said. Were she and Mirna still on for that? They watched a few Blue Stallion competitions over the last year, but this was supposed to be shit watching, like Eurovision was, and she was really looking forward to that. Mirna's insults for subpar dives were a treat.

"Well, they had some cancellations recently. And their organizer is apparently a lot more "progressive" than I am..." As he said the last word, Franka imagined how much he rolled his eyes. "So they had an idea to invite two of the best female cliff divers in this country."

"Are you...?" Franka tried to ask, but the heavy feeling in her stomach and all the adrenaline overtaking her body made it hard for her to form words.

"Yes. The train for Sarajevo leaves tomorrow at 6:39 a.m. Be there, win a place at the podium and show us all how good you are," he said. "If you don't, have fun watching the rest of us dive on the twenty-third," he added, almost matter-of-factly, but Franka couldn't help but picture a supervillain smile on his face.

"How long have you known this?" she asked.

"Since Monday," he said. "If you won't play fair, neither will I. Are you in or out?"

"You asshole," she said. "You know we are in."

"Okay, see you in the morning, bright and early."

The moment he hung up, she called Mirna. Mirna answered, her voice gruff as if she had just woken from a nap, or...she was having an intense crying session.

"Hello," she asked, probably confused because they would always send messages to each other instead of calling.

"Mirna, we are going to Sarajevo!"

Chapter Fourteen

Kad ja pođoh na Bentbašu

Mirna had not slept a moment last night, but when she met Franka at the train station, she smiled and pulled her into a hug. Franka couldn't find out Mirna was chugging painkillers like candy for the past twelve hours, or that she was moments from fainting. As far as everyone was concerned, Mirela Lakić was as healthy as a real, actual horse.

Her mood wasn't helped by the fact the light in their hallway went out again, so she almost died when she tripped while putting on her shoes. She left them a message that it needed to be changed, but she knew she would probably have to do it on her own when she got home on Sunday.

Franka wasn't the only one to meet her at the train station on that sunny morning. Aca and Bakir would also compete in Sarajevo today. Thank Allah, it was the two of them and not anyone else because Aca was genuinely nice, while Bakir had spoken about twelve words in the twelve years Mirna had known him, so they were the perfect company for today.

Mirna and Aca exchanged their needlessly complicated handshake, as usual, that thankfully didn't include her bad arm, while she shared a polite "Hi" with Bakir. They both greeted Franka, too, even if they kept looking at her like she was a very foreign, possibly slightly radioactive jewel. But Franka didn't mind one bit, if she even noticed. The joy on her face could only be likened to a child from the tropics seeing snow for the first time after hearing about it their whole life.

"You have been to Sarajevo, right?" Mirna asked her, smiling at Franka's eyes that were filled with excitement. The train stopped at the station and the tired-looking conductor checked their tickets.

"Of course I have. But I've never been on a train!" Franka said, looking around the gray and green interior of the Talgo train as if it were a luxury yacht. "The US is not really in love with trains. We love our cars and our planes. But this! This is awesome, Mirna!"

"I love trains!" Mirna said, not about to ruin her fun with the fact Bosnia actually had shitty trains compared to the rest of Europe. Let the kid enjoy herself. "You are going to love this."

The entire trip, Franka didn't even blink, glued to the window, watching Herzegovina turn into Bosnia, as they passed by almost the whole Neretva River, Jablaničko Lake, and amazingly green forests, while the three of them tried to catch some sleep.

But while Aca and Bakir were long gone by the time they left Mostar, Mirna could only close her eyes and hope her face didn't betray how the rest of her body felt.

It was anxiety, plain and simple. They were suddenly asked to dive in a place they had never dived before, in front of lots of people. In fact, this was her first diving competition ever. Of course, she was nervous, but that didn't mean anything was wrong with her. That shoulder pain? Psychosomatic, of course. If she didn't think of it, it would go away. She would be okay.

But her body was fighting a battle against her, making it hard to even think straight. She wasn't going to quit. Never. Not when she was so close.

They arrived at the railway station too late to give Franka the time to appreciate the architecture. The cab took them straight through to the old town. They didn't even go to the hotel. Maybe they should have gone there a night early, but Emir probably didn't want to pay for an extra night.

Bentbaša dives weren't nearly as big of a deal as Mostar ones, but people gathered to watch anyway. Most of the other divers were already ready, waiting for the four of them.

As in Mostar, no one would dive without a checkup. Aca and Bakir came out of the small makeshift tent at the top of the hill they would dive from in a matter of minutes.

"See ya soon," Aca said, gleaming with pride like he had already won the thing.

When Mirna and Franka entered the tent, the doctor smiled at them. He was nice, too nice even, very young and full of enthusiasm for his job. A few minutes later Franka was proclaimed to be perfectly healthy, which caused the smile on her face to widen even more.

"You are good to go," the doctor told her with a kind smile. "Mirela, you're next."

She didn't even correct him. She didn't have the strength. As soon as he tried to check her pulse, the exam went to hell.

"Are you all right Mirela?" he asked, his eyes narrowing. "You have to be honest with me. Your heartbeat is through the roof like you ran a race," he said in a calm voice. He checked again but kept shaking his head no like she didn't already feel her heart slamming against her ribs as if it were about to break them.

"I'm fine," she snapped, as beads of sweat began to roll down her forehead and her back.

"You don't look fine," he said. "Franka, is she fine?" he asked, turning his attention to her. Franka's eyes, those beautiful eyes, stared at the two of them. She took a step backward, away from Mirna and the doctor. "Is she?" the doctor continued because he wouldn't get an answer from Mirna. She was too stubborn to admit anything was wrong, as she shook her head no again.

"She got injured last night," Franka finally spat out, unable to deal with the doctor's probing eyes. Mirna's heart might as well have been thrown off the cliff into the depths of the river. Red, almost painful heat took over every molecule in her body at Franka's betrayal.

No, Franka, how could you do this?! Muscles in Mirna's body tensed up, like a car ready to pounce at her like a cat, to fight her, just to prove she was fine.

But one look at those flustered, beautiful eyes caused that anger to dissipate. At least, her anger at Franka. Her friend was doing the right thing.

"Is that true?" the doctor asked Mirna. She looked up at Franka, her eyes already filled with tears, and nodded. What was the point in trying to hide it anymore?

"It's okay, only a bruised shoulder," she assured him desperately, fighting for this one chance. She could do it. Even tired and in pain, she was better than most of the guys here. She had to prove herself! "I'll be fine."

But she lost this battle. It hurt so bad, and she hadn't slept a moment. She hadn't eaten anything and couldn't bring herself to change that. She was in no state to jump into anything but a bed.

The doctor insisted on checking her shoulder, only to reveal what Mirna had already known.

"Mirela, I'm sorry, but I cannot in good conscience let you compete today," he said after a short examination. The bruise on her shoulder wasn't nearly as bad as the one she got when diving off the Old Bridge, but it still made movements painful and strained. If she landed on it, God knows what would happen. "I know how much this dive means to you, but I'm afraid that if something goes even a tiny bit wrong you will wreck your shoulder for good. And medically speaking, you look a mess. There is no way you can get into the zone. You will get injured. But if you take it easy and don't dive from fifteen meters like a madwoman, this should heal in a week or so. You should be perfectly ready to dive in Mostar," he assured her with a friendly smile.

"Unless I make the podium here, I won't get to dive in Mostar," Mirna said. Tears pooling in the corners of her eyes blurred her vision as she tried her best to wipe them without making it painfully obvious she was doing that. She hated crying. It always made her feel so weak. The rational part of her brain knew that wasn't true, but she couldn't help her feelings.

"That's bullshit," Doc gasped. "I have seen your videos. You have to compete!"

"That's the deal we made," Mirna said, her voice breaking. After all this time, was her anger going to do her in again? The uncertainty of Franka's existence in her life that had been bubbling up for months, and her inability to deal with it finally reached a crescendo yesterday, took the form of anger, and caused her to lose her cool. No wonder she'd injured herself.

"We never said who has to win," Franka said, her voice growing stronger with every word. She stood above Mirna, like even the concept of fear dissipated from her body. "I'm still competing."

Mirna looked up at her, those green eyes full of fire. Franka grabbed her hand and smiled.

"I'm going to do this, Mirna," she promised. "I'm going to get us to compete in Mostar, the way you wanted to. You'ave trained me for a year. Please, let me prove myself to you," she said.

Mirna's heart beat faster, but her brain began to relax. Her faith was in the hands of this woman, this perfect specimen of a human. She had nothing to worry about. That didn't mean it didn't hurt. She really wanted to dive too. She wrote to organizers of the Benbaša dives last year also, but she was a minor without parental permission, so no one was going to let her compete, even if she wasn't a girl. But she would dive in Mostar. Franka would make it happen.

"Okay, Franka. I trust you," she finally said, returning her smile, as weak and feeble as it was.

The pain of her shoulder was secondary to the pain of her inability to compete. It would pass. The doctor agreed it wasn't a big injury, so he gave her medicine (a cold bottle of Bosnian Cola to serve as an ice pack and some painkillers, Allah bless him) and told her to lay low.

"I can't wait to see your dive in Mostar," he said with a smile. Franka would make his and Mirna's wishes come true.

Even if she wasn't going to compete, Mirna had to know what she was missing. She climbed to the diving board atop a cliff overlooking the city and stared west, as the many bridges of Sarajevo crossed Miljacka one after the other. It wasn't as high as the Old Bridge and the river was muddy brown as opposed to Neretva's amazing blue-green hue, but Mirna's heart still ached for a chance to dive.

"Next year," Franka assured her, and Mirna tried her best to believe her. She tried to return her smile, but it didn't work. Her lips simply refused to make the right motion.

Omer, the main organizer, sighed when she met them a few minutes late, shaking his head like his heart was broken even more than Mirna's was.

"I heard the news, *srećo,* and I am so sorry!" he said. He was shorter than Mirna, meeker than Emir, but despite his peculiar language choices of calling her "luck," he at least tried to be nice, even if his tone crossed boundaries to condescending. Right now, she appreciated his words. "We have been looking forward to having you dive with us for weeks. The first two female competitors! Amazing press!" He pointed out, his eyes wide with ideas of future brand deals. Of course, he used the male version of the word competitor.

"Well, it's next year for me," Mirna promised him, putting at least some of the golden-child persona back on, no matter how much energy it drained from her. "But you have Franka, and you are in for a treat."

She thought she would still be angry and fight the doctor and the organizers, but most of all Franka, for betraying her with the truth. Instead, the storm in her mind passed, and she could sail the seas safely again. It was what it was. She didn't have the strength to be angry anymore.

Maybe she couldn't compete. Maybe Franka would disappear into thin air at any moment. Maybe. But she was here now, by her side, bringing her a sandwich and a bottle of water.

Lying to herself and letting self-doubt and fear take over only led to this disaster in the first place. If she was honest, she wouldn't have been distracted, and if she wasn't distracted, she wouldn't have made that stupid dive.

She could only eat her sandwich and wait for Franka's dive.

Mirna went back to the audience on the other side of the river and sat on her own jacket under a tiny sapling that could generously be called a tree. She leaned against her backpack that they hadn't had time to drop off at the hotel and waited. The day was hot and moist, and she wanted nothing more than to dive, if for nothing else than to alleviate the heat. The rest of her group was already on the cliff above the small dam. When they noticed her sitting in the shade, they waved at her. She did the same.

"Welcome, ladies and gentlemen, to this year's Bentbaša diving event!" the announcer, Mr. Omer himself, said. The crowd was big, but it was nowhere close to the numbers Mostar pulled. It was probably for the best. Franka was the first one to dive and she didn't need any more pressure than she already carried.

"Twenty people will be competing today, diving from a height of fifteen meters from a platform on a cliff," Omer announced. "We have competitors from four countries as well as someone special. For the first time in the history of this amazing competition, we have with us a female contestant!" He all but squealed with excitement, with as much enthusiasm as if he got the Queen of England to compete as opposed to simply a girl. "Please, everyone, welcome our first diver for today: Franka Garcia from Mostar!"

Franka was high up on that platform, above Mirna and the rest of the world. To Mirna, she looked like a mythical creature that might have seemed small and unassuming, but which still made the planet turn.

Franka's smile was strained, like she was going through the motions without feeling the joy she was supposed to portray. She didn't strut on the board like she did at her most confident. Instead, she walked slowly, like she was afraid it might break. Despite the act she put on for Mirna, she was still only human, and anxiety did its thing.

Still, Franka did dive like Mirna had never seen her move before, so graceful and light, as if she were about to fly. It was far from the typical dive most people expected to see. She was like a vila, a superhuman creature that demanded admiration. Or maybe Mirna saw her that way.

It wasn't her best dive. The landing was a bit off, and her movements in the air were stiffer than they usually were. Nerves got to her; that much was obvious. It was her first competition; what else could be expected?

"Very good first showing for our debutant," Omer said, reading the score on the upper levels of average.

Maybe. It really depended on other divers.

But Mirna didn't see most of them. After Aleksandar Janković, eighteen, Mostar, made his dive that scored lower than Franka's, just like Bakir's did, her eyes begged to be closed. The summer sun beamed down on her, making her even drowsier.

She wouldn't miss anything. Guys from Jajce were next, and they weren't anything special. She decided to close her eyes for a little while, just a few minutes. It would all be okay.

"Amazing job, everyone!" Omer yelled after what must have been seconds. "And with that, we have our official winners. First place: Danilo Bulatović from

Montenegro. Second place goes to Zlatko Fazlagić from Bihać! And the dark horse of this competition wins the bronze in her first-ever event: Franka Garcia from Mostar!"

Every last bit of sleep left Mirna in an instant. She jumped up, only to realize other viewers had formed a small buffer zone around her so she wouldn't get trampled. She missed the whole thing!

But as she repeated Omer's words in her head, her heart began to beat faster. Franka ran to her, arms wide open, and pulled her into a hug.

She did it! That amazing woman did it. The Swallows would compete in Mostar!

"You slept through it, didn't you?" Franka asked, still locked into Mirna's embrace, her voice tittering with laughter. Mirna looked at her sheepishly and was just about to say something when Franka added, "I'm not mad, silly. I'm glad you got your rest."

At that, Mirna brightened and picked Franka up.

"Yes! You and I are going to conquer Mostar!"

Chapter Fifteen

Sarajevo ljubavi moja

Franka could carry the whole city of Sarajevo on her back. She could take on the whole world with her own bare hands if that's what it would take. Nothing could stop her today.

She did it! She won third place. Emir had to shut up and let them compete. He could suck it. The Swallows of Mostar won!

Mirna pulled her into a hug and lifted her in the air like she was a very small cat, but Franka didn't mind because it was her.

"You did it, you brilliant woman! I knew you would do it!" she yelled. "I could kiss you!"

"Then do it, you coward!" Franka said, but Mirna must not have heard her from the sounds of Aca and Bakir yelling in joy like they were the winners. She brought victory for the team and the club she was now apparently a part of, so they finally had a reason to celebrate.

"Awesome!" Aca said. "I can't wait to see you in Mostar!"

"We are going to kick your assess!" Mirna yelled, her cheeks red from excitement. It was her win as much as it was Franka's. She had taught her everything she knew, so she had bragging rights.

The award ceremony was rushed and a bit amateurish, but for the most part, Franka didn't care. She got her cheap-looking bronze medal she could throw at Emir's head. Or give it to Mirna, or hang it on her wall, depending on her mood.

The organizers kept trying to get her to stand in the middle like she won the whole thing. Danilo, the actual winner, and Zlatko, the runner-up, were less than thrilled by that idea and Franka had no intention of getting the ire of a Montentegrian and a Krajišnik, both known for their short tempers, on her. But no matter how much she tried to fix the misunderstanding, Omer and the rest of the organizers kept pushing her in the middle.

"We are so proud to have a woman come so far," Omer said to the two guys who obviously didn't share his enthusiasm for #girlpower. "It's good for the branding!"

Later, Franka and Mirna would learn Omer had a degree in marketing and that his girlfriend ran a mildly popular Quickgram page on feminism so it would all come together in her mind perfectly. But even then, Franka understood she was mostly here to make them look good and modern, and that they would have paraded her around almost as much if she splashed from that diving board. They were lucky that both she and Mirna were actually really good at this. But their luck must have run out as neither of them were at all interested in being used as a marketing pawn. That's why she got Mirna and the guys and dragged them away from Bentbaša at the exact moment she finished all the duties she had to fulfill.

Their hotel wasn't that far away, a bit down the river, next to the Emperor's Mosque. It was an old Austrian building, probably older than all the houses in her American suburb combined, quite charming, even if it had seen better days.

"Two singles and one double," the clerk said, checking what Emir must have booked for them.

"It's supposed to be two doubles," Mirna said. She insisted on carrying Franka's backpack in her hand, even if she couldn't carry her own on her bruised shoulder, so Aca and Bakir took both and designated her as "the adult" instead. It was only then that Franka realized she was in fact the oldest one here, as Bakir and Aca had only turned eighteen this year. Weird. Since they were both so tall and had beards, she assumed they were old, immortal Slavic gods. Why was everyone in this country so big!?

"Take it or leave it," the clerk said, not too interested in arguing with them. Two more people were already behind them, waiting to check-in. "They have already been paid for, and we have a no-refund policy."

"We'll take the double!" Aca volunteered before anyone could say anything. "Bakir and I, I mean."

"It's only polite," Bakir said, possibly his first words of the day.

"Oh, thank you," Franka said, with the most polite, yet artificial smile she was capable of.

Damn it, she had plans for that double room with Mirna. Did Emir really have to mess even this one up too? When was she going to get this chance again, for goodness' sake?

"Only the best for our winner," Mirna said, her smile like that of a corporate saleswoman. "Come on, we're wasting valuable Sarajevo time here," she added and led the way to the rooms.

Franka's room was nothing to write home about. A queen-sized bed seemed clean enough, a bathroom for her to wash off the last traces of that filthy Miljacka water, and a window overlooking the place where they shot Franz Ferdinand a century ago.

She didn't even dry her hair, counting on the warm summer air doing that for her, as she put on her favorite oversized T-shirt (black, with Spike Spiegel on it) and forwarded a picture of herself at the podium to her mom and Isabella, so they would know she didn't drown. Everything else could wait. Mirna was waiting for her.

Thank God for summer and heat that brought back Mirna's crop tops and skirts, as she was sporting a black turtleneck that revealed her inhumanly perfect belly and a long bright yellow skirt ("Two marks at the thrift store, can you believe it? And it even has pockets!").

"When was the last time you were in Sarajevo?" she asked.

"Whenever I've been here, it was either the airport or the American embassy," Franka admitted.

"It's my first time alone in Sarajevo too," Mirna said, her eyes shining.

"Come on, let's explore together then!" She grabbed her hand before they started running together. Franka wasn't sure why they were running, but she knew it felt like the right thing to do.

Sarajevo was amazing. Not too hot, not too cold, a bit touristy, but because she was a tourist here, she didn't mind it that much, and neither did Mirna. As they walked through the Barčaršija Old Town, the smell of freshly ground coffee and cinnamon took Franka back in time to the time when the Ottomans ruled the country. Storefronts were filled with the same kicky knickknacks she could buy at Džidže, just with "Sarajevo" written on them, but they felt different here for some reason. It was all in her head, but tonight, she let the magic carry her wherever it wanted.

Since Mirna didn't eat beef, traditional Bosnian ćevapi—small rolls of grilled mincemeat Sarajevo was famous for—were out of the question. Instead, they had a satisfying and cheap dinner at a semi-famous place that only sold chicken and pasta, as every restaurant should. It was Mirna's treat, as was the ice cream and an assortment of nuts from an equally semi-famous store chain.

"Tonight, you deserve everything you want!" she announced. Franka allowed herself to be pampered, but she wanted one thing and one thing only. She would have to wait to get it.

Organizers of the diving event invited them to an official party after the competition that Bakir and Aca decided to attend, but both Mirna and Franka were done playing along for today, so they got to spend the evening on their own.

Even if Sarajevo was half the size of Atlanta, tonight, to Franka, it might as well have been New York, filled with endless opportunities and wonders to see. They popped into a local pub that for some reason hosted a "Norse night," which consisted of cheap mead and poor waiters wearing plastic-looking horned helmets.

"You know, actual Vikings didn't have horns on their helmets. That would have been so stupid," Mirna added after the first mead, chatty and in a great mood like Franka. They both made a silent vow to stop at the second shot (which was already watered down), so they wouldn't get hammered like they did on New Year's Eve. Franka wanted to remember this night. She also wanted it to last for a little while longer after they called it quits at the pub.

More relaxed than she would have been otherwise, but still aware of exactly what she was doing, when she got back into her room, Franka brushed her teeth like she was going to the dentist. She wore her best black bra and panties under her pajamas. Maybe nothing would happen, but it didn't hurt to be prepared.

She wasn't 100 percent sure what her plan was. Knock on Mirna's door and start smooching her? Confess her undying love to her? Get on one knee and propose? She would let the moment decide. She had to give it a go. Tonight, she could do anything. She was the third-best cliff diver in the whole city!

The hallways were pitch black as Franka left her room and locked the door behind her. A blackout maybe, or they were trying to save a little bit of money on lighting. Room 209: that is where Mirna was. When they were saying goodbye, she smiled at her as she entered. How could she forget that?

But when Franka knocked, no one answered. She tried again, only to be met with the same lack of response.

"Mirna, it's Franka," she finally said to the door. "I'd like to talk to you." Mirna didn't answer.

Franka's heart fell from that diving board into the murky river below. Maybe she didn't understand this properly. Maybe Mirna really did want them to just be friends?

Why was being into girls so unnecessarily complicated? Boys weren't much easier to decipher, but at least it was usually easier to figure out if they were pals or "gal pals."

As she walked back to her room, she wasn't even looking where she was going. She stared at her own feet and at the wooden, creaky flooring, her head full of thoughts of the last year that she so thoroughly misinterpreted.

The next moment, she was on the floor, having slammed into something with all her weight and strength.

It wasn't something, but someone. Mirna fell on the floor next to her, as they knocked into each other in the dark hallway.

"I was looking for you," Mirna said, her voice a whisper as if she didn't believe what she was seeing.

"Me too," Franka said as Mirna helped her get up. "I thought you were asleep," she lied.

"I couldn't sleep without seeing you first," Mirna confessed. Even in the relative dark, Franka could see her blushing, trying to look away like she was suddenly spooked by the fact this was really happening. Or maybe Franka was projecting because that was how she felt. Still, she wasn't going to stop. She liked where this was going.

"Come on, let's go to my room," Franka said, proud of the confidence in her voice. "We can talk in private."

"I would love that," Mirna said, her smile infectious.

Franka barely managed to open the door because her hands were shaking so much. It was a good kind of anxiety, no matter what happened. Mirna took her hands into her own and helped her guide the key into the lock with the most loving smile on her face.

"Hey, it's going to be okay, champion," she said.

"I only won third place," Franka reminded her. Mirna would have won the whole thing, Franka knew very well, like she'd do next week.

"Well, you are the champion of my heart."

"You can be smooth when you want to be," Franka said as the door finally opened. Her own heart was threatening to beat straight out of her chest, but she knew what she had to do.

The moment the door closed behind them, she pushed Mirna against a wall and started kissing her. The fresh taste of mint made her smile against her lips. She must have been planning this as much as Franka was. She could have kissed her forever. Her lips were so soft and her touch so sweet and loving.

But when Mirna pushed her on the bed, despite how much her entire body burned with desire, Franka moved away from her.

"Why now?" Franka asked.

Mirna stood above her, her breathing heavy as she looked down at Franka. Her spaghetti-strap shirt revealed that her shoulder was a sickly shade of purple. It really was for the best that she didn't dive today. It didn't mean she looked any less amazing and beautiful. But Franka needed answers first. "After almost a year, why are you here now?"

"Because I'm done lying to myself. I'm done being angry and counting days until a bad thing happens. I wrecked my shoulder because of that. I don't want to do that again. So, I'm accepting what I feel and what I need. And I need you," she said. She sat on the bed next to Franka, her brown eyes so kind and loving.

"Will you freak out and ignore me for two months again?" she asked. She couldn't do that again. This time, it would hurt even more and she wasn't going to live through that again for the sake of one night.

"No. I want you in my life, Franka. For as long as you'll have me," she said. "Besides, we were too drunk on New Year's Eve to make the right choice. No matter what we felt at that moment, if we did anything, we would have both regretted it. But now I'm sober, and I still know what I want," she admitted. "That is, if you want me. Ever since I saw your eyes when I rescued you from that river, I knew I would fall for you. You kept proving how amazing you are day after day. I was too scared to accept that. After what you did today, I couldn't pretend anymore." Her cheeks were already bright pink by this point. No matter how honest she sounded, talking about her feelings didn't come easy to Mirna.

"It was just a dive," Franka said, rubbing the back of her neck, but Mirna shook her head no.

"When you told the doctor I was injured, even though you knew it would upset me, that was the amazing part," she said. She sighed and closed her eyes for a few moments before she finally found the words to continue. "I really couldn't dive today, but I know myself well. I am one stubborn donkey, and I would have injured myself even more. But you didn't let that happen. You called me out on my bullshit. And for that, I couldn't be more thankful," she said with a smile that was so soft and loving that Franka's vision suddenly turned blurry.

"Goddamn it, woman, are you trying to make me cry?" Franka asked, on the verge of ugly sobs of joy.

"I would never do that, Franka Garcia," Mirna said, wiping the tears off her cheek with a soft touch. "I care too much about you."

"I care about you too," she said. She could have said something more, but this was enough for one night. They had better ways to spend their time than talking about their feelings.

She pulled Mirna into a kiss, soft and full of passion, and let her hands explore her body as Mirna did the same.

On this summer night, they had all the time in the world for themselves.

Chapter Sixteen

Da zna zora

Franka's breathing was soft and rhythmical as she lay in Mirna's embrace. Mirna stared at her, too scared to move because she didn't want to disturb this little piece of perfection. Bright summer light broke through the windows covered in gaudy beige curtains, letting her know it was probably too late to continue sleeping in, but Mirna needed to keep this fairy tale going for as long as possible.

Her shoulder still hurt, but not nearly as much as before. Maybe this whole thing healed it. The bruise was a gnarly shade of purple that looked kinda cool, despite the pain it caused.

After a short while, Franka finally opened her eyes and looked up at Mirna. Those eyes would be the death of her. Or her life, if she'd let them.

"Did that really happen?" Franka asked with a smile like she wasn't lying half-naked in Mirna's embrace. She didn't move away, only snuggled closer, as Mirna's whole body had never felt lighter and the smile on her face never more sincere.

"I sure hope it did," Mirna said before they burst into laughter that, sadly, didn't last long.

The phone buzzed in the distance and one phone call took them back to the real world.

"Hey, Mirna, are you alive?" Aca asked when she answered, his voice filled with worry. "I knocked on your door, but you didn't answer. Breakfast is almost over, and we have to leave the hotel by ten."

"Ooh, sorry, I slept in a bit," she said, as in the background Franka hastily put on a T-shirt that she found halfway across the room. "I'll be there in a few."

"We'll talk more about this soon. I promise," Franka said, handing over her bra that she picked up from the floor. Mirna planted a kiss on her lips and got dressed in haste. When she snuck back to her own room, she was only seen by four people, all of whom looked mildly amused, but since none of them were an Aca or a Bakir, Mirna counted that as a win. But as she brushed her teeth just enough to say she did it or shoved her stuff into her backpack without any rhyme or reason, she couldn't stop smiling.

Nothing about them had changed. She and Franka would continue doing the same things they usually did—with some extra kissing on the side. But at the same time, everything was different now. Because she was honest with herself and with Franka, everything weighing her down was gone, and she was ready to fly.

They met again in the hotel restaurant, where Mirna grabbed one of the last pieces of toast, butter, and a cup of coffee she poured approximately half a kilo of sugar into, while Franka chose a sausage and one solitary egg that somehow escaped everyone else's attention.

"We'll get something good later," Mirna promised her, in one of the rare moments they could look at each other without giggling.

Aca and Bakir were already gone by the time Mirna and Franka evacuated the hotel at 10:15 a.m., after being yelled at by housekeepers. They would meet back up at the train station at five with Aca and Bakir, so they had the rest of the day to themselves.

First, they went to a bakery older than the USA and came out with a small mountain of croissants and pastries. Both of them were functioning mostly on a fuel of sugar and spite, given that they had slept about three hours in total.

Neither of them ever had the chance to take the cable car from the city center to Trebević Mountain, so that was their agenda for the day.

As soon as they boarded the gondola, the whole city of Sarajevo appeared in front of them, from Old Town all the way to Ilidža. In an act that reminded Mirna she was still very much a teen, they spent most of the ten-minute ride making out, only stopping to take a few selfies. They weren't even for the Swallows account, but it was probably written in the law somewhere that one must take a selfie in the cable cars in Sarajevo.

They had a lot of kissing to make up for since Mirna wasn't able to admit her feelings to herself for too long, so neither of them minded that they came out of their cable car feeling slightly dizzy.

The fresh mountain air helped fix that little issue as they made their way to the old bobsled track lost in the woods. It was made for the Winter Olympics in 1984, but decades of neglect, not to mention war and occupation of the city, had made it fall into disrepair.

They walked around in nature, holding hands a lot more openly than Mirna would have dared in Mostar, and enjoying their first real date.

"Are we…like…you know…" Mirna tried to ask as they sat on the half-destroyed concrete tube and listened to the birds chirp. Why was it suddenly so difficult to form sentences? Mom was right. Romance does make one stupider.

"Girlfriends?" Franka asked, once again the more clear-headed one here and looking very smug for it.

"Yes! That!" Mirna said, making Franka burst out laughing, but Mirna didn't mind. She was done playing it cool. She liked Franka Garcia, and she wanted the whole world to know it.

"If you want us to be," she said in her fake serious voice. "And if that goofy grin on your face is any indication, you do."

"Of course I do," Mirna said. She wanted to officially call this wonderful woman her girlfriend! "If you haven't deduced that from my inability to form complex sentences."

"You are very cute when you lose the golden-child mask," Franka said, making Mirna frown.

"It's not a mask," she insisted, even if it wasn't the truth, but it made the banter more fun. "I am just that great, and you know it," she said.

"You are absolutely amazing, to be fair," Franka said before she looked around, figured they were alone, and pulled her down into a kiss.

They spent the afternoon in nature, getting lost in space, and more importantly, in time, so when they finally returned to the city, they had to get a cab to the train station because they were running late. They were the last ones to board the train, where Bakir and Aca waited for them, after calling Mirna's phone about a hundred times.

"We're here. We're here!" Mirna yelled when they finally met as the train began to pick up speed and leave the city of Sarajevo behind.

"Good, glad to see you," Aca said, relief washing over his face. "I thought you decided to move here."

"Nah, Mostar is my one true love," Mirna said, giving Franka a significant look that made her smile.

After about five minutes, Aca was already out cold, sleeping like he had never slept before. Bakir joined him, leaning against his shoulder for most of the ride. It was kinda adorable.

Mirna and Franka covered themselves with Franka's jacket because they were "kinda chilly; it must be the water," but they actually wanted to hold hands. They kept glancing at each other, sharing their little secret so well kept they only learned about it yesterday.

151

To the surprise of everyone, Emir didn't so much as acknowledge their existence.

"I thought he might send us a message or taunt us in some way," Mirna said, checking her phone for the millionth time. Many other people had already sent their congratulations, so the news obviously spread, but Emir was nowhere to be seen or heard from. "Not that I'm complaining about the silent treatment. It's better than the alternative of his asking us to climb Mount Everest if we want to compete just because it's us."

"We already won," Franka said with a smug smile on her face. The post of Franka's winning dive was making rounds on their accounts and causing quite a *splash*.

"You did," Mirna reminded her. Her heart beat faster, but for once, it wasn't angry. The desire to prove her worth lit a new fire in her. "I didn't get to compete. But that's okay. I am jumping a swallow off that bridge, and I am going to win. After all this, I have to."

"You will," Franka assured her, squeezing her hand under the jacket. Together, they could do anything.

Soon, the train reached Mostar and it dropped them off at the station before continuing on its track to Čapljina.

"See you on the twenty-third!" Aca said as they said goodbye. "Can't wait to kick your assess!"

"You wish!" Franka said, but she still high-fived him. They weren't yet in the "complex handshake" territory, but they were getting there.

And then Mirna and Franka were alone again. The street was unusually empty for this time of the day, but it gave them more chances to talk.

"Do we, like, tell people?" Mirna asked, because she really didn't know what the right answer was. She might have been more open than most queer people in Herzegovina were, but she still knew where she lived. It was something they both had to agree on because it would affect both of their lives. It had to be a joint decision, at least in a town as small as Mostar, where everyone knew everyone else, and all their dirty laundry.

"I don't know," Franka said, her eyes narrowed in thought. "If we were in Atlanta, I wouldn't bat an eye, but you know the situation here better than I do. What did you do with previous girlfriends?"

"We were usually 'friends' who were very touchy," Mirna confessed. Also, her longest relationship lasted a full two months, mostly because Mirna couldn't bring herself to break Simona's heart like that, until Simona did that for her by sending her a message on Quickgram and blocking her on all social media.

Simona conveniently forgot they were still in the same class. "But that was high school. I don't want to hide you. You mean so much to me."

"What's the possibility of someone beating us up?" Franka asked a direct and pragmatic question.

"Equally high on both sides of the town," Mirna said. It was the truth they both knew already. The fact nothing happened to them on New Year's Eve was a miracle.

"How about we take it one step at a time? We can tell people who need to know, and we'll take it from there," Franka suggested. Mirna agreed.

"One day a time," she said. They said goodbye at Mirna's garden, sneaking in one more kiss under the pomegranate tree before Franka left.

Their issue was partially resolved about half an hour after Mirna walked into her house, still tasting Franka on her lips.

Mom was closing up the shop for the day, so it was only Ado and Grandpa when she came in, watching some Turkish soap opera both had gotten really invested in recently. She sat next to them as they all stared at the intense scene of Ezel trying to break up with Zynep for her own good, even though he still loved her. If Mirna hadn't developed an allergic reaction to the Turkish language from all the tourists she had to deal with, she would have enjoyed it even more.

"We are very proud of you two," Grandpa said as Mirna grabbed some of the zeljanica pie with spinach Mom made for lunch. So good!

"Thank you," Mirna said, stuffing her face with the amazing pie. "I mean, it's mostly Franka. I just trained her for a year," she added, less than modestly.

"So, you and Franka, how long has that been going on?" Ado asked, making Mirna choke on her pie. She may have been expecting that question, but not that directly.

"What are you talking about?" she asked, her cheeks already turning bright red, confirming his assessment.

"Pay up, old man," Ado said triumphantly as Grandpa frowned and handed him a ten marks bill. "We are so happy for you two," he added. "And for my shiny new *cener*."

"Franka is like family to us and we're glad you finally see what we have been seeing for months now," Grandpa said, smiling at her, but giving Ado a very judgmental look. "I thought both of you would chicken out and not confess."

"I, on the other hand, knew right away," Ado said. "Just like I know everything," he added in an ominous tone of an ancient prophet. He mouthed the words "New Year's Eve" and gave her a long and significant look, only confirming her suspicion he was, in fact, an *evlija*, a powerful prophet, but only in the area of gossip.

As Mirna went to her room to retire for the evening before they could continue with questions, the light in the hallway shone brightly, bringing a smile to her face. Maybe she really didn't have to do everything on her own.

In the end, as she was about to go to sleep, her phone rang; a familiar number that made her growl as she answered.

"It's 11:00 p.m., Emir," she said.

"I know. I know, but I had to call," he said, sounding almost apologetic. "I'm so sorry I'm calling so late. Emil is with me on the weekends, and we lost track of time. I just returned him to his mother."

Mirna didn't say anything, but her pissiness subsided a little. She couldn't be pissed if Emil was involved. The kid did nothing wrong.

"I'm calling to say I got the good news," he continued. "And Franka winning is good news, Mirna, it really is. You two did something amazing, and I hope you're proud of yourself."

Mirna didn't answer him right away, more certain with each new word that she misread the caller ID. This was not the Emir who had been brawling with two teenage girls for a year. "Thank you," she finally said. "It was mostly Franka, though," she added because it was true.

"I hope your shoulder is feeling better," he added, with the tone of voice she expected from an older brother, one she never had.

"It's going to be okay by Saturday," Mirna said, still too confused to function at her full capacity.

"Glad to hear that. You have to understand I was only harsh on you for your own safety. After your dive in August, I wanted to make sure you would never injure yourself again. I care about the safety of my contestants," he explained, sounding sincere for the first time in his life.

Then why did you dare my thirteen-year-old brother to dive when he wasn't ready? That question stayed in Mirna's head. Maybe this was a once-in-a-lifetime opportunity to start things fresh with Emir Kapo. She would be a fool to not try at least, even if it meant keeping some observations to herself.

"I am happy to officially invite you and Franka to the competition. We can't wait to see what you girls have to offer," he said, and she could hear his smile through the phone. "Since it's only the two of you, you will be competing with the rest of us."

"That's what we wanted," she said, letting herself be a little smug. She deserved it. She knew this would happen ever since Franka's victory woke her up from her nap, but hearing his confirmation after all this time made her heart beat a little bit faster.

"But I'm not calling only to let you know something you already know. I need a favor. Or, to be more precise, my Aunt Bisera needs one," he said. "She got really into cliff diving lately. She doesn't want to try it, but she is very interested in the history of it and things like that. She'll explain everything to you in person. But first, she wants to do a short promo video for this year's event. It will take, like, an hour at most. You'll need to say a few lines and that's all, and it will really mean a lot to me and to her."

"Oh," Mirna said. "Okay, I guess." She had no reason to deny him, especially if she was trying to turn over a new leaf.

"Awesome. You're really doing me a big favor. See you at the bridge at eight thirty-ish? Great. See you there," he answered himself before she had the chance to.

If Mirna had any idea what she would learn on that morning, she would have told Emir to *odjebe*.

Chapter Seventeen

Tajna

Franka's new and shiny bronze medal fit in very nicely with the rest of her room. She hung it on the wall above her desk to complement the little Old Bridge Mirna gave her, then stared at it for at least five minutes with a dumb smile on her face.

With Mirna's help, over the last few weeks, she finally unpacked the last of her boxes, including hers and Dad's favorite records like King Crimson, Queen, and of course, Zdravko Čolić (that one was Mom's), to show off and make the room feel lived in.

Mirna also got her a few throw pillows to make her bed homier and helped her pick out a rug that "really ties the whole room together, y'know?"

It looked more like *her* room now, not just a place where she slept. Mirna had a few of their photos developed, so Franka taped them on the walls over the desk to help her study. And she was keeping the whole place a bit cleaner than usual. Maybe collecting plates on one's bedside table wasn't the best idea. Her room was never going to be as wonderfully neat as Mirna's, but it was good enough for her.

After she was done hugging her and fawning over her as if she'd brought home an Olympic medal, Mom suggested a movie night, so Franka set up Bella's subscription channel and made popcorn (one thing she could make!) and tried her best to enjoy the movie.

But no matter how well-planned the murder on the screen seemed, Franka couldn't concentrate on the movie. The conversation she had with Mirna played in her mind again.

She might as well do it now, right?

Mom followed the events on the screen with half a mind, occupying herself with a costume for the play her students, who were in the summer drama school with her, would perform at the end of August. The gender-bent, steampunk, dystopian, but condensed version of *Hamlet* sounded amazing. Maybe if she had done that when Franka was still in school, she would have actually joined her.

Inspired by Mirna and Franka (as well as Bisera's interview), Mom insisted on making it with the kids from both sides of the city, including the girls from the local Madrasa. One of them was her Hamlet, so Mom was currently modifying her costume to go along with her hijab.

Mom had left the city during the War when it seemed like the world was on fire and never would heal again because the people of this town were too different from one another. Those memories were with her all through her life in the US, even if they never transferred to Franka for the simple reason Franka was a "real" American, but it was still nice seeing her work through those prejudices and finally accept this city as her own once again.

As a gruesome murder took place on the screen, Franka finally spat it out. "Mom, I think you should know I'm dating Mirna!"

The sentence burst out of her with so much passion, as if she were chasing an Oscar or an MTV movie award. The rest of the scene played out in her mind in an instant: loads of crying and hugging and promises of love, like she hadn't come out years ago with no one batting an eye. Of course, reality was a bit different.

"Weren't you dating already?" Mom joked, barely looking away from the stabbing on the TV, causing Franka to throw a "*la familia es todo*" pillow at her. "I'm kidding. I'm kidding. Thank you for telling me, kiddo. I'm glad you can be honest with me. I am very happy for you. Mirna is a great gal."

"She is amazing!" Franka squealed, unable to hold in her excitement for her amazing girlfriend.

"That Mirna, she brings out the Franka you were before Andres died. I missed that Franka a lot," Mom said, putting down her needle and facing her. She was tall and willowy in build, pale and blonde, unlike Franka who took after her dark-skinned, dark-haired dad, but their eyes were the same. Franka knew that, of course, but it was like seeing it again for the first time. "Especially since we moved to Mostar." She was silent for a moment again, like she was choosing her words carefully. "I know the move left your life in shambles. It took you away from all your friends and your aunt, but we really had no other choice. I think you know that," she finally said, taking a deep breath, like those words had been stuck in her throat for years.

Franka nodded. This conversation has been a long time coming.

"You hated it here more than I did," Franka said. Mom had tried to hide it over the years, smiling and saying how good they had it here. Compared to being homeless in Atlanta, it was good, but Franka assumed that it was likely Mom was as miserable as Franka when Franka wasn't around.

"It's true. Mostar has only brought me so many bad memories, even before the War. I wanted to escape this house long before the first bullet was fired," she said. Franka didn't want to push her to talk about it further. Maybe one day Mom would open up and tell her the whole truth, and Franka would listen to her and offer comfort like Mom comforted her, but for now, it was still too painful.

"I didn't know how to help you, Franka. I still don't. Andres was always so much better at understanding you. All I could do was provide you with a roof over your head and a meal on our table," Mom said. She looked around, avoiding Franka's gaze like she was ashamed of her perfectly justified choices. "But luckily, that young lady did what I wasn't able to do and got you out of your funk."

"Mom, don't blame yourself for what happened," Franka said. "It really wasn't your fault. No matter what, I would rather have a middle-class life in Mostar than be poor and homeless in Atlanta," Franka assured her. Even as an emotional sixteen-year-old, she understood that much. That's why she didn't complain about it out loud, only kept it all inside. She didn't want to bother Mom. She lost Dad too. "I know you love me so that made it all easier. Even if I didn't show it enough, knowing you were there for me really meant the world to me."

Mom pulled her into a hug, her eyes filling with tears.

"I love you, Franka," she said. "I don't think I say that enough."

"I love you too, Mom." It felt great to say it out loud after a forever of hiding her feelings inside.

"And Bella also loves you quite a lot," Mom added. "Something is waiting for you in your bedroom. Hint: it's under the desk lamp," she added in a playful voice.

Franka ran to her room, jumping over two, three steps at a time, inches away from breaking her neck, but she was too excited to slow down. And there it was, just as promised, under her flamingo-shaped novelty lamp that didn't actually give off enough light: a return plane ticket to Atlanta.

"Bella wanted to see you," Mom said, catching up with her a few moments later, smiling as she leaned against the door. "She asked me if you would be free next month, and I said you would. She wanted you to come earlier, but I knew you wouldn't want to miss the competition."

"OMG! Thank you, guys! You're amazing!" Franka yelled.

"Don't thank me. I've done the bare minimum of keeping my mouth shut, that's all," Mom said. "And in return, Bella wants one thing from you: tomorrow, 7:00 p.m., you are to sit in your room in front of your laptop and answer her video call," she said as she took out her phone and read Bella's message: "And tell her to wear a nice shirt. Maybe something blue or green. It brings out her eyes. And please tell her to brush her hair. At least so that she doesn't look like she just got out of bed."

"What is she planning?" Franka asked, slightly puzzled. Mom mimed locking her lips and threw the imaginary key over her shoulder.

"That is for me to keep quiet about and you to discover tomorrow," she said with a cryptic smile, and Franka knew she wouldn't get anything out of her.

The next day, she and Mirna didn't meet for their morning practice.

> **Mirna**: I have decided to be a bigger person, and I am sucking up to Emir Kapo and his aunt. God forgive me for my sins that I shall elaborate on soon.

Her message was followed by a whole barrage of gifs of people praying.

> **Franka**: Go ahead, honey. If you get big enough, you can squash him like a bug. See you at two.

Franka went right back to sleep until the tender hours of the afternoon like God intended.

A few minutes after two, Franka finally got to the bridge. She leaned against the wall, breathing heavily, trying to catch her breath. Of course, she was late because she had run there. Warm but persistent summer rain ruined their desire to dive today. It was probably for the best, giving Mirna's shoulder an extra day to recover.

They did have one more thing to do, arguably more important than practicing. But something peculiar happened: Mirna was late.

In all the time they had known each other, Franka had come to the conclusion Mirna ran on an internal atomic clock because she was always on time. But now, Franka sat by the bridge for almost ten minutes, checking her phone, before Mirna ran down a flight of stairs that led to her house.

"I was at the library," she said, wheezing, as she bent over to catch her breath, the giant backpack she carried threatening to topple her.

Franka gave her a bottle of water, which she drank whole within seconds.

"Library? Was it one of those 'you actually didn't finish all your exams' dreams you took too seriously?" Franka teased as Mirna came back to life, breath by breath.

"That was one time!" Mirna insisted with a chuckle that seemed fake instead of genuine. That spark was missing from her eyes. No matter how good her mask was, her eyes always gave her away. "But nah, I was doing some research and got lost in it."

"Have you heard of YA books? Or beach reads? Or crime novels?" Franka asked with a smile before she realized Mirna wasn't smiling at all. If anything, the flared nostrils and balled-up fists made her look like she was about to fight someone to the death. That someone wasn't Franka because Mirna smiled again a few seconds later.

"The heart wants what it wants," she simply said.

So Franka didn't say anything about her future trip. Other things occupied her mind more. That afternoon, they finally officially signed up to compete. Two competitions would take place simultaneously, one for those who would do a feetfirst dive, and the other for those brave souls who dared to do a swallow. Franka made her decision a few days ago.

"I can't do a swallow," Franka finally admitted. "It just... Maybe I could, but I would rather do one good dive instead of half-assing two." Maybe next year. The image of Mirna's shoulder still haunted her, and she wasn't going to risk it. Not on her first Mostar competition.

"I'll do the swallow. Only swallow," Mirna said like she was preparing to drop nukes.

"Are you kidding me right now?" Franka asked. "You are brilliant in both. Why would you limit yourself like that?"

"I have to," she said, too stubborn to be argued with. Once Mirna made her decision, Franka knew everything she said would just bounce off her.

"It kinda sucks I won't get to compete against you," she said after a while. "I wanted that rivalry back. It was really fun," she added, making Mirna smile.

"Well, one of us had to qualify higher than the other, like in college. Where I won, if my memory serves me correct," she said, like she wasn't exactly sure if she had straight A's in her second semester.

"You won that one," Franka admitted with a frown, pretending she didn't love that for Mirna. "But will you win this one? What's better, hard work or natural talent?"

"I guess we'll have to see this weekend. The betting odds are slightly in my favor," Mirna said. It was true, at least what Grandpa Džemal said. They were both on the bottom, but despite Franka's third place in Sarajevo, most people trusted Mirna's years of experience slightly more. People still didn't believe they could actually make a splash in this competition.

"We'll just have to practice even more," Mirna said.

"Smooching time must not, and cannot, bite into our practice time," Franka said, seriously and firmly like it was a business negotiation.

"Oh, my lovely girlfriend, don't think I will go any easier on you," Mirna promised her. "We are still practicing like it's the Olympics!"

"That's what I like to hear," Franka said with a laugh. "I won't let you win because you are cute," she assured her. Even if she wanted to, her competitive spirit would never, ever let her.

"I would be insulted if you did," Mirna said, and Franka knew it was the truth because it was the same for her. "I am winning this thing fair and square. You'll just have to settle for second place, I guess," she added, with that playful smile Franka had learned to love so much.

That evening, she did what Bella had asked her to do: put on a nice dark blue, button-up shirt, even though it was very hot in her room, and sat in front of her laptop. At exactly 7:00 p.m., as promised, Bella called her. But she wasn't alone.

The man on the other side of the camera looked like every other white man in the position of middling power, with neat salt-and-pepper hair, a strong chin, and dark glasses that hid light-blue eyes.

"Good evening," Franka said in her most polite voice as she stared at her aunt who looked like she was about to explode if she didn't speak right now.

"Franka, this is Mathew Jonson, a friend of mine. And a friend of your dad," Bella said in her sweetest voice.

"Nice to meet you, Mr. Jonson," she answered, content with staring blankly at the camera and smiling until further notice.

"Your aunt has told me so much about you, I had to meet this wonderful young woman as soon as possible," he said in a corporate voice and an even more corporate smile, like he wasn't enjoying this exchange much more than she was.

"I didn't want to tell you in advance because I knew you would get all worked up and you also had your diving competition. I wanted you to focus all your attention on that, but Matt is here to conduct an interview with you," Bella explained quickly, trying to speak normally, but her voice trembled with excitement.

"Just a formality, nothing to be worried about," Mr. Jonson said with a polite smile that finally reached his eyes. "Isabella and I met at my brother's birthday party a few weeks ago. My brother is the guy who gave you the pro camera you're using. Always the adventurous type." Franka finally smiled for real. That camera did so many great things for her and Mirna. "We started talking and we realized I went to college with Andres. We were quite close friends, but since he went into the industry, and I remained in academia, we drifted apart," he explained. "Still, you have my condolences for your loss, dear Franka."

"Thank you," Franka answered, trying not to focus on the way he pronounced her name, like Frank, with an extra *a*. That's how everyone in the States always pronounced it, and she had gotten used to it when she was there, but now it grated at her ear like nails on a chalkboard.

"I am a Vice-Dean at Emerson Clifford University. You may have heard of us," he said.

"In Birmingham, right?" Franka asked. She was tangentially aware of the school in question. It was never at the top of her lists (Emory University all the way!) because jokes were that it was almost as expensive as an Ivy League but with all the quality and prestige only marginally better than a community college. Also, if she was going to move from Atlanta or Georgia, she would have liked to go somewhere a bit less quintessentially Southern than Alabama. But she was too confused by the existence of this conversation to question anything at this point.

"I'll give you two some privacy; how about that?" Bella asked and disappeared out of the frame.

"So, how can I help you, Mr. Jonson?" Franka asked.

"Tell me about yourself, Franka."

Most of the talk went by in a blur. She talked about her accomplishments at both high schools, her language studies, and her first year of college. After a few initial minutes of panic and confusion, Franka relaxed and eased into the conversation as if Mirna were next to her and they were trying to impress a gullible journalist.

"You really are very special, Franka," Mr. Jonson finally said after what Franka realized only now was an hour. "It was a pleasure talking to you."

"Likewise, Mr. Jonson. I'm so glad Isabella had the foresight to bring us together," she said, at least partially honest.

"Me even more. You might be just the person we were looking for," he explained with a smile.

"Oh, really?" she asked, trying to keep her breathing normal, even if her heart was beating like crazy.

"How would you like to attend our school?" he asked. "We have a new program for minorities and foreign exchange students, and right now, you fit into both categories. We have a growing science department and you can major in any number of fields that would allow you to continue your studies and become a pharmacologist like Andres was, if that is what you want. It is all a bit unorthodox and rushed, but we have a few unexpected openings, and we would like to fill them with fresh new faces. So, what do you say?"

"I...I'm very honored, sir," she said the only thing she could, her hands shaking with excitement, but her brain too stunned to think.

"Think about it for a little while, of course. I know you have started a lot already in Mostar, but this could be a fresh, yet familiar, new beginning for you. How about you get back to me by the twenty-fifth?" he suggested. "Classes would start in the third week of August, so you would have plenty of time to make other arrangements if you choose to join us."

Okay, okay, everybody stay calm! This was happening! It was really happening! I would go back to the US! About two and a half hours from Bella! We could spend every weekend together! And yeah, the school wasn't that great, but it was probably better than the one I'm attending now.

Still, one by one, questions pooled up in her brain. The biggest one didn't have to do with leaving Mirna and Mostar behind. It was far more pragmatic.

"I'm sorry I have to be so direct, but what about the tuition fee?" she asked after a brief pause. Mr. Jonson fixed his glasses, looking away from the camera.

"Well, sadly, we wouldn't be able to cover the cost of your tuition," he said like this was the one question he was dreading.

"How much?" she asked. "Give it to me straight, please. I appreciate the honesty."

He smiled.

"I like you, Franka. You ask the right questions." Of course she did. It was her future they were talking about! "Your tuition for the undergrad studies would be about fifty thousand."

"Plus fifty thousand for graduate studies?" she asked, doing the very simple math familiar to anyone who wanted to attend a private college in America.

"Give or take," he confirmed. "You can take out a loan, of course."

One hundred thousand dollars in debt by the time I am twenty-five! The American dream.

Here, she could get a diploma that was valid in all of Europe in five years for about nine thousand dollars or even significantly less now that she would have most of the cost covered by the country for being a good student.

When she was in the US, a loan seemed like the natural and only choice, unless she got really lucky and got a rare full scholarship. But now she knew it didn't need to be that way.

But as Mr. Jonson left and Bella came back into the frame, her smile wide, happier than Franka had seen her since Dad died, a choice never seemed so difficult.

Chapter Eighteen

Laži me

The local librarian was an old lady, probably the age of the bridge itself, gray and wrinkly like a fig, but just as sweet. Thick glasses covered most of her face, but they didn't hide her friendly smile.

"I like seeing bright young kids like yourself asking about their history. So fun," she said when Mirna ran into the library for the fourth day in a row with her hair wet and still smelling like Neretva. "Splendid."

Mirna didn't feel splendid. If she wanted to read dusty, old newspapers from the last century, she would have studied journalism. But before she said or did anything, she had to make sure Emir had been telling the truth.

***

On Monday morning, Mirna had been the last one to arrive, even if she wasn't late. Looking back on it, it should have been a clear sign she would have been better off not going at all.

Bisera had looked larger than life in her deep-blue blazer, while her cameraman, unfortunately named Srećko, seemed even less alive in the bright morning sun. With them was Emir, who smiled at her when he saw her, and Safet, aka one of the other guys who had made the most dives off the Old Bridge.

"It's so nice to see you again," Bisera said when she saw Mirna, pulling her into an overly familiar hug only a middle-aged woman could be capable of. "Let me congratulate you on your success. Amazing job, girl, we are all proud of you."

"I didn't actually compete," Mirna answered her, but Bisera wasn't listening one bit. She had her own story to tell.

"I would like to apologize for how my nephew treated you two," she said, looking at him like he was a five-year-old who bit someone in kindergarten. "Emir is a nice kid, I swear. He is just very stubborn and passionate about this sport." Mirna didn't say anything, even if Bisera made him sound like a child, but

167

Emir didn't seem to mind as he gave them both one of those "live and learn" sort of shrugs. "Kind of like you," she added, and Mirna couldn't disagree. "Thank you so much for doing this on such short notice. I have a really cool idea. We are going to have Safet, as the symbol of the past, Emir as the symbol of the present, and you as the future all inviting us to come and see this year's diving. It's going to be great!" she said.

The shoot went as well as could be expected. Without Franka by her side, trying to impress Bisera wasn't nearly as fun, but she said her line, "We invite you to join us this Saturday for a competition unlike anything you've seen before," with as much passion as she could muster.

"Come on, let me treat you all to coffee for being great sports," Bisera insisted after it was all done.

Mirna, still determined to make this work, didn't say no to her offer as Bisera ushered them all, sans Srećko, who was politely asked to take the footage to the editor to be done as soon as possible, into a coffee shop right next to the bridge.

"It had to be Džemal's granddaughter. Your grandpa was always a bit cocky. Training a girl, so weird," Safet said as soon as the waiter got them their drinks. He looked at Mirna like he didn't actually comprehend what he was seeing, but didn't like the view regardless. Old men like him weren't usually outright malicious like the younger guys could be, but they still didn't like women in spaces where there usually weren't any.

"Well, someone had to give us a try," Mirna said with her most polite smile, even if she hated the dismissal in his voice like Grandpa was trying to train llamas to dive off the bridge and not two perfectly capable, healthy, and athletic humans.

"Back in my time, you couldn't prove yourself as a man and date a girl until you jumped off the bridge. I don't know why a girl like you would even bother," he continued.

Don't mention you're gay. Don't mention you're gay, Mirna repeated to herself. She really didn't need to bring it up right now, no matter how funny it would be.

"I don't know if girls will ever be strong enough to compete," he added, a tad dreamily, like he wasn't aware Mirna was taller than him.

"My friend Franka won third place in Sarajevo," Mirna said. She took out her phone and showed him Franka's dive. It was far from her best, but it still looked impressive enough for Safet to frown in confusion and nod.

"I guess," he said. "We'll see how you do in the real thing." To Mirna's great delight, he looked a tiny bit interested in finding out more, and that was all Mirna could ask for.

As suspected, Bisera didn't bring them here out of the goodness of her heart. She had a proposal to make.

"I was never that much into diving myself, I have to admit," she said. "But you girls and Emir have really gotten me interested. I will never dive. I'm too much of a coward, but it is a part of our culture and history, and it deserves to be documented. And you two girls and you, Safet, are a part of it. First female competitors! How exciting."

"Sure," Mirna said. She really didn't want this to be as big of a deal as it was. She wanted to compete. Making history was a side gig.

"What I'm working on is going to be big. I want to make a documentary about our cliff divers, our history, present, and the future. I have already asked a few people to participate, but I also want you two," she said to Mirna and Safet. "How about another interview?" she asked. "Our viewers loved you last time. You really stole the show. This time, we would talk mostly about diving and the history of it."

"I would like that," Mirna said, this time at least partially honest. She knew so much trivia about this sport; it would be a shame if most of it stayed in her head. She tried not to info dump to Franka too much, even if Franka didn't mind. Bisera's idea sounded like something that someone should have done a long time ago. Why wouldn't she want to be a part of it?

"Wonderful!" Bisera exclaimed. "You and Emir are such wonderful kids! It was all his idea anyway, and he helped me do research, especially into old divers."

Emir smiled at his aunt and then at Mirna.

"Did you know Franka's late grandfather won once? In the seventies?" he asked.

"Wow!" Mirna couldn't stop herself from saying. "She never mentioned that." Did Franka even know that? Mrs. Romana didn't seem like one to share wholesome family anecdotes like that, even if she had warmed up to Mostar again.

"Yeah, Emir was so surprised when he found that out," Bisera said.

"Matej Gaćina," he said with his best polite boy smile, despite the funny name.

"Oh, I remember that old bastard," Safet said as his expression turned into a sour frown. "He didn't compete many times, but he was a great diver. A terrible man though," he added.

"What do you mean?" Mirna asked before she could stop herself. She didn't want to sound like she was gathering gossip, but Franka only mentioned her grandpa to make fun of his last name, so if Mirna could get more info, she wasn't going to say no to that offer.

"He had a bit of a temper problem. And he drank. A lot. He almost drank that house away. No wonder that daughter of his never visited. Unlike your grandpa, I never liked him," he said. "Emir, son, how come you didn't ask Džemal for this? You know that man likes to talk about diving like no one else."

Emir looked as if the Eid holiday had come early, like he had been waiting for this exact moment his whole life. His smile caused Mirna's fight or flight response to kick into high gear, as if it knew she was about to be mauled by a beast. He smiled at her, his face losing even the tiniest bit of honesty. It was pure smugness.

"Oh, you didn't know?" he asked. "Mirna's grandpa only competed once. And he came in second to last."

Mirna froze. Emir was lying. Plain and simple.

"Wait a minute, kid," Safet backed her up. "That can't be true. I remember that competition. He really didn't do well. I think he ended up breaking his arm." Emir nodded, not fazed by Safet's words one bit. "But there was also... No, that was Dušan. And..." He tilted his head in confusion, trying to access memories of times long forgotten, and Mirna knew he would remember more. Her grandpa was a local legend for goodness' sake! Everyone in this city knew him. Emir was a lying liar! "He was always there by the bridge. He gave me the best advice to improve my swallow, but now that I think of it, I can't remember a single dive of his," he finished, like he wasn't exactly sure why. Grandpa never went in depth with his stories, but he had enough of them to assure Mirna and the rest of the town of his legendary status.

"I checked the archives when I was helping Aunt Bisera. It was only that year and never before or after," Emir said as Bisera nodded. "Never. Not a single time," he added, looking at Mirna and no one else.

"I know; we were surprised too," Bisera said.

"Did you know that, Mirna?" Emir asked in his sweetest voice, like he was trying to cause her pain. "You must have known your grandpa wasn't actually a legendary diver?" Mirna tried to keep her face as neutral as possible, but she knew she would fail as every single neuron in her brain was now on high alert.

"Oh, I guess you didn't know," Emir said, looking her in the eyes, taunting her. "That is unfortunate. That your grandfather, who taught you everything you know, never even came close to winning while Franka's grandpa was a legend. But it doesn't matter, right?" he asked, still with that innocent look on his face. To Bisera and Safet, he may have seemed to just lack tact, but Mirna understood his maliciousness right away.

"Emir was very surprised when he learned that. Džemal seems like such an important member of the diving community," Bisera said, failing to realize exactly what her nephew was doing.

"Very interesting," Mirna was somehow able to say, even if the world around her came to a standstill.

"But it doesn't matter, right?" Emir said. "It's a coincidence that Franka's grandfather was a champion and she won bronze at the first competition she ever attended after only a year of training while you didn't even get to compete?"

Safet, who must have caught on to what he was doing, gave him a look to cut it out, but Emir didn't even notice. This was his petty victory, and he wasn't going to let it go so easily.

"Maybe talent runs through some families more than others," he added and shrugged.

"So, Monday, the twenty-fifth, around eight a.m. under the Old Bridge. Does that work for you and Franka?" Bisera asked, seemingly oblivious to what Emir's words did to Mirna, who still stood frozen, unable to move from her chair or look at anything other than Emir's smug grin as her mind tried to figure out what this all meant for her but was unable to come up with any real answers.

"Sure, sure," Mirna said to hide how shaken she actually was.

She wasn't sure how she got home that day. She knew she had said bye, with a generic excuse she had to help her mom or something, and all but ran away from that place.

And then she went to the library to try to find out the real truth. Emir was lying. That was the only possible option.

Mirna must have missed something in the past four days of constant research. Džemal was a local diving legend, for goodness' sake. No matter how much she and Ado teased him, it wasn't just he who said that. All the other guys agreed. He wouldn't have been respected as much as he was. This was Mostar. People remembered those kinds of things, right?

"Strange," the librarian said. "No one had looked at those archives for decades and now you are the second person to ask for them this month. It was some lad before you. I think he's one of those diving guys. Emil. Or Edin. Very polite."

The pressure in her skull rising, Mirna made herself put her head down and go back to reading. She didn't want to say anything to Franka or Ado or

Grandpa before she was sure. There had to be an answer. Emir must have been lying and made Bisera go along with his story to make her lose her cool and waste valuable time on this stupid quest. She would find plenty of evidence of what happened in the 70s and 80s and prove them both wrong.

But she found nothing. Just as Emir said, her grandpa had competed once, came in second to last, and never went back to the bridge again. She did find that Matej Gaćina, Franka's grandpa, won in the late 70s, with a perfect swallow, so that part was true.

When she reached the 90s on Thursday afternoon and everyone stopped caring about bridge diving, Mirna had to admit defeat.

Her grandfather had only competed once.

As she came out of the library, her mind filled with a mist of anger and disappointment, she tried to rationalize it by making a list of possibilities:

1. A lack of competitive spirit resulted in only one record of his dives

2. He did jump, as many times as he said he did, but never in an official capacity.

3. The archives were wrong. God only knew it was a miracle she found what she did, especially after the War.

He was her grandpa, as competitive as she was. No way in hell he wouldn't have competed every year he could. Safet didn't say he didn't remember him competing, but diving at all. And archives weren't so barren that only he and he alone was missing.

So what if he didn't compete? What if he only jumped once or even never in his life? Why did that matter? Those were *his* accomplishments. Mirna was making her own.

But then again, everything she did, every minute she had spent practicing, every fight she had been in because they wouldn't let her compete or train, even her and Franka— everything lay on the foundation of the fact her grandpa was a prolific jumper. She had carved this path out for herself based on what he taught her. Not only taught—inspired, encouraged.

If the foundation was so shaky, could the house she made be any better?

Izmir's nose had made such an awful, crunching sound when her fist made contact with it. He had fallen on the floor, and Mirna had frozen, looking at her own hand and then at the boy cowering under her, his face bloody, his eyes overflowing with tears. In the aftermath of that—the yelling of the school principal and her parents, and the later interview with Unbounded High School—Mirna knew she had to find a way to dive. She had sacrificed so much to prove them wrong, all because her grandfather had told her she could do it. If Grandpa wasn't the one to encourage her to keep diving, she probably would have never punched Izmir. She would have gotten into the Unbounded High School. She would have gotten a scholarship for some really good school. Her entire present and the future would have been different.

Maybe that's why she'd injured herself twice this year. As that thought entered her mind, a sharp pain shot through her shoulder, even if it had been quiet before.

***

She wasn't sure how she got back home that afternoon as the hot summer sun burned everything it came in contact with, making her dizzy and weak, almost as much as the news she discovered did.

Grandpa wasn't home when she got back. Thank Allah. She wasn't ready to have that conversation. She couldn't even look at him.

Adnan. The perfect person for this conversation. Mom had made him take a day off, and Grandpa took his place at Džidže.

"Dude, I have to talk to you." She knocked on his bedroom door to find him behind his computer, playing video games instead of scheming for a change.

"Shoot," he said, taking off his headset. "The post of Franka's jump is really making rounds. People are excited to see you two compete."

"Yeah, cool," she said, making him frown. Not because she wasn't appreciating his hard work and hustle, but because he knew her well enough to recognize it wasn't just that.

"What happened?" he asked. "Was it Emir again?"

"Yes. But no. Kinda. I mean, not his fault. It's Grandpa," she finally spat out.

"What did that old man do?" he asked, now in his therapist mode that could so quickly spiral into "*mahaluša*" mode.

"I did some research and he..." she began, but he cut in.

"Jumped off the bridge like once?" Ado asked in the most casual tone of voice imaginable. "I know. He got kinda tipsy and talkative when he came back from the New Year's Eve party. We started talking, and he confessed to it. I didn't want to tell you because, well..." He pointed to her, waving his hands around. Mirna's face must have been completely red by this point. "I knew it would upset you."

"Can you blame me?" she asked, but he shook his head no, way too cool for Mirna's liking, as if he was doing it on purpose.

"So what, Mirna? It should have been obvious to both of us for years now. He never went into detail about his own dives. He was bad at explaining how it feels or what exactly you should do. It was us who didn't want to believe it."

"He lied to us," Mirna said. Ado shook his head again.

"Maybe because I'm not a diving prodigy nor the golden child, but what some old man did forty years ago doesn't dictate what I can or cannot do. And I love that man! Weren't you the one going on and on about how we don't need to be defined by what our ancestors did in that interview of yours? Or does that only go for when they did bad things?" he asked, all but rolling his eyes because he knew that would really make her pissed.

Mirna wasn't listening to him anymore. She wanted to, but his words didn't make sense. Of course he wasn't upset. Even when he was into diving, he wasn't nearly as into it as Mirna was. Maybe because he didn't have to fight as much as she did. He was a guy. Whether or not he was from a long line of divers, it wouldn't be weird if he was into the sport. No one in Emir's family before him showed interest in it and he still became who he was. But for Mirna, it was different. To even think about diving, she had to have someone to implant that thought into her mind.

She texted Franka the partial truth.

> **Mirna**: Hey, darling, I have to help Mom with some housework tonight, so I hope you don't mind if we don't hang out this evening.

That evening, she went into her parents' bedroom to iron and fold a ridiculous pile of laundry, theirs and clients' alike, because ironing was a better option as opposed to thinking. Maybe that's why she fell asleep that night easily, only partially faking crankiness and tiredness to get out of hanging out with the rest of the family.

She had barely spoken to Grandpa since that conversation with Emir. She couldn't look at him with the same eyes. He must have noticed something was off because he seemed to be avoiding her too. He wasn't there during their practice the whole week, and now Mirna knew why. He couldn't teach her anything.

She arrived at their final practice on Friday morning ahead of the scheduled time. She wasn't going to give Franka any reason to doubt anything was wrong. None of this was Franka's fault, and she wasn't going to take it out on her.

There Franka was, at the exact time they had agreed to, her black hair bouncing as she ran down the steps. She smiled at Mirna and the whole world seemed to be in order for once. She smiled back and pulled her into a hug.

What a fool she was for not doing this all the time. She had to restrain herself from pulling that gorgeous woman into her embrace every time they were alone together, even in the Partisan Cemetery, no matter how in poor taste it might be, for months. She was so scared it would all end, and Franka would just disappear one day without a trace, that she wouldn't let herself do it.

The idea still lingered in her mind. Especially whenever Franka mentioned her cool aunt. But she wouldn't let herself be eaten by fear and doubt. She would have Franka for as long as she wanted her, and she would make every moment count.

"Come on, let's do this one last time!" Franka said, still smiling as she took her hand and led her to the river.

But Mirna's heart wasn't in the practice. She wasn't even diving angry anymore, but a piece of her was missing. Her movements were stiff, robotic, and so, so careful, as if this were her first time diving. The fear she hadn't felt even when she was a kid now overtook her. If she dove like this, Mirna wouldn't even get close to the podium, but maybe she wasn't meant to do great things anyway.

They called it quits earlier than Mirna anticipated, but her head really wasn't into it. Only thing she could do was injure herself, and now really wasn't the time. Today, her shoulder only hurt when she thought about it. The pain was in her head, just a consequence of the storm of emotions in her brain, the reluctance caused by what she knew now.

When she got home, she was alone for a little while. Everything was at peace. She didn't need to fix anything, make lunch, or mow the lawn. She did some of those things already, but not on her own. It was just her and their creaky old house.

Mom was at the store, and Ado went out to his friend's house. Dad would come back in a few days, finally. She did miss him a lot when he wasn't here, but he had been working like this since Mirna was a kid, so that was all she knew. He would always come back.

Mirna could have done many things when she was home alone, for once in her life. Instead, she lay down on the couch in the living room and stared at the TV, where a Turkish telenovela played, because she just didn't want to think anymore. Thinking got her into this mess to begin with.

"Hey, little one." Grandpa's voice dragged her back to reality, kicking and screaming. She didn't notice him coming, so she stared at him like a deer caught in headlights. "Have you been avoiding me?" he asked, a question so honest she could only answer with the truth.

"I have." If she was going to get hit by this car, she would at least take him with her. What was the point in dragging this out even further? "On Monday, Emir Kapo told me something I knew couldn't be true, so I spent the rest of the week trying to prove him wrong. But I couldn't. He was right. You are not a legendary diver. You only competed once," she said, surprising herself with how calm her voice was.

Now Grandpa was the deer, his eyes wide, like he was getting ready to run away in an instant. But he wouldn't get away. Mirna wouldn't let him. Tomorrow was the competition, and she needed answers.

"It's true, Mirna," he said, his voice weak, like he didn't want to say those words but knew he had no choice. "I was like you and Adnan, watching divers from the shop. I jumped a few times, but I was never good at it. I'm afraid of heights, and I didn't have it in me to become a pro. I was pretty abysmal at it, to be honest."

"Then why lie about it?" Mirna asked, breathing deeply to keep the pressure inside her from rising. She had to stay calm. Getting angry now would get her nowhere.

"You were a kid, Mirna. You would have believed anything I said. I exaggerated what I actually did, and you never questioned me," he admitted, even if it didn't make sense.

"But I'm not the only one. Every driver in this city knows you. Based on what?" she asked.

"Based on me always being around and giving good advice. These young divers, Mirna; they weren't here when I was their age. They don't know the truth," he said. She wasn't the only one he tutored. If it wasn't for him, many more guys would regularly get injured, but he was always there to stop them from doing something stupid.

"And the old guys? Did you lie to them?" she asked, and he shook his head no. Mostar was a small town. They all knew each other. Safet and guys like him should have known the truth.

"I did dive, Mirna. Just not as many times as I said I did. We all exaggerated things to one another. I have seen more dives than anyone in this city. I have sat for decades in that store and watched them. I know what makes a good dive. And I still think I have a lot to teach you. Nothing has changed, darling. I promise you that." His voice was breaking more and more with every word he spoke, his eyes wide.

But everything was different, even if Mirna couldn't put into words exactly why. The world of last week and the world she lived in now were two dramatically different places, not for anyone else, but for her.

"Tomorrow, you are going to compete. You will make history, despite what I did or did not do," Grandpa said. He looked her in the eyes, pleading, but they both knew it was too late. "Please, don't let my failures distract you from your goal. You have done so much to get where you are. You can make this last step."

But what if she couldn't? What if she was like him, better suited to watch as others competed and achieved greatness than to do it herself?

She couldn't answer him, couldn't think or speak. All she could do was leave this house and seek salvation with the one person who would understand her: Franka.

NEIRA FAZLOVIC

Chapter Nineteen

Prokleta je Amerika

Mirna's dives weren't bad. They simply weren't as good as they usually were. She wasn't going to injure herself and she would get a decent score, but not nearly as good as she was capable of. As they practiced on that Friday morning, it was only the two of them. Grandpa Džemal was nowhere to be seen, and even Ado didn't seem as enthusiastic as he usually was.

"Everything okay at home?" Franka asked as Mirna got out of the water after a dive she could have done without a year of extensive practice.

"Yep, perfect," Mirna said with a smile that seemed a tiny bit off. By this time, Franka understood her well enough to see the difference. But she wasn't going to push it. She'd kept her plans to return to the US to herself because she didn't know how to tell Mirna, so she wouldn't complain if Mirna had secrets of her own.

"Mirna, I think I'm done for today," Franka said after a short time. In reality, she could have gone on for hours more. Her body had never felt better. She would never be a child of Neretva like Mirna was, but she did amazingly well. Mirna wasn't into it today, and the more she pushed herself, the greater possibility she would injure herself again.

To Franka's utter surprise, Mirna didn't fight her at all. Only yesterday, she would have made a joke or placed a bet or said something to reinforce her power and superiority as a diver, but now she nodded and simply agreed with Franka.

"Probably for the best," she said with that slightly artificial smile that made her look like a doll. "We did all we could. We'll just see how it goes tomorrow."

But Franka had one last trick up her sleeve to make Mirna smile again.

"Hey, since I know you will spend hours trying to decide on the perfect swimsuit, can I suggest the yellow one?" she yelled as they said goodbye. Mirna turned to her, slightly puzzled. "You look like our own little sun in it."

Mirna smiled and ran to pull her into a hug.

"You can't say corny things like that. If you make me cry, that will ruin my reputation."

With the knowledge that she at least made Mirna smile, Franka skipped back to her house. With Mom out, she took a shower and prepped her own suit. White, of course. That one didn't have turtles on it, so there was at least a chance all those Slavic deities she would compete against would take her seriously.

But Franka couldn't devote all her mental energy to diving like she wanted to. Her thoughts wandered back to the university offer she got. Even now, three days before the deadline, she wasn't any closer to making her decision. It was all so much and so sudden.

Mom wasn't that helpful either.

"It's your choice, Franka. Your future, so I won't make you pick anything you don't want to. I will miss you so freaking much, but if you choose to leave, you have my blessing," she said, even if the tears pooling in her eyes made it so obvious how much it would hurt her to see Franka leave.

For once in her life, Franka wanted someone, anyone, to make the choice for her. Mirna's usual plan of making a list of pros and cons didn't make this any easier. Nothing helped! How could anyone expect her to choose the path for the rest of her life in a week, at age nineteen? That wasn't fair, for goodness' sake. But the deadline was creeping up on her and she had to make a choice that would dictate her entire future. No matter how hard she tried, she simply couldn't find a way out.

Around five, when Mom came back, delivered a veggie burger to her, and went out again, Franka got a message.

Mirna: "Can I sleep at your place?"

Franka: "Sure thing. Mom won't mind."

Did the two of them being officially a couple change anything? Mom was raised Catholic, and while it only occasionally showed, it was still something to consider.

Mirna came by not even ten minutes later, her eyes puffy and blood-shot, strains of her golden hair sticking out from her messy ponytail, like Franka had never seen them before.

"Did something happen?" Franka asked. For some reason, her mind went straight to Mrs. Emina causing a scene because she found out about the two of them.

"It's... What would you do if what you thought was true all your life was a lie? Something that made you who you are?" Mirna asked, her voice already breaking.

A stupid thought came into Franka's mind. *Did Mirna just realize she was switched at birth?*

"It really depends on what we're talking about here," Franka said the only thing she could.

"Grandpa Džemal lied to me," Mirna finally spat out, tears already pooling at the corners of her eyes. "He lied to the whole city. He only jumped off the bridge twice in his life. He's not the expert he told us he was."

"Oh," Franka said, her breathing back to normal. "That sucks. You scared me there for a bit."

"Sucks?" Mirna asked, her voice teetering on the edge of anger that Franka was quick to recognize. "Just that?"

"I mean..." Franka scrambled to find the right words that would take her through this minefield. She tried to make her voice as calm and neutral as possible because everything she said would probably sound like an insult to Mirna now that she was so upset already. "I hate that he lied to you all this time, but you sound like your entire life has been a lie."

"Because he's a fake, I feel like I'm a fake too," Mirna said, surprisingly calm, but her voice broke, like she didn't want to say anything else even if she had to. "Like, I've based so many of my life choices on his words and his legacy. If he could do it, I could do it too. But maybe I can't."

Franka shook her head no. *Preposterous!*

"You can't? Mirela Lakić, the girl who jumped in dimije to save a stranger? The first woman to jump in a pair from the bridge? You? You can't do it?" she asked. She didn't want to be this direct, but she had no choice. Mirna didn't answer her, shaking her head no like Franka's words and all the rational evidence bounced right off her. "I've been watching you for a year now, and just because your grandpa couldn't do it doesn't mean you can't. You have proved you can."

"I didn't," Mirna argued. "You are the one who won third place."

"You would have won first place if you competed!" Franka said. Yes, Franka was supposedly the one with the "natural talent," but Mirna was still running circles around her.

"But I got injured. Twice. That didn't happen to you," Mirna said, still finding a counterpoint to every compliment Franka could give her. "Ado got injured too. Maybe we, as a family, weren't meant for this."

Franka now had no choice but to laugh.

"And my Colombian ass was genetically predisposed to dive off Ottoman bridges in some special way? Ridiculous," she said.

"Your grandfather won in the 1970s," she said. Franka paused for just a second.

"Huh, who knew?" she said. "Mom never mentioned that." No wonder she was so skeptical about Franka's new hobby since it reminded her of that awful man. "It changes nothing."

"It does! You are a legacy child," Mirna said, making Franka laugh again even if she knew it was in poor taste. But Mirna must have known how ridiculous she sounded.

"What legacy? I met the man twice, and he was an asshole. If he wasn't, I would have known about the dive already. My mom hates him, even though he was her father. Are you telling me he had more impact on me than your amazing grandpa had on you?" she asked. Regardless of everything that happened or didn't happen fifty years ago, Džemal still had taught them so much in the past year. "We are human, Mirna, not racehorses. We're not bred for this sport."

Mirna took a deep breath and sat on Franka's sofa like her spirit was broken.

"It's...it's like everything I knew has been shaken," she said, looking so much smaller than Franka had ever seen her. Franka couldn't look at her like that, so she pulled her into a hug. Mirna didn't resist and instead hugged her back.

"I've noticed. Your diving was subpar today. You can do so much better. I've seen you soar and you weren't there today," Franka said. She looked Mirna in the eyes to make sure she heard her words. "Please, love, don't let this crush your spirit. You aren't your grandfather. I'm not mine either. We are our own people, and we get to do things our own way. Circumstances of our birth define many things, but not this, Mirna. You proved that yourself, and you'll do it again tomorrow."

Mirna didn't say anything. The slight frown on her face revealed that she didn't fully believe it, and Franka knew she wouldn't. She could just hope it would be enough to get her to consider her actual worth.

"I guess you're right," she said after a pause. "That's what Ado said too. And Grandpa. But it might take me a while to process that. I've given up so much, and I don't want it to be for nothing."

Franka smiled and hugged her again.

"It won't be. I assure you! You're going to kick their assess!" she tried to hype her up, but only got a small smile out of her. "Come on, let's watch

182

some Blue Stallion diving compilations. I've heard someone's wife won again," Franka said with a smile. They had been saving the Blue Stallion footage from Portugal for Sunday, after Mirna's birthday party, but now seemed like a better day. Mirna nodded and smiled again. She could never say no to her wives.

Having read Franka's message that Mirna was sleeping over, Mom got back from work with a batch of ice cream and popcorn and reminded them she was downstairs if they needed anything.

"Just down the stairs," she emphasized as Franka closed the door right in front of her face.

She didn't need to worry. Franka and Mirna cuddled up against each other, letting Franka's fan cool them off a bit, and watched one of Mirna's wives (this one from New Zealand) win her competition.

Despite everything, Mirna calmed down, smiling and joking, having fun. Sadness still showed in her eyes, but she might be able to keep it at bay until tomorrow when she would kick ass and prove to herself she really was worth it. And then it all got so much worse.

When Franka returned from the bathroom before they went to sleep, Mirna was leaning over her desk. Franka could only see that golden waterfall of hair, but her stomach still dropped to her toes.

"Is this...?" Mirna asked, finally looking up. She took the piece of paper in her hand gently, like she was afraid she might tear it just by touching it.

"A ticket to Atlanta," Franka said in the most robotic voice she was capable of.

"I've never seen one," Mirna said with that fake, jovial tone of voice that hid so much more. "I've never been on a plane. Weird." She was trying to look cool like it was a small bit of paper that didn't mean anything. But it meant so much, and they both knew it.

"Bella bought it for me," Franka finally confessed, avoiding Mirna's gaze. "I'm leaving on the second of August."

Why was this so difficult to say? She hadn't even made up her mind yet. But no matter what she chose, she had to talk to Mirna about it sooner or later. She owed her that much.

Mirna looked at her, like her heart was already broken, her shoulders drooping, her eyes dull.

"How long will you be staying?" she asked.

"I might not come back once I leave," Franka said the words she had been dreading to say for days. "I got an offer to attend school there. I have to get back to them by Monday."

"Oh, good for you," Mirna said, trying to smile, but her breathing was shallow and her eyes wet with tears she must have been trying so hard to keep from falling.

"I might not take it," Franka said quickly. "I haven't made up my mind yet. It's not a particularly great school. That's why most people have never heard of it. The tuition would probably be over fifty thousand US dollars for undergrad. Just for tuition with nothing else included. I can't live with Bella because it's, like, a two-hour drive daily, and that isn't practical. By the time I'm a pharmacologist, I would probably be over two hundred thousand dollars in debt. Probably a lot more, with the cost of living, textbooks and everything else." She said everything in one breath, all her pros and cons list, like she should have told Mirna from day one. Mirna was the rational one. She would have helped her make the right decision.

"But that's normal for the US, right?" Mirna asked, her voice so calm it verged on artificial.

"If you're going to some really fancy school like Harvard, it's normal. For most others, it's not that much," Franka explained. Two hundred thousand dollars was so much money. After losing everything when Dad died, something in Franka simply couldn't commit to that kind of debt again. But maybe this was the only way to create the future she had dreamed of in that old life. "I'm not sure what I'll choose. I could see Bella on the weekends and probably get in touch with some of my old friends. But I still don't know. I haven't made up my mind."

"What a peculiar situation," Mirna said, still too emotionless.

Franka didn't say anything. She had dreamed of returning to the US for such a long time. All her friends were there and her aunt and everything she once cared about. If Bella had offered her this chance last year, she wouldn't have hesitated for a moment. She would have left her mom and been in Atlanta already.

But now things had changed. She was happy here. She had a college she loved and was doing great in, friends, a hobby, and most importantly, she had her: Mirna Lakić, the amazing woman who was still looking at her, with brown eyes already filled with tears.

This time Mirna didn't get angry. Franka wanted her to. Maybe Franka could make sense of her own emotions better if Mirna got angry and demanded that she stay, fighting for her and what they were starting to build here.

No, instead, Mirna turned quiet.

"I haven't made up my mind yet," Franka repeated quickly. "You have to understand, Mirna. It's not an easy decision."

"I do understand you. That's why it hurts so much." Mirna didn't say anything else for a little while as they sat on Franka's bed, posters of long-gone bands staring at them.

"I'm not going to tell you to stay," Mirna finally said. "It's your future we're talking about here, and if it's somewhere far from here, I can't blame you for leaving to chase it. I don't know what I would do if I got the same offer. But if you decide to stay, just know you have someone who cares about you." She put her hand on Franka's, gently, as if it were the first time and she might move it at any second, spooked by Mirna's presence.

"I know. That's what makes it so difficult," Franka sighed. She wasn't any closer to making her choice, but at least she didn't have to lie to Mirna anymore. Maybe tomorrow would bring a breakthrough. She could only hope.

"But you are here tonight," Mirna finally said. Her smile was weak, but it was true, as she squeezed Franka's hand in hers. "I won't let myself regret not making every minute count anymore."

"I'm here tomorrow. We're going to compete, my love, and we're going to win," Franka promised her as she pulled her closer into a hug that she never wanted to end. "Happy birthday, my bird," she said, as the clock struck midnight. "May all your dreams come true."

"Maybe they won't be able to," Mirna said, burying her face in Franka's embrace.

NEIRA FAZLOVIC

Chapter Twenty

Poslednja pesma o tebi

Even though they set an alarm, Franka's mom woke them a few minutes before seven.

"Rise and shine, my swallows," she said in English, coming into the room without knocking, as if she expected to find something. All they did the whole night was cuddle. Neither had the strength for anything juicer than a kiss.

"Good morning, Mrs. Garcia," Mirna said, her eyes still half closed. Warm summer sun entered through the window, helping her wake up. It was going to be a beautiful sunny day. Perfect for diving and saying goodbye.

"Happy birthday, Mirna," Romana said with a warm smile. "Now, come on. I got us some breakfast."

"Did you make it yourself?" Franka asked, still refusing to fully open her eyes.

"Like always, sweetie," she answered, immune to her daughter's teasing. "With the help of the bakery and the Konzum store."

Mirna didn't feel like eating, but she needed the strength. Her insides were hollowed, but not by hunger. She kept looking at Franka because now she knew for sure how limited their time actually was. In the end, she was right. Franka was about to disappear from her life like she was never even part of it, but Mirna still wouldn't have changed the last year for anything, no matter how much it would hurt.

"It's the anniversary of the Old Bridge reconstruction, so there will be even more people than usual," Mirna said to distract herself as she slobbered some pretty decent cheese spread on the still warm bread rolls.

"Well, that's good, right?" Romana asked. "More people get to see how cool you two are."

"And we are very, very cool," Franka said, her eyes still crusty with sleep and her chin smeared with plum jam. She looked at Mirna and smiled, and Mirna smiled back, even squeezing her hand under the table, but the pit inside her stomach didn't get any smaller.

187

She would dive today with Franka. Maybe for the last time. She didn't get to see her dive off the bridge except on video and that could never capture the real deal.

What a wonderful way to say goodbye. Franka might as well fly off instead of landing in the water. So Mirna had no choice. She had to make the best dive of her life. For one jump, she had to be perfect. Maybe the Swallows of Mostar wouldn't exist anymore, but they would go out on a high note.

After breakfast, they got dressed in Franka's room, mostly in silence, as their nerves were starting to kick in. They said goodbye to Romana and went out into the warm summer day. The city was filled with people, more than Mirna had ever seen. Or maybe it simply felt different now, when she would be diving in front of them.

The two diving competitions weren't the only things happening today, of course. They had junior divers jumping off the small diving board below the bridge, the race in floats and, of course, a competition in swimming across the river. In the past few years, that was the only thing she was allowed to compete in.

"I won two years ago," she whispered to Franka, who shook her head and smiled.

"Why am I not surprised one bit?" she asked.

"They weren't too happy about it either, but sixteen-year-old Mirna could be just as annoying as the nineteen-year-old one, so since they weren't going to let me dive, this was a compromise we both agreed on," she explained with a smug smile. "They were all so pissed that I bested them. It was amazing."

"You devious woman," Franka said with a smirk.

"But it's obvious I needed a partner to fulfill my true plan and undermine the entire bridge-diving community," she said. "Maybe it was I who busted that fence last year," she added in a conspiratorial tone of voice, making Franka laugh. Of course, she hadn't, but if she could thank that German tourist who did, she would.

"See, you are capable of winning these things when they let you compete," Franka said, sounding a bit like she was her mom explaining the moral of the story to her students, but Mirna didn't mind. "Why should diving be any different?"

Mirna didn't answer her right away. Last night, some of her anger was washed away. She didn't have the time to be angry anymore. Franka was here, maybe for the last time ever, and if nothing else, Mirna had to do well for her.

The part before the actual dive required a lot of waiting. In addition, to the buildup of anticipation, both Mirna and Franka would dive last in their categories, which made the wait so much longer. But Mirna liked it that way. She had Franka by her side, and she wasn't going to waste a single second of the little time they had left together.

This time, the medical checkup went perfectly. Her shoulder was fine, and it would remain that way, like the rest of her.

"So you are competing after all, unlike your grandpa?" Emir asked her, cornering both of them after they were pronounced healthy enough to compete. Behind him was his usual little companion. Emil gave them a small smile as a hello. "Maybe you'll score as low as he did."

Mirna shook her head.

"I wouldn't count on that if I were you. I am really good at this sport," she said with the confidence she was yet to possess, but he didn't need to know that.

"Don't expect any points based on your gender," he said, making Mirna laugh.

"If anything, you'll take some off for that," Franka said, but both Mirna and Emir shook their heads no. Despite everything, Emir cared about this sport more than anyone else in this city, and he would never let its integrity be damaged.

"I would never do that, Franka. No matter how many headaches you have caused me. Your score will be based only on your performance. And after all you both put me through, it better be a damn good one," he said and left.

Still following his dad, Emil turned around, smiled and said, "Good luck."

"I think he might grow a soft spot for us one day," Mirna said, looking after them.

"Then he'll promptly remove it, like a tumor," Franka said, reaching a far more plausible conclusion.

As they made their way to Džidže, where they would wait for their chance to dive, Mirna was almost knocked on her butt by a sudden gust of wind coming her way. Or maybe it was the very small child hanging around her waist who must have made her way through the crowd. Mirna was not a child person, but the little girl with dark eyes and dark hair in two long braids was kinda adorable, even if she had never seen her before.

"Look, Mom! Here she is!" the girl yelled as a woman in her thirties ran after her.

"I am so sorry," she said, trying to separate her kid from Mirna without much luck, because the girl seemed to be glued to her. "She has been following your posts for months now, and she is a bit obsessed," she explained, making Mirna smile. She just knew that somewhere, not too far away, Franka was hiding and laughing her ass off. "Iman, please," she pleaded, like Mirna's mom had pleaded with her a million times, and it was equally effective.

"It's okay," Mirna said. She picked up little Iman, which wasn't that difficult because the girl couldn't be more than five years old. She gleamed with joy, like it was the best day of her life, her eyes wide with excitement.

"I want to jump like you!" Iman squeaked, smiling. "And be a *vila* too."

Her mom gave Mirna that sympathetic smile that said: "Yes, I know, and I have tried to explain it to her, but it didn't work." Even if Mirna didn't mind the adoration one bit. If anything, she was flattered.

"Well, Iman, I'm sure you'll get to dive as soon as you are old enough. You and many other girls. I will make sure of that," she promised. For the first time, she didn't beat herself up for taking Emir's challenge to "prove" she and Franka were "good enough." His sexism was bullshit, but maybe future generations wouldn't have to fight so hard. He would keep his promise. She would make sure of that, even if she had to call his aunt on him.

"Thank you!" Iman said, planted a kiss on Mirna's cheek, and jumped out of her arms, only to be chased by her mom.

"I have some competition for your attention, or so it seems," Franka said, coming out of hiding after avoiding the hurricane named Iman.

"Prospective divers love me, what can I say?" Mirna said. Franka smiled as she led them through the crowd that was already forming.

"We're making history here, Mirna. Not your grandfather, not mine either. The two of us and no one else," Franka said, looking her in the eyes to make sure she understood her.

Mirna was finally beginning to.

Aca and Bakir, as well as most of the divers from Mostar, greeted them with excitement. A few were still on the sidelines, like they were too good to interact, but Mirna didn't care. They would either come around to them sooner or later, or they would keep ignoring their existence. The choice was up to them. Their fellow divers from other cities across ex-Yugoslavia also greeted them. Some kept looking at them like two aliens from planet Venus had joined the competition, and they were the only ones seeing anything weird about that, but for the most part, they kept their mouths shut.

In total, thirty-eight people would compete. Twenty would do a feetfirst dive while the other eighteen would do the swallow. The jury of five men sat on the wooden dock under the Old Bridge, behind small traditional wooden tables, ready to hand out points, looking ever so slightly bored. They could award each contestant a score of one to ten each for a maximum total of fifty points.

Grandpa Džemal had been a part of the jury a few times, but of course, not this year. Despite everything, the man really knew what made a good dive. Even if he had been offered the job, Mirna would have made him say no, just so no one would be able to tell her she won because of anything but her own merit.

But that didn't mean her family wasn't involved in the whole ordeal. As they made their way to the top of the bridge, Ado was frantically waving at them from below, where he stood, dressed in his costume, holding a microphone and a stack of papers with notes on them.

"I can't believe he weaseled his way into the announcer gig," Franka said, shaking her head.

"I can," Mirna said, trying to hide her smile with a fake frown. Despite everything, she was proud of him. He really did do a pretty decent job, even if Mirna didn't pay much attention to what he was saying. Generic intro, welcoming everyone, number of people competing, and of course, the mention of how special it was they had actual human females competing. What a surprise! At least Ado made his generic speech a bit more bearable by adding a slight tinge of sarcasm.

Before every diver, Ado read their name and a few pieces of information about them, bringing his own little flair to the announcement and making the audience laugh.

This year, everyone brought their A game to the competition. Mirna might have attributed it to the fact she was supposed to compete against them, but she hadn't seen this many high grades in a long while. Every year, she would watch them dive, hoping and praying she would be allowed a chance, too, so she was an expert on how it usually went, but this year they were better than usual. Maybe they didn't want to lose to two girls.

The guy from Slovenia really killed it with his feetfirst dive, when he landed pretty early on, and he was obviously the one to beat today. All the swallow dives were good, too, but Mirna was pretty certain she could beat them with a bit of luck and concentration.

Next to her, Franka had bitten her nails to the bone without even realizing it as she watched all those guys, most of them twice her size, as they performed feats she probably didn't even know about last year.

"Are you nervous?" Franka asked as the time of their dives came closer. According to the schedule they had, Franka was supposed to be up in a few minutes, so she did the last few stretches, just to be sure. Mirna didn't doubt her at all. She would kill it, for sure.

"Why would I be?" Mirna asked. Nervous? No, not even a bit. But another emotion was buried in her heart, one that didn't belong on this sunny day filled with laughter and excitement: overwhelming sadness, capable of taking over every part of her body if she let it. But she wouldn't. Today was hers and the bridge's birthday. She wasn't going to ruin their day with sadness. "I have nothing to worry about."

"You really are something special," Franka said.

Maybe Mirna should have been nervous. If she didn't make the best dive of her life, she would be the laughingstock of the city. All those *seronje* who thought women couldn't dive would have their bigoted beliefs reinforced. It wasn't fair she and Franka carried the burden of representing all the women in the world, while they could splash around for fun. But today wasn't about them. Today was about her and Franka. One last dive for the two of them. This was all they worked for, all the hours of practice, of care, of jokes and rivalry, of friendship and love, rolled up into one single dive. Mirna would make sure it was perfect, her swan song.

"And you?" she asked, even if the answer was fairly obvious.

"A bit," Franka admitted. "Mostly because there will be so many people. They don't matter. I'm not jumping for them today. I'm jumping for myself. And for you. I wouldn't have been here if you didn't do a stupid thing and jump after me last year," she said. "Because of you, I know how much I'm worth and what I'm capable of. And for that, I am very thankful."

"Are you trying to make me cry again?" Mirna asked, her heart a restless sea of emotion she could only hope to tame one day. She pulled Franka into a hug because she couldn't help herself. This woman was beyond words.

"Maybe," Franka said with a smile. "Now, watch me dive for us."

But as she made her way through other divers and the organizers at the bridge, she suddenly came to a halt as if she were frozen in the moment. Mirna ran up to her just as a familiar voice announced the reason for Franka's reaction.

"And now, a special surprise competitor for the swallow dive category; straight out of his early retirement, everyone, please welcome our one and only EMIR KAPO!" Ado announced, sounding equally as surprised to be reading those words as everyone was to hear them.

They were the truth. Emir was climbing onto the bridge, but he wasn't the man they saw entertaining the crowd a few months back. He reminded Mirna of herself, like he was diving angry. He didn't pay any attention to the cheers of the audience or to his fellow competitors trying to high-five him. He climbed that wall without saying a word to anyone.

"I can't believe this," Franka said. "Is he doing this to spite us?" she asked. Mirna didn't answer her. *Maybe he is.* Or maybe they had reawakened his love of diving and competing. She didn't know the man well enough to say for sure.

Despite everything, Emir was a living legend for a reason. When he jumped off the bridge, it was obvious he was a league above anyone who had come before him. Elegant yet strong, it was the most amazing swallow Mirna had ever seen. By her side, Franka looked down at the dive in shock and surprise, unable to say anything.

They weren't the only ones impressed. Moments after he landed in the water, before he even swam out, the jury had already given out the points.

"And we have a new first place!" Ado announced, like it wasn't painfully obvious to everyone who had seen it. Emir got out of the water, refusing the towel offered to him, without smiling or reacting to the audience in any way.

"Well, *jebi ga,*" Mirna said. If she wanted to beat him, she needed a miracle. Emir got a near perfect score, forty-nine points. She had seen him dive before, but this really was something special.

"*Jebi ga,*" Franka repeated her swear word, nodding. "I'm up next. I guess I have to win, since you probably won't," she said, smiling at Mirna like she did last year when they did the interview. Mirna understood right away. This was a challenge. If a miracle was what she needed, then that was exactly what she would pull off. "Wish me luck," Franka added.

Mirna ran, pushing her way through the crowd to get under the bridge. She would cut it close with time needed to get to her own dive, but she wouldn't miss Franka's dive for the world. This was the first and last time she would get to see it. People must have noticed she was in a rush, as they moved out of her way without much hassle. By the time Ado was announcing Franka, Mirna was already at the shore.

"And now, for the first time in the history of this competition, our first female diver, who came here all the way from Mexico, please welcome Franka Garcia!" he yelled.

"Colombia!" Franka yelled what he already knew very well from the top of the bridge so loud that most of the audience heard her without a microphone, making the whole crowd laugh.

"Colombia," Ado repeated with a chuckle. But Franka didn't mind. Today, she was a Mostarka. She wasn't nervous anymore. In fact, she was smiling, waving at the audience, getting them to cheer her on even more than they might have otherwise. She was playing this game to win, Mirna noticed with a smirk.

And then, Franka asked them all for a moment of silence as she stood atop the bridge. She was so tiny in comparison, but in that moment, she seemed like a giant to Mirna.

While everyone held their breath, Franka took that step forward and flew.

It was unlike anything Mirna had ever seen. Her body contorted into a double somersault before she straightened up again just before she landed in the water feetfirst, making almost no splash as she did. Neretva took her into her embrace.

Tears. Mirna was crying. She only noticed when her sight turned blurry. She hated goodbyes. Her Franka, her swallow; she would be gone soon. No matter how much Mirna wanted to be happy for her, Franka's leaving still hurt. She was only human. And no matter how perfect this dive was, it was the last one they would ever get to share.

But Franka wasn't getting out of the water. She stayed in for longer than any other contestant, so long that Mirna was about to jump in after her before she finally surfaced, smiling like she won the whole thing.

The frowns on the faces of a few judges made it obvious she wasn't going to win the competition, but that smile on Mirna's face as she helped her out of the water told Franka she won Mirna's heart. And no matter how much it would hurt once she was gone, Mirna was happy that she did.

Chapter Twenty-One

Vraćam se majci u Bosnu

Every cell in Franka's body screamed in pain as the cold water embraced her, but it was only for a few moments before they acclimated to the familiar feeling of Neretva. This river would never hurt her. Mirna made sure of that. Franka opened her eyes and found herself in the beautiful blue world.

She did it! She dove off the Old Bridge, the first woman in history to ever compete. It was so amazing. She flew like Mirna had last year, adrenaline leading her without much thought. Finally, she was a real Swallow of Mostar.

The blue around her was mesmerizing, and for a few moments, she imagined it was clear enough that she could see all the way to the Adriatic Sea. She didn't want to get out. Getting out meant facing choices.

"Swim!" she reminded herself when her lungs began to ache for oxygen.

And she did. Once she surfaced, Mirna would be there to meet her. That was all she needed to know. Seeing her again might make the choice easier.

Mirna wasn't the only one waiting for her. The crowd noises reached her even underwater, but once she had surfaced, their cheers became so much clearer. The small boat was already there, and Franka realized she had been underwater for long enough for people to get worried. Probably not the best choice, at least for her score.

"Thank you, everyone!" she yelled at the audience, smiling, remembering the game she was playing with Mirna. But it wasn't just an act this time. She wanted to acknowledge these people. The crowd chanting her name was unlike anything she had ever felt! "It's an honor to compete!"

"I thought you might have drowned," Mirna said when Franka was back on the shore, then pulled her into a hug, even though Franka was completely wet.

"I thought about faking it so you would come and rescue me, to make you even more famous," Franka joked, kinda sorry she only now thought of that. It would have made a cool story.

"Not fair. You have to rescue me from time to time," Mirna said with a smile.

"How was it?" Franka asked. For most dives, the jurors would vote in a matter of minutes, but they still hadn't handed out Franka's points. But Mirna was incredibly good at guessing how many points any dive would get, a talent one could only get from standing on the sidelines year after year and bitterly watching and analyzing every dive.

"You were magnificent in the air," Mirna gushed. "I have no words for how amazing you looked. I knew you were good, but that was something else. The crowd loved you."

"But?" Franka asked, as Mirna's frown made it obvious she had more to say.

"I mean, I wouldn't be surprised if they deducted points for how long it took you to come out of the water," she said. Franka chuckled. She fulfilled the goal she set for herself already, so the actual numerical value her dive earned didn't really mean much anymore.

Mirna was right, of course. As the jury finally showed their points, Franka knew she wouldn't win. That guy from Slovenia was still in first place with the amazing dive he made. But the familiar feeling of disappointment never came. She'd had too much fun to be bothered with such silly things as victory. She'd won a long time ago.

Mirna was quicker at math so she was the first to calculate the total number of points.

"Third place!" she yelled. "I am so proud of you, you amazing woman!" She lifted Franka up and pulled her into a hug before dropping her gently, but way too soon. It was her turn to dive, and the organizer on the bridge was pointing at them and mouthing a very juicy swear word.

"*My people, is that possible?*" Ado yelled, losing his mind with excitement when he was handed the official results. "First female competitor in history, and she already won third place in her category!"

As the crowd cheered on, Mom ran to her, holding her phone up where she was on a video call with Bella. She pulled her into a hug, ruining her perfectly decent white blouse in the process.

"Are you okay?" she asked, wrapping her up in a towel before she had a chance to object.

"Never better!" Franka yelled. "Third place!" She translated the results to Bella who screamed with joy.

"Amazing job, kiddo!" she yelled from the phone. "I knew you could do it!"

"Thank you, thank you," Franka said. She looked at that woman, halfway across the world, smiling like she was the one who won, as Mom pulled her into a hug again, and in that moment the choice became a bit clearer. But she didn't have the time to think about it.

"Mirna Lakić!" Ado pulled her back to reality, genuinely excited to get to say her name. "Most of you from Mostar already know her well, but we won't blame her for being the less awesome of the Lakić siblings. Can she pull off what Franka did now?"

Of course, she could. Franka had no doubts about that. Even from a distance and without her glasses, she could see Mirna's smile still shone like a torch atop the Old Bridge. How could she miss it? It lit up half the city.

Franka thought Mirna would try to make the crowd go wild like she had, to continue their little competition and prove how amazing she was in front of everyone. But she was calm, smiling, looking down at where Franka stood with her mom. She wasn't diving for the crowd. Mirna was diving for herself.

To win, she had to be better than Emir Kapo, who'd made a jump unlike anything Franka had ever seen. But Franka knew Mirna had it in her. She only had to show everyone.

The crowd was silent now. Franka's feetfirst dive was one thing, but diving a swallow was a whole different beast. It was much more dangerous, so they all held their breath, waiting for Mirna to close the competition with her dive.

And what a closer it was!

Mirna's dive was the one last dance of a bird who was scared she would lose the one she loved. She spread her arms wide like she wanted to embrace the whole city, and she flew, like Franka had never seen her do before. Her landing perfect, she swam to the surface a few moments later, that infectious smile still on her face.

The crowd was screaming her name and words of support, but Mirna wasn't paying attention to them. When she got out of the water, she went straight to Franka and pulled her into a hug.

"I love you," she whispered into her ear. "I don't want you to go away without me saying that."

"I love you too," Franka said and pulled her even closer. They stayed, locked in an embrace, both wet and a bit cold, blind to the world around them. The competition didn't matter anymore. Just this moment, just the two of them.

But when the crowd once again erupted into chaos, the competition came back to them.

"I can't believe this! She's tied with Emir Kapo!" Ado yelled, losing even the last shreds of what little professionalism he had. "That's my sister, everybody! Mirna, *carice*, you showed them how it's done!"

When Franka and Mirna finally turned to face the world, Ado was really telling the truth. Mirna got the same score as Emir Kapo.

"You amazing woman! I am so proud of you!" Franka yelled. Mirna stared at the score, her mouth open in shock and absolute glee before she squealed in joy and lifted Franka again. "But it's a tie. What happens now?" Franka asked. The answer came to her long before Mirna could say anything.

Emir stormed by them, and his steps seemed to shake the ground he walked on, fuming with anger as he approached the jury, ready to fight them if that was necessary.

Before he could reach them, a small boy broke away from his mom, made his way through the crowd and ran to him. He grabbed him by the leg and looked up at him, his smile genuine, like Franka had never seen.

"I'm so proud of you, *babo*!" Emil said to his dad. "You're my winner!"

Emir froze like he was seeing his kid for the first time. The boy who looked like him was still smiling, and Emir took a deep breath before picking him up and putting him on his shoulders.

He approached the jury and talked to them for a few moments, and Franka held Mirna back so she wouldn't interfere before they called Ado over.

"It is official, my dear audience," Ado announced a few moments later, grinning ear to ear. "The winners of this year's competition are both Mirela Lakić and Emir Kapo!"

The crowd turned even wilder than before, but Mirna just took a deep breath and smiled. They did it. They made their wish come true.

The next few hours were a vaguely fun blur of people and events, but Franka wanted nothing more than for the crowd to dissipate, leaving only her and Mirna alone in this world.

As a reward, Franka got 100 marks and a copper carving of the Old Bridge (the same one sold at Džidže), while Mirna got 250 marks and the same carving, just bigger. She would cherish it as her child, she promised. They weren't going to get rich off this, but it was something.

As expected, the time after the official award ceremony and before the concert involved one chicken sandwich each (courtesy of Mrs. Emina, God bless her heart) and loads and loads of pictures with the other winners and interviews with the news station. For one day, in this city and this city alone, they were the most important people around.

The interviews were the perfect chance for the two of them to return to their rivalry.

"I hope other young women, all over the country, can see what we did and know that they are good enough!" Mirna passionately proclaimed to the national journalist, who nodded her head, moved by the performance.

"I want little girls all over the world to dare to dream. With hard work and perseverance, everything is possible," Franka assured the journalists from a news portal.

Once again, they hogged the spotlight from the other competitors, especially the winners in Franka's category, a Slovenian and a Serb who kept frowning in all the photos and grumbling to themselves, but this time neither Franka nor Mirna minded that much. They would get over it. And it's not like either of them wanted the media to make a spectacle of them. If they had treated Mirna and Franka like regular competitors from the start, none of this would have been necessary.

After a series of very stilted and fake photos of all six winners smiling with their prizes, Emir turned to them.

"You really did well," he said.

"Thank you," Mirna said. "You were great too. But why didn't we just dive again for first place?" she asked, cautious of her own words and what they might bring to her.

Emil ran to his dad again, and Emir picked him up with a smile on his face.

"I promised him we would do something that he likes this afternoon. Diving against you again would take too much time. Besides, you proved that I have nothing to worry about when it comes to the future of this sport," he said, shrugging, like he finally realized the Sisyphean act of fighting two teenagers.

"You looked so cool, Mirna!" Emil said from his dad's shoulders, eyes wide in excitement for cliff diving for the first time in his life.

"Can't wait to see you dive one day," Mirna said with a smile, but Emil shook his head no.

"I'll leave that to you and *babo*," he said. Emir sighed but smiled afterward.

"There's always time for you to change your mind," he said. His battle for a legacy wasn't over, but maybe he didn't need to push it on a child who only wanted his attention. "Now, kiddo, let's go. I think I promised you a movie."

"And popcorn?" Emil asked.

"Of course." They blended into the crowd and were gone as another small bit of pressure lifted from Franka's heart. Maybe they would be okay.

"Character development," Franka whispered into Mirna's ear, making her chortle.

They didn't get to talk much in those few hours. Everything was happening all at once, and everyone wanted a piece of their attention, so they didn't get to be alone for a minute.

The best they got was during the concert of the traditional Sevdah music under the Old Bridge, where they stood next to each other, holding hands in the crowd as Mirna sang along to old songs that Franka didn't know but started to fall in love with anyway.

"Mirna, I have been looking for you the whole day," Grandpa Džemal said. He stood behind them, looking somehow smaller and older than he had before.

"Oh," was all Mirna could say, like she wasn't sure what was supposed to happen.

"I know I hurt you," he said. "I broke your trust, and that was a shitty thing to do. But I never meant for it to go this far. I was too much of a coward to fess up to it. What I did or did not do doesn't dictate what you can do. You have proved that today, Mirna! You are our gold!"

Mirna pulled him into a hug.

"I know you meant well. But it will take me some time to process it all; you have to understand that," she said. Džemal nodded.

"I know," he said in a calm voice. "And, Franka, I'm sorry to you too. You also deserved the truth."

"It's okay," she said. "You know I'm not my grandfather, and Mirna is not you either."

"We are our own people," Mirna said with a smile.

"And 'your own people' is late," Ado tapped her on the shoulder, making her jump in fright.

"Ooh, I forgot!" she said, already on her way before Franka could say anything. How was this girl so fast, on land and in water? "See you soon!"

"What happened?" Franka yelled, but Mirna was already gone.

"The winners are supposed to dive off the bridge carrying torches tonight. Emir let Mirna do it for both of them," Ado explained. "We really, really like diving off that bridge," he added, a tad dreamily.

"Ooh, that will be so pretty!" Franka said. She would get to see Mirna dive again. What a treat!

"But not as pretty as this," Ado said, showing her a sizable stack of money, that smug smile on his face bigger than the bridge itself.

"Who did you rob?" Grandpa asked, and Ado grabbed his chest in a fake pantomime of hurt.

"No one. Except for all the dumb guys who decided to bet on Emir when they realized he was competing. But I knew what would happen. You with the bronze, Mirna and Emir tied for first place and me with riches!"

"Are we sure he isn't an *evlija*?" Grandpa asked.

"Quite frankly, no, not really," Franka answered him.

"I can't wait to see you girls dive again next year. I see good things in your future," he added in a dramatic voice.

Franka smiled, but this time, the idea didn't make her stomach feel like it was full of gravel. In fact, she liked the sound of it. Next year. What an awesome concept.

As Ado was temporarily relieved of his announcer duties ("The crowd loved me, they'll be begging me to return next year! Begging, I tell ya!"), it was up to the singer to announce the divers.

The young man from Slovenia was the first one to jump, carrying two lit torches, sparking around him like he was an otherworldly being. His dive was something else too. Grace and power, all in one. Franka really was a beginner in this sport, and that was awesome.

"I guess that is my goal for next year," she said, more to herself. She could pull that off, but she needed to practice.

Then, it was Mirna's turn. In the darkness, only the golden light of two torches illuminated the night sky. She was still smiling, now wearing her black wetsuit, because of course she found a place and time to change. Tonight, she was the guardian of the Old Bridge, or the reincarnation of it. Her dive wasn't as technically perfect as it was today, but it didn't matter. It was still as impressive, and the crowd agreed. She put out the candles for herself and the Old Bridge. What a way to celebrate their birthday.

It wasn't that dive that made Franka sure of her choice, but as Mirna got out of the water, she knew she had to tell her tonight. Still, she couldn't speak to her just yet with all these people around, as the band played a love song for the Bridge itself, to close out the night.

"Let's stay here," Franka whispered into Mirna's ear when the band said goodbye.

"Of course," she said, her smile still as wide as the bridge itself.

The night came to a close, and the crowd slowly but surely dissipated. In the pitch-dark the lights illuminated the bridge, so Franka wasn't scared. For the first time since this morning, they were finally alone together. They sat on the rock next to the river that moved past them, cold and green, like it always was. No one else was here. It was like the bridge stood only for the two of them. Mirna was still in her wetsuit, wrapped up in a towel, but the night was warm, so neither of them were worried.

In all the hustle and bustle of the day, Mirna didn't even get a piece of cake for her birthday. They would have a small party tomorrow, but Franka still found time to get her a muffin from a store and put a candle on it. It was way past midnight, but the thought still counted.

"For Mirna and for the Old One!" Franka cheered.

"I'm sure the bridge is as thankful as I am," Mirna said with a smile.

"You were so amazing," Franka said. They sat by the river, all alone in the old town and maybe the whole universe. "You earned your victory."

"You earned a higher position too," Mirna said. "Out of all the competitors, no one looked that good in the air. The jury just didn't know what they were looking at."

"I don't mind. I won this competition the moment you rescued me from the river last year. If that didn't happen, I would still be that sad, directionless person I was before." She spoke her truth. "While I was under water, it was like I saw the world much clearer. I think I made my choice."

"About America?" Mirna asked, her voice already breaking, ready to receive the news she dreaded so much, no matter how supportive she tried to be.

"In the end, there is only one thing I can do," Franka said. "I'm going to Atlanta, but I will come back," she promised. Mirna stared at her, still processing her words, not breathing, like she didn't believe what she was hearing. "It's really stupid of me to plunge myself into all that debt when I don't have to. And my mom would miss me too much. She needs me. And I still need her. And you... Well, I can't let you go to the gym alone again," she said with a smile.

"Please don't do this for me," Mirna said, shaking her head. "I could never forgive myself if you missed something like this for my sake."

"It's not just you, Mirna. Believe me," Franka assured her. "You're amazing, but so is my mom and so is this messy, divided city and my college. In Alabama, I would only get an American diploma for a college that doesn't seem that great. I would be closer to Bella, but I couldn't even see her every day. I would start over and come out on the other side two hundred thousand dollars in debt. I don't know if it's worth it. I know Bella loves me and wants what is best for me. Going back there may seem like the perfect ending, but it's not."

"Neither is Mostar," Mirna said with a sad smile. "I love this city more than anyone, but it's far from perfect."

"I know that," she said. "But I have a chance at happiness here. No, actually, I already have it, right now, with you by my side. And I want to stay. Because I love you and I love this mess of a place."

Mirna pulled her into a hug that evolved into a kiss. Her lips were so sweet, still tasting of the chocolate muffin they shared, and Franka never wanted this to end.

The Old Bridge above them stood as a silent witness of the love they shared for each other.

NEIRA FAZLOVIC

Epilogue

Iznonit će stari za one što ga vole

Five people followed Mirna carefully, only a few paces behind her, listening to her every word like it was gospel.

To a group of civil engineers, the story of how a four-hundred-year-old bridge was reconstructed from rubble to perfection in a span of a few years probably *was* gospel. Mirna doubted anyone before had studied all the detailed descriptions, pictures and diagrams of the techniques used in that feat that were framed and hung in the museum with so much care, so this was one batch of tourists Mirna didn't mind guiding.

Even though Isabella Garcia was taller than Franka—like basically everyone in this country—she and her niece looked remarkably similar. Bella and her posse of civil engineers arrived in Dubrovnik a few days ago and made their way to Mostar in time for this year's diving competition. Then they would go on, covering the Balkans, as they were especially interested in Yugoslavian architecture, while Isabella would stay and spend time with Franka and her mom.

But that was tomorrow. Today, they had a day to relax and have fun.

The city was buzzing with excitement already as they walked out of the underground museum and into the warm summer air, right next to the bridge.

"So cool!" Isabella squealed, her voice filled with childlike joy and wonder like her colleagues.

As the engineers took an excessive number of photos of the Old Bridge, Mirna stared below, where juniors were practicing. Emir Kapo had kept his word. Ten boys were joined by three girls. One of them jumped off the board, landing gracefully on her feet as Mirna looked on. New talent was hiding in this city, and Mirna couldn't wait to see it reach its full potential.

All the girls had her phone number in case anyone was being mean to them, or at least meaner than to the boys. And the boys also knew they could call her and Franka if someone was acting like a jerk. They deserved to train in peace too. Old habits change slowly, but they could still change. Maybe the likes of little

Emil could have a safer experience, even if he seemed more interested in movies than anything else.

She waved to Grandpa Džemal, who waved back from his usual chair that he always put by the river. Tomorrow morning before the competition, he would take their guests under his wing and talk to them about the old Old Bridge, which they were looking forward to hearing about, because Isabella apparently exclusively hung out with nerds.

He took over the role of the supervisor of the practices, a job he mostly made up and consisted of him sitting under the bridge and commenting on how people jumped and sharing tips and tricks to improve their technique. No one questioned him because he was Džemal Topalović and he had a new title: the man who saw the most dives off the Old Bridge, so he could do whatever he wanted. Besides, the kids liked him a lot.

"My darling guests, how are you enjoying your stay so far?" A familiar voice brought Mirna back to the top of the bridge. Ado approached them, wearing his brand new, custom-made *čakšire* and a red fez of an unbelievably vibrant shade. "If you want any souvenirs, may I interest you in amazing 3-D printed replicas of the Old Bridge, handmade by local artists?" he asked with his most charming smile.

His hustle was still on and doing well. He would even be the announcer again tomorrow because people really did love him. Džidže were selling like halva. Thankfully, Mirna wouldn't have to inherit the family business and could be an academic, like God intended.

Ado was still in charge of the Swallows of Mostar social media accounts, which were now mostly for fun, as they should have been from the start. It really was fulfilling to share their successes (and a few failures) with others all over the world. Every time they got a message saying someone dared to dive because of their posts, Mirna was reassured she was doing the right thing.

The guests, tempted by the promises of unique džidže, approached the store, leaving Mirna on her own. To be fair, those little bridges really did look cool.

But Mirna wasn't alone for long. From the other side of the bridge, a small figure approached, her dark messy bob giving away her identity before anything else. Franka smiled and ran to meet her. The ice cream she had been licking was walnut-and-fig flavored, which turned out to be Franka's favorite taste. Unlike Mirna, Franka didn't feel like spending hours in a museum, reading about highly technical details of bridge reconstruction. A shame, really, because the engineers were able to explain technical things Mirna never understood before.

Mirna took her hand and pulled her into a hug. They weren't yet at the public kissing level of comfort, but those who really mattered accepted them. Those who didn't, now knew for sure most of the divers in the city would come after them if anything happened to their champions.

Mom and Dad took it better than Mirna had thought they would.

"Mirna, son, I have been in Germany for ten years. It's normal there. Why shouldn't it be normal here?" Dad asked her as they hugged. "As long as you are happy, I'm happy too."

"After your diving off that bridge, I don't know if anything can surprise me anymore," Mom said, shaking her head, but she continued inviting Franka over for dinner and treating her like one of her own.

Even their friends at college, at least the ones they thought were deserving of knowing, were pretty cool with it.

"Yeah, I know, I know. I was both with you in high school and there for New Year's Eve. You weren't exactly subtle then. Good for you. Now, help me with these smears. I don't get these colors!" Selma said, making Mirna smile and explain the differences between gram-positive and gram-negative bacteria to her again.

Ivona apparently started crying with joy and support when Franka told her, because she had recently watched *Love, Simon* and was still processing it. Both Mirna and Franka decided to accept her emotions and support, no matter what caused them.

The year went by too fast, even though it was a fun one. The second year of college was even tougher, but together, they made it work. They were done with the exams already, just like last year, so they had another free summer.

After Franka had returned from Atlanta in September, armed with all the spices and produce she could legally carry, they went back to the gym and to diving practice, and this time the mood was different everywhere they went. Jumping off the bridge gave one a certain kind of social status in Mostar, and both felt it deep in their bones. People were nicer to them. Of course, as usual, a few jerks refused to change, but they were a minority, and now, their friends would sometimes call them out.

Five women would compete tomorrow. Mirna and Franka, of course, a Croat and Macedonian, plus the infamous firefighter (one of Mirna's wives) who sounded pretty hurt Mirna and Franka hadn't let her in on their little plan last year.

"I would have loved to help you!" she assured them.

The organizers suggested forming a competition for women only, which Franka was quick to refuse.

"*Šta je, pičke?* Are you afraid of women?" Franka said in the middle of a pretty serious meeting. Mirna was equally horrified both for ruining her precious innocent Franka and proud that she had taught her well.

The notion was quickly dismissed.

"How are the engineers treating you?" Franka asked.

"They are very enthusiastic about bridges in general and this one in particular," Mirna said. "Bella more than most."

"That's my aunt for you," she said. "Mom is meeting them at the bus station after. They made plans to see the Dervish monastery, Blagaj Tekkija, and want to take the bus for a more authentic feel."

For now, they were still busy with Ado and all the amazing things he was trying to sell them. The rest of the other wonders of nature and architecture Mostar had to offer could wait a bit. Since Mirna couldn't jump from it, it was slightly less interesting.

"You cannot judge national monuments based on whether or not you can dive off them," Mirna told her when they were in Jajce that spring, enjoying the country and also making arrangements for the competition in August that they were suddenly more than welcome to attend.

"I can and I will," Mirna assured her, making her burst into laughter.

"Excited for tomorrow?" Franka asked, leaning against the fence, watching as a new group of tourists approached.

"Very much so," Mirna said. "It's been too long." She smiled at the river below them, as if it were calling for her.

"Yes, these are the famous Swallows of Mostar," Ado said in English to the new group of approaching tourists. The group started snapping pictures of them like Mirna and Franka were more famous than the bridge itself. Mirna did what she did best and smiled.

"We are big fans!" one of them yelled. "You are the reason we came to Mostar."

"That's nice to hear," Franka said, her smile equally wide. They weren't the first ones to say it, but every time they heard it felt equally nice.

"Could we see you dive?" one of them asked, his eyes enormous with hope and excitement.

"But..." Franka was probably going to say they would see the dive tomorrow at the competition, before Ado cut in.

"You have to pay, you know that?" he asked, like he was their manager. "These women would risk their lives for your entertainment. They deserve substantial financial compensation."

"Of course, of course," their leader said, taking out his wallet while the others shortly followed. They must have seen how the interaction was usually done. They looked rich enough that it wouldn't financially ruin them. "Is fifty okay?"

"Euros or marks?" Franka asked, her forehead scrunched up in contemplation of the offer.

"Euros, for each of you, of course." Mirna and Franka exchanged knowing looks and smiled at each other. Money and a dive! An offer with literally no downside.

"Don't tell Mom!" Mirna said to Ado as she took off her shirt and shorts to reveal the swimsuit underneath. Franka did the same and they both laughed at the other's willingness to dive off the bridge at a moment's notice.

"That's gonna be a five euro fee to keep my mouth shut," Ado said, gathering the money from the tourists who stared at them with awe. "Same for you, Franka."

"And five for me, if you don't want Romana to know!" Isabella added but didn't try to stop them. Instead, they all approached the edge to get a better view.

"Take it, you little *lihvari*," Franka said with a laugh. She and Mirna climbed up the stone fence of the bridge together. Most of the time, guys who dove for money had to make a show of it to collect enough to make it worth the risk, but now, thanks to Ado, they didn't have to wait. They could simply do it.

They high-fived each other, synchronized their dive, and let the river take them.

The cold Neretva water had never felt so welcoming.

Acknowledgements

Writing seems like lonely work, but given how difficult this acknowledgment section is to write it's anything but.

Yes, I wrote the novel, but so many people helped me in one way or another, so I didn't do it alone.

I would like to thank my friends, Nadi, Boris, Vedo, Nai, and Emir, for being here for me, listening to my silly rambles about bridge divers from Mostar, and for helping me through some tough times.

A big thanks to my friends on Balkan Writers Discord (especially Petra) for bullying me to submit my manuscript to NineStar Press. Without you, this book would still be stuck on my computer.

To someone special: you saved my life, cared when my brain told me no one else did, but now I'm so happy to be here and have you as a part of it. Leila, thank you for being in my life. Hopefully, you will be in many future acknowledgments and I will make your life better like you do mine.

To my wonderful editor, BJ! Thank you for taking a chance on this story.

To all my beta readers, including Natalie and Uma for making this book better with your feedback.

Great thanks to the city of Mostar itself, for inspiring this story and making me feel like I was home. I hope I did your people justice and that I'm allowed back in. Special thanks to Jasmina for providing me with Mostar info only someone who grew up next to the Old Bridge would know.

If you're interested, you can find the songs that the chapters were named for on this link: open.spotify.com/playlist

And last, but not least, to my roommate and bestie, Karl: This book wouldn't have been possible without you.

About the author

Neira Fazlovic is a writer of books about lesbians, ghosts and science. Veterinarian by trade (and soon to be a PhD), she has been writing since she was thirteen. She is a great fan of cats, typos and Bosnia and Herzegovina.

Email

Fazlovic.neira@gmail.com

Twitter

@neirawrote

Website

www.neirawrites.com

We hope you enjoyed this book!

Thank you for supporting our authors. If you have a minute, we would truly appreciate your review.

www.ingramcontent.com/pod-product-compliance
Lightning Source LLC
Chambersburg PA
CBHW071106100726
47908CB00008B/2285